MW00616489

FRENCH QUARTER
FRIGHT NIGHT

FRENCH QUARTER
FRIGHT NIGHT

Ellen Byron

**SEVERN
HOUSE**

First world edition published in Great Britain and the USA in 2024
by Severn House, an imprint of Canongate Books Ltd,
14 High Street, Edinburgh EH1 1TE.

severnhouse.com

British Library Cataloguing-in-Publication Data
A CIP catalogue record for this title is available from the British Library.

ISBN-13: 978-1-4483-1265-8 (cased)
ISBN-13: 978-1-4483-1266-5 (e-book)

All Severn House titles are printed on acid-free paper.

Typeset by Palimpsest Book Production Ltd.,
Falkirk, Stirlingshire, Scotland.
Printed and bound in Great Britain by TJ Books,
Padstow, Cornwall.

Praise for the Vintage Cookbook mysteries

"Plenty of suspects and plenty of fun"
Kirkus Reviews on *Wined and Died in New Orleans*

"Byron, author of the award-winning 'Cajun Country' mysteries, combines setting, vintage cookbooks, recipes, and family drama in another delectable cozy"
Library Journal on *Wined and Died in New Orleans*

"The characters feel like old friends. Everything about this story keeps the reader invested . . . you won't be disappointed. This book will keep fans excited and looking forward to the next installment"
thecozyreview.com on *Wined and Died in New Orleans*

"Fans of Byron's award-winning 'Cajun Country' mysteries will enjoy her return to New Orleans with an engaging, fun cast of characters"
Library Journal on *Bayou Book Thief*

"Cozy fare served up Crescent City style"
Kirkus Reviews on *Bayou Book Thief*

"Lots of twists and turns will keep you guessing right up to the hilarious end. Beware reading while hungry"
Libby Klein, bestselling author of the Poppy McAllister Mysteries, on *Bayou Book Thief*

"A cast of exceptional supporting characters, all as quirky as the city . . . *Bayou Book Thief* is the start of what I am sure will soon become one of my favorite series and I can't wait for my next visit"
Vicki Delany, National Bestselling author, on *Bayou Book Thief*

About the author

Ellen Byron is an Anthony Award nominee, bestselling author and recipient of multiple Agatha and Lefty awards for her Cajun Country Mysteries, Vintage Cookbook Mysteries, and Catering Hall Mysteries (as Maria DiRico). She is also an award-winning playwright and non-award-winning writer of TV hits like Wings, Just Shoot Me, and Fairly OddParents. Ellen was the 2023 Left Coast Crime Toastmaster but considers her most impressive achievement working as a cater-waiter for Martha Stewart.

A native New Yorker, Ellen is a graduate of Tulane University and lives in the Los Angeles area with her husband, daughter, and a rotating crew of rescue pups. Visit her at www.ellenbyron.com

Dedicated to Severn House Publishing for giving me the chance to solve more mysteries with Ricki and the gang at Bon Vee Culinary House Museum.

CAST OF CHARACTERS

The staff at Bon Vee Culinary House Museum:

Miracle 'Ricki' Fleur de Lis James-Diaz – Proprietor, Miss Vee's Vintage Cookbook and Kitchenware Shop at Bon Vee

Zellah Batiste – artist and café manager; also works at Peli Deli, her family's business

Lyla Brandt – Executive Director

Eugenia Charbonnet Felice – President of the Bon Vee Foundation board; niece of the late owner of Bon Vee, Genevieve Charbonnet

Olivia Felice – Eugenia's granddaughter and Ricki's intern

Theo Charbonnet – Eugenia's nephew and self-titled Director of Community Relations

Cookie Yanover – 'Recovering children's librarian' now working at Bon Vee as the Director of Educational Programming

Benny and Jenny – senior-aged twin docent/tour guides

Virgil Morel – former executive chef at Charbonnet's restaurant; current cooking world hottie; co-owner of the Bayou Backyard, a popular hangout

Mordant – haunted history tour guide and Bon Vee handyman

Law Enforcement:

Nina Rodriguez – detective

Samuel Girard – detective

Assorted others:

Blaine Taggart – A-list movie star

Miranda Fine – his assistant

Jason Bergen – intern-turned-assistant

Nat Luna – Blaine's older half-brother, bodyguard, and sober companion

Mooni Benson – Blaine's aunt and personal cook

Delia Frontenac – Blaine's interior designer

Lakshmi – Blaine's spiritual advisor and masseuse

Bob 'Bobby' Grimes – a PI

Gordy Fine – Miranda's brother

Chess Villeneuve – Miranda's ex-boyfriend from high school

Britni Sanchez – Miranda's ex-friend from high school

Paige, Sarah Jane, and Toni – other ex-friends

Father Gabriel – priest at St Aquilinus

Ky Nguyen – co-owner, Bayou Backyard

ONE

uhwaa ha ha!

M Ricki James-Diaz bolted up from bed at the sound of the evil laugh, which triggered warning barks from her canine companions Thor and Princess. She grabbed the baseball bat she kept at the side of her bed, a birthday gift from her father who worried about his daughter living alone in scenic but sometimes dangerous New Orleans.

Muhwaa ha ha!

The maniacal laugh came again. Heart racing, Ricki swung her legs over the side of the bed and planted them on the ground. She held the bat high above her head, ready to take a swing. Thor, a tiny Chihuahua mix mutt, emitted a deep-throated growl while Princess, a hefty Shepherd mix, whimpered. All three tensed, on alert for what might come next.

Muhwaa ha ha!

A glow came from the cell phone on Ricki's nightstand. Fearful it might be a taunting message from whomever was threatening her, she grabbed it with her free hand, adrenaline pumping.

A cartoon vampire flashed a bloody grin, then let out a maniacal laugh as the words 'Happy Almost-Halloween!' danced across the phone screen.

Ricki let out a disgruntled grunt. 'Seriously?' She dropped the bat and called up a telephone number for Cookie Yanover, her friend and coworker at the Garden District's Bon Vee Culinary House Museum, where Ricki was proprietor of Miss Vee's Vintage Cookbook and Kitchenware Shop. 'Cookie, I love you, but why are you GIF-ing me in the middle of the night?'

'It's not the middle of the night,' her friend protested. 'I sent that at exactly one minute past twelve o'clock. I wanted to remind you of the Hallo-month Breakfast Kickoff tomorrow.'

'It's not like I can forget. I've gotten reminders from everyone at work. During *normal hours*.'

'It's New Orleans, chere. Not normal *is* our normal. Get used to it.'

'I'm trying. But right now I'm sleepy and grumpy.'

'Hey, that's two of the seven dwarfs. Grumpy, Sleepy, Bashful, Dopey, Doc, Sneezy . . . who's the seventh? I can't remember.'

'"Happy," which I'm going to be as soon as I hang up and go back to bed. I'll see you tomorrow.'

Ricki ended the call. Another GIF popped up on her phone, this time a monster. Ominous music played as the screen read, 'Have a good night! I'll see you *in your dreams!!!*' She shot back an eye roll emoji and turned off the cell's sound. Then, she maneuvered her way around the two dogs, who'd already gone back to sleep.

As Ricki pulled the covers up to her chin, she thought about the difference between Halloween in New Orleans and her former home, Los Angeles, where the holiday barely registered on people's radar once their kids had grown and flown.

She'd been born in the 'Big Easy' and spent her first eight years in the city, adopted by Josepha James, the NICU nurse who cared for her after Ricki's mystery of a teen mother disappeared from Charity Hospital. When Josepha married Luis Diaz – a grip in town working on a movie – she and Ricki relocated to the San Fernando Valley, where he was based. Now, twenty years later, Ricki returned to the city that had always felt like the home of her heart, looking for a fresh start after a career disaster and the death of her estranged actor husband.

Ricki was excited about spending her first Halloween in New Orleans since childhood. Her quirky gift shop was a dream come true. She'd made wonderful new friends and loved her rented shotgun home in the Irish Channel, likening its bright, over-the-top décor to living in a Mardi Gras float.

But there were times – and this was one of them – when she wondered if she'd ever truly shed the twenty years she'd spent in SoCal and fully adopt the *laissez les bons temps rouler* spirit of 'The City That Care Forgot'.

After walking and feeding her pooches in the morning, Ricki paid homage to the fall season by slipping into a vintage 1970s orange jumpsuit she'd found at her favorite resale shop, Good

Neighbor Thrift Store. She pulled her mass of thick light-brown curls into a high ponytail held in place by a brown scrunchie. After making sure the doggy door was accessible and bestowing kisses on Thor and Princess, Ricki headed out the door.

Kitty Kat Rousseau, her landlady and next-door neighbor in the attached double shotgun, leaned out her front window to wave at her. 'Happy almost Halloween!'

'Thank you.' Ricki noted the sixty-something hospice nurse's Wonder Woman headpiece and bustier. 'Getting an early start on the holiday?'

'I wear a different costume every week of the month. My patients love it. This week I'm . . .' Kitty Kat flexed her arms, revealing unexpected and impressive muscles. 'Wonder Woman.'

'You're that every week,' Ricki said with a warm smile. 'To me and your patients.'

Ricki made the short drive from her home to Bon Vee Culinary House Museum, the largest and most magnificent mansion in a district filled with spectacular historic homes. Built in 1867, Bon Vee was Italianate in style, featuring a showpiece curved portico graced with a half-dozen Doric columns. An intricate three-story gallery of cast iron added additional beauty to the east side of the home, which nestled among an acre of gardens ranging from a formal parterre to a lush and colorful array of tropical blooms. *I will never, ever get tired of this*, Ricki thought, drinking in the sight.

She parked her Prius in the small area allotted to staff and exited the car. As she crossed the verdant lawn, still wet with morning dew, Bon Vee's resident peacocks Gumbo and Jambalaya shrieked at her like they did every morning. Then suddenly something brushed her ankles.

Ricki shrieked. She whipped her head around, catching only a glimpse of a fast-moving blur. She shuddered. 'Please tell me that wasn't a rat,' she muttered as she strode towards the carriage house, which housed the staff offices and conference rooms upstairs in the estate's former staff quarters.

Ricki's Bon Vee friends were already there, helping themselves to donuts shaped like bats and ghosts and a carafe of coffee sporting the label *Ghostly Boo*.

'It's "boo" instead of "brew,"' Cookie explained through a

mouthful of donut. With her petite stature and shiny blonde pixie haircut, she looked more like a kid than an adult as she inhaled the donut.

'Boo, not brew. Cute.' Instead of claiming a whole bat donut, Ricki cut one into quarters and took a fourth, mindful of the weight she'd put on via a diet of deliciously rich Creole dishes.

'Cookie's proud of herself for that.' Ricki's friend Zellah said this in a tone tinged with amusement. An artist who also ran the Bon Vee café, Zellah liked to use herself as a canvas, painting decorations on various parts of her body. Today, beautifully detailed pumpkins gleamed from each cheek and she'd wrapped her hair in a tignon whose pattern also featured pumpkins.

'I did everyone a favor and created a spreadsheet of Halloween events in the city.' This came from Theo, the sole male in the room and self-styled Director of Community Relations, a job that allowed him to write off much of his socializing as 'business expenses.' For Ricki, Theo bounced between friend and frenemy, somehow always managing to redeem himself right when she was ready to throttle him. However, since her quest to find her birth family recently revealed Theo to be a long-lost cousin, she leaned toward cutting him slack.

'And . . . send.' Theo pressed a button on his laptop with a flourish and helped himself to a donut hole frosted to look like an eyeball. 'Check your inboxes for a Hallow-month schedule. You're welcome.'

Ricki sat down in one of the antique chairs surrounding the massive Victorian dining table, which served as the conference room centerpiece. She scrolled to Theo's email and perused the attached document. 'Yowie. This is a lot of events. Like, a ton of them. Every. Single. Day.'

'If you brag you're the most haunted city in America, you better bring it on Halloween,' Zellah said.

'Count me out of almost everything.' Lyla Brandt, Bon Vee's executive director and Ricki's immediate boss, took a glum sip of coffee. She adjusted one of her ever-present headbands, all of which somehow ended up sitting off-center on her salt-and-pepper bob. The good news for Lyla was that her errant teen daughter Kaitlyn had found something she was good at besides circumventing her parents' rules: volleyball. Unfortunately for Lyla, who'd never met a sport she liked or understood, there was a downside to Kaitlyn's newfound passion. 'Kaitlyn's travel team won't stop winning. We've got tournaments every weekend this month. If they keep going the way they're going, she may be playing volleyball through *November.*' Lyla's lower lip quivered.

'Sending love and sympathy,' Ricki said as she continued to scan Theo's spreadsheet. 'I see there's something happening at the BB.' She used the nickname for the Bayou Backyard, an indoor-outdoor bar on Tchoupitoulas that was up the street from Ricki and the group's favorite hangout. 'What's the Halloweenie Bar Crawl Challenge?'

'Only the best event ever,' Cookie declared, backed up by enthusiastic nods from the others. 'A bunch of bars join up all month for the challenge. Each bar also offers a contest where if you win, you and your group get comped for your entire bill. If you lose, you're a "Halloweenie."'

Theo held up his phone. 'You can download a Halloweenie app that's like a passport. You get a virtual set of vampire fangs for each bar you visit and if you go to all of them, you get a T-shirt that says, "I'm a Bar Challenge Halloweener."' He puffed out his chest. 'I've got five of them.'

'I bet you do,' Zellah said to Ricki's amusement.

'Speaking of the BB,' Cookie said to Ricki while sneaking one of the eyeball donut holes Theo had commandeered, 'any update from Virgil? Will he be here for Halloween?'

Ricki's good mood dissipated. Virgil, her across-the-street neighbor and co-parent to Thor and Princess, was a famed chef and part-owner of the Bayou Backyard. He was also on the verge of a romance with Ricki when he left town for his role as a judge on the reality show, *America's Next Top Southern Chef.* Aside from the occasional short text checking on their joint pets, Ricki hadn't heard from him since he departed. *I don't need a man, I'm perfect the way I am.* Ricki repeated the mantra to herself a few times. She'd found it helpful in pushing back against the loneliness that sometimes dogged her.

'I don't think Virgil's going to be in town,' Ricki said, dodging the first question about whether he'd been in touch with her. 'I doubt the show gives him time off to celebrate Halloween.'

Eager to change the subject, Ricki reached for the last donut hole, earning a 'Hey, those are mine!' from Theo. She ignored him. The donut holes had given her an idea. 'You guys, what if we set up a haunted house at Bon Vee? The old-fashioned kind where it's dark and there's spooky music and people put their hands into a bowl of grapes they think are eyeballs or spaghetti they think is brains?'

The others responded with an excited chorus of yesses. An enthusiastic Cookie bounced up and down in her chair. 'OMG, how much do I love this idea?! We can do two versions, one scary, one a super tame version for kids.' Cookie, who referred to herself as a recovering children's librarian ran Bon Vee's educational programming. 'I can supervise that.'

'Ooh, we gotta bring Mordant in on this. I can't wait to tell him.' Zellah rubbed her hands together with anticipation. Mordant led haunted history tours around New Orleans clad in a nineteenth century undertaker's outfit. He supplemented this with handyman jobs around Bon Vee. He'd been besotted with Zellah since first laying eyes on her and the two had recently . . . *finally*, in his eyes . . . started dating.

'Bon Veevil.' Everyone turned to look at Lyla, who dropped the title gem. 'That's what we can call it.'

Impressed, Theo nodded. 'Excellent. But we have to make sure we spell it in a way that people know how to pronounce it. "Bon Veevil" could make people think of boll weevil. If we put a dash after the V, they'd think it was "Bon Vee-evil."'

The group debated this. They'd landed on Bon *Veeevil* when Eugenia Charbonnet Felice entered the room, silencing the chatter. This was not intentional on Eugenia's part. The tall, aristocratic doyenne simply inspired respect. Not only did she basically run the place as president of the house museum's board, she was also the niece of Genevieve 'Vee' Charbonnet, the late revered New Orleans restauranteur. Determined to save Bon Vee, a home built and eventually lost by profligate Charbonnet ancestors, Miss Vee had bought the dilapidated mansion decades earlier and restored it to beyond its former glory. Turning the home into a culinary house museum after she passed was Eugenia's way of paying homage to the local icon and aunt she adored.

The same DNA tests that linked Ricki to Theo had also

connected her to Eugenia – and revealed Ricki to be the great-granddaughter of Miss Vee, a woman once assumed to be childless. But even that impressive genealogical credential didn't stop Ricki from sometimes being tongue-tied in Eugenia's presence.

'Apologies for missing the Almost Halloween celebration,' the board president said. She held up a stack of mail with a perfectly manicured hand. 'The paperwork involved with running an historic non-profit never seems to end.'

'We're out of donuts, but Ricki had a great idea,' Lyla piped up. She'd been Ricki's champion since day one, earning the shop owner's eternal gratitude. She pitched the possibility of a haunted house to Eugenia, ending with, 'And we can call it Bon V*eeevil*,' which she delivered in a dark, sonorous tone.

No one drew a breath while they waited for a thumbs-up or down from Eugenia. As she stood there contemplating the idea, it occurred to Ricki she resembled a Greek statue – if the statue had been carved to honor genteel Uptown landed gentry who favored the beige Chanel suit they would be able to wear for time immemorial because it never went out of style.

'I like it,' Eugenia announced. The Bon Vee staff's collective sigh of relief was strong enough to send a few napkins on the table wafting off into the air. 'We'll host it the last two weeks of the month. We can create a path through the first floor where people can see themed tableaus inside a few rooms on the first floor but focus most of the event outside. Bon Vee will offer limited tours during the day, but if Ricki is willing, we can keep the gift shop open during evening tours. Out of respect for the residential neighborhood, there will only be two slots per night, one at six p.m. and one at eight p.m. We'll close from four thirty to five forty-five for a staff dinner break and to prepare for the tours. I'll make arrangements with St Aquilinus for guest parking. I'm sure the Charbonnet family's donations over the last century and a half have earned a bit of good will. And Garden District residents will receive free admission with proof of address. Any questions?'

There was a beat, then a chorus of no's from the staff.

Eugenia gave a nod, then began deftly slicing open mail with an antique letter opener. 'Ricki, since this was your idea, you take the lead on it. But I expect everyone to pitch in and make this the fundraiser Bon Vee truly needs.'

She extracted what appeared to be a business letter from an envelope. She glowered at the letter and blurted a profanity made more shocking by the fact it came from her. 'Did Eugenia just drop an f-bomb?' Cookie whispered to Ricki, who responded with a wide-eyed nod.

'Everything OK, Aunt Eugenia?' Theo asked, concerned.

'No, it is not OK.' Infuriated, Eugenia thrust the letter out in front of her, wrinkling her nose as if it smelled. 'It's another complaint from the lawyers representing our mysterious new neighbors next door.'

Someone had recently – and unexpectedly – bought Duncan-Sejour, the mansion next door to Bon Vee and the second largest home in the Garden District. Since the buyer listed for the sale was an LLC and not an individual, no one knew who the new owners were, but they'd already created enmity with a string of complaints in the mere weeks they'd owned the place.

Eugenia gave the paper in her hand an angry shake. 'Every letter they send threatens legal action. Now they're saying we're exceeding the limit of our trash allowance by one bin and threatening to "take action".'

Eugenia mimed air quotes, then crumpled the letter into a ball and dropped it in a trash can. 'I'm not going to waste my lawyer's time with this. I've made sure Bon Vee meticulously observes the requirements for maintaining the non-profit culinary house. If the new owners of Duncan-Sejour are worried about garbage in the neighborhood, they'd best start by looking in the mirror.'

'Did Eugenia just literally trash-talk?' Cookie said under breath to Ricki, who responded with another wide-eyed nod as the Bon Vee matriarch marched out of the conference room.

Theo watched his aunt leave. 'Uh oh.'

Cookie eyed him. 'What?'

Theo pursed his lips. 'If the Duncan-Sejourers are threatening legal action over a trash bin, they're gonna go into overdrive when they hear we're planning a haunted house.'

TWO

Theo's concern proved prescient. News of the upcoming haunted house dates sparked a flurry of letters threatening a smorgasbord of legal repercussions if Bon Vee didn't cancel the whole event. Fortunately for Bon Vee, the threats from an upstart newcomer had the opposite effect on the closeknit Garden District community. Supportive flyers blanketed the neighborhood and local businesses trumpeted the news on their websites.

Ricki ignored the drama. She had a haunted house to create and a business to run. She and her cohorts kicked off their hunt for spooky props in Bon Vee's attic, a creepy location in and of itself. 'Great-aunt Vee did this place up for every holiday,' Theo said. 'There has to be a crate of skeletons and fake crows around here somewhere.' As he pushed aside ancient steamer trunks and furniture detritus, he spoke through one of the masks they all wore to protect against questionable dust particles dating back almost two centuries.

'I was hoping I could find a costume,' Cookie said, 'but I don't think Miss Vee ever dressed as a hot nurse or hot flight attendant.'

'You need a costume that's in keeping with the theme,' Ricki said. 'If you're going to be a hot anything, make it a hot ghost or witch.'

Cookie stiffened. 'Not a witch. Never a witch. No witches. *Ever.*'

'OK,' Ricki said, taken aback by Cookie's reaction. 'Sorry.'

'No worries.' Cookie resumed her usual cavalier attitude, but Ricki sensed it was a cover. 'Hey, you know how you thought we should do a Halloween-related cooking class for the kids? I'm officially approving it as Director of Educational Programming.'

'Thank you.' Ricki opened a battered old trunk, waving away the cloud of dust it generated. 'Except I can't get anyone to run it because Virgil is MIA and no one can cook except Zellah and she's too busy running the café.'

'We never needed to cook 'cuz our moms and grandmamas did,' Theo said. 'Ah, found the crows.' He held up an old crow, extracted from a bag of them. He brushed off the feathers it shed. 'And you're one to talk, Ricki. Your whole business is selling cookbooks and kitchen junk and *you* don't cook.'

'True,' she admitted. 'I love the history of the cookbooks and how they're a window into our past. The cooking part, not so much.'

'Anyhoo . . .' Cookie regained control of the conversation while unearthing a bag of skeletons and assorted fake bones. 'I thought of a project that doesn't require cooking. Marshmallow ghost lollipops. We get bamboo skewers, the kids stick marshmallows on them, and then use frosting to make ghost expressions. You know, like that famous painting, "The Scream."' Cookie affected a horrified expression, mimicking Edvard Munch's legendary work.

It was Ricki's turn to stiffen. 'No!' She blurted this, then tried to back off. 'No witches for you, no marshmallows for me.'

Theo shot Cookie a look. 'Thoughtless much?'

Cookie winced. 'Ricki, I'm so sorry. I wasn't thinking about the whole Chris thing.'

'It's OK. Don't worry about it. Really.' Ricki managed a smile. 'Let's get this over with before we catch an old-timey disease from whatever's floating around in the air here.'

Ricki tried to concentrate on mining the trunk in front of her for haunted house paraphernalia. But she couldn't shake the memory of getting the awful call from her estranged husband's best friend Blaine, who delivered the terrible news that Chris had died. A frustrated actor, Chris had found fame on the internet as Chriz-*azy!*, an influencer whose motto was 'No stunt too stupid!' Or too dangerous, as it turned out. Egged on by Blaine, Chris wound up choking to death after stuffing his mouth with too many marshmallows in response to a dare.

Ricki pushed aside a pile of old, homely drapes and saw what appeared to be a black gown cut on the bias. She carefully extracted the gown and held it up to show the others. 'I found a costume.' She gestured to the silky bell-cut black sleeves whose jagged hems matched the jagged hem of the dress. 'I think this is a female vampire's dress.' She leaned into the trunk and pulled out a matching full-length black cape lined in blood red with a stiff high collar. 'It's definitely a vampire outfit.'

'If it fits, you found your haunted house costume,' Cookie said.

'I wonder if there are any accessories in here.' Ricki rummaged through what was left in the trunk. 'Nope. Wait. What's this?' Ricki reached in and removed a faded and battered navy-blue leather ledger – a bookkeeping journal from Charbonnet's, the family's legendary restaurant that was still a hugely popular destination in the city's French Quarter. She opened the journal carefully, mindful of the brittle pages crumbling into decades-old confetti.

'That doesn't help us with the haunted house,' Cookie pointed out.

'I know but it may help me track down my great-grandfather.' Ricki gently turned a page. 'It dates back to the early 1950s. That lines up chronologically. Miss Vee told Eugenia he was an Irish busboy. Maybe there's a name in here.'

'Let's put a pin in the genealogy search, OK? The sooner we're done here, the sooner we avoid catching bubonic plague or yellow fever or whatever freakish diseases are lurking in the walls.' Theo eyed what appeared to be a large sack. 'Why did Aunt Vee have what looks like a crash test dummy?'

'No idea, but I'm sure we can use it somewhere.' Ricki closed the book and stood up. She heard a scuffling sound and froze. 'Did you hear that?' The others nodded. 'This place is either haunted or got mice. Let's make tracks.'

The three grabbed their respective hauls and hurried out of the attic, the bookkeeping journal tucked under Ricki's arm.

Given the deadline bearing down on Bon Vee's haunted house, Ricki shelved the Charbonnet's restaurant bookkeeping journal and spent the next week and a half alternating between running her shop and helping to morph Bon Vee's elegant parlors, library, and dining room into Halloween tableaus. The staff managed to do this while deflecting a barrage of complaints hurled at them from whoever now owned Duncan-Sejour.

Still, the situation had everyone on edge, particularly the newest docents, a retired set of twins named Benny and Jenny. Tours at Bon Vee were led by a combination of volunteer docents and paid tour guides, who were mostly knowledgeable locals who could use the small amount of extra cash it added to their coffers. Both groups were a mixed lot of quirky personalities. Benny and Jenny were proof positive of this.

'Did you see this? Did you?!'

Benny, his round face bright red with rage, thrust a letter in Ricki's face. He and Jenny had been assigned to help Ricki stock a recent collection of cookbooks donated by the estate of a local gastronome. But the two had marched into the shop with a different agenda: complaining about the enemy next door.

With their short, rounded bodies and matching grey haircuts, the twins, who were in their mid-sixties, were as close to identical as twins of different genders could be. They'd vowed to wear a different costume every day in October and so far had managed this odd feat, culling their wardrobe from a wide array of matching costumes they stored in a climate-controlled warehouse. Today they were dressed in identical scout uniforms.

Ricki read the letter, which documented a noise complaint registered with the city. 'They're saying the tour guides are too loud and are disturbing the peace? That's nuts.' Angry on the guides' behalf, Ricki shook a fist in the direction of Duncan-Sejour, which stood behind a row of ten-foot-high hedges across from the Bon Vee parlor that now housed Ricki's shop. She handed the letter back to Benny. 'Give it to Eugenia. She's already sent a stack of complaints to her lawyer, who's nice enough to handle them all pro bono.'

'Did you know Duncan-Sejour wasn't even for sale?' Jenny mirrored her brother's anger. 'Our mama knows someone who knows someone who knows the Duncan-Sejour real estate agent. A secret buyer made an offer too good for the owners to refuse. They signed a contract saying they can't reveal the name of the buyer who's hiding behind that LLC corporation thing.'

'I hadn't heard that,' Ricki said, wondering how old the twins' mother could possibly be and giving her props for still being keyed into the New Orleans gossip grapevine.

Benny held up the letter again. 'We're not the only ones who got trouble from them today. They sent a food inspector to shut down the café.'

'*What?!*' Furious on café owner Zellah's part, Ricki shouted this.

'Shhh.' The twins each held up an index finger to their lips, Jenny adding, 'Just in case sound travels through the shop windows.'

'Would you mind running the shop without me for a little while? I want to go see if Zellah needs any backup.'

'No problem,' the twins responded in unison.

Ricki strode out of the shop, down the antique Oriental rug that ran the length of the mansion's main gallery. A woman, on a mission, she ignored the rainbows cast by the crystal prisms dangling from a massive chandelier and threw open the French doors that led outside at the end of the hallway. Peacocks Gumbo and Jambalaya, who usually loved bullying the staff, sensed her anger and stood down.

She found Zellah boxing up sandwiches in the café, which was housed in Bon Vee's former pool pavilion. Miss Vee had replaced the pool with a slate patio decades earlier after a few too many guests danced into it during her famous liquor-soaked Mardi Gras parties.

Ricki craned her neck to search the café area. 'Where's the health inspector? I want to make sure he knows he was dragged out here on false pretenses.'

'No worries. He knows. But I appreciate the support.' Zellah held up pastry in a wax paper bag. 'He left with a veggie muffaletta and two of these pecan hand pies. It's been slow today, so I'm boxing up the rest of this to bring over to St Aquilinus.'

'I'll help you carry it.'

Ricki hefted a cardboard box of goodies and the women headed down the side yard to the street. 'We have to do something about Duncan-Sejour but I don't know what. Considering we haven't done squat to antagonize them and they're still making our lives miserable, I'm afraid confronting them could only make things worse.'

'Truth. Best to leave it to Eugenia and let her throw her "my family's been in N'Awlins for two hundred years and you don't get to mess with me" weight around. Speaking of the grand dame . . .'

Zellah gestured to the Bon Vee front entrance, where Eugenia was waving to them. They paused to let her approach.

'Ricki, I wanted to get back to you about the Charbonnet journal.' Eugenia smoothed down an invisible wrinkle on her St John knit skirt. 'The investigator I hired to help locate your birth parents was going to take a look at it but he was felled by a minor heart attack. His wife blames it on too much rich food.'

'Him and the rest of the city,' Zellah deadpanned.

'I'm on the hunt for a replacement,' Eugenia continued. 'I've seen a man around the neighborhood who has the look of ex-law enforcement. I assume one of our neighbors hired him for a bit of extra security, given the rise in crime. I keep missing him, so if either of you see him, would you mind getting his card? If he doesn't do investigations himself, he might be able to recommend someone.'

'Absolutely,' Ricki said. She hesitated, then said, 'And thank you. For helping me.'

'Of course. We're family.'

Eugenia cleared her throat to divest herself of emotion, then turned and headed back inside.

Zellah stared after her. 'Am I seeing things or was there a hint of a glimmer of humanity in the Ice Queen?'

'Hey, that's my cousin you're talking about,' Ricki said with a grin.

Zellah shook her head, bemused. 'Lord help you.'

They crossed the street to St Aquilinus, where a grateful Father Gabriel accepted Zellah's donations. 'I'll share these with the "grungy attendees" at our twelve-step meetings,' he told the women as they packed the goodies into the worn refrigerator housed in the church's modest parish room.

Ricki pursed her lips. '"Grungy attendees," huh? I can guess where that description came from.'

The priest sighed. 'The new residents of Duncan-Sejour don't seem to understand that the meetings bring in a bit of much-needed extra income, given that church attendance isn't what it once was. But also, the meetings are important to the community. Yes, there are income-challenged attendees. But there are also upscale locals who need the meetings. Addiction doesn't make class distinctions.'

'No, it does not,' Ricki said, her response heartfelt. Many of Chris's performer friends had struggled with alcohol or drug abuse.

The women left St Aquilinus for Bon Vee. Ricki glanced across the street and noticed a middle-aged man leaning against a car. He wore jeans and a sport coat that didn't close over his generous gut and his jaw moved with a rhythm that indicated he was chewing gum. 'I've seen that man around lately. I think he may be the security guy Eugenia mentioned. I'm going to ask.'

'Go for it,' Zellah said. 'I'm done for the day and I promised Dad I'd take the late shift at the deli.' Zellah's family owned the Peli Deli, a beloved local convenience store-cum-sandwich shop.

Ricki crossed the street. She gave the stranger a small wave, which he acknowledged with a nod. 'Hi, I'm Ricki James-Diaz. I run Miss Vee's Vintage Cookbooks and Kitchenware, the gift shop at Bon Vee. The board president has seen you in the neighborhood and wondered if someone hired you for private security.'

'They did.' The man took a foil gum packet out of his pocket. He spit a wad of gum into an empty foil packet, then popped out a new gum square. 'Smoker quitting gum. It ain't the same as the real thing.' He popped the new square into his mouth and extended a hand to Ricki. 'Bob "Bobby" Grimes. Private security and investigations.'

'Ah.' Ricki hid her amusement at the Southern predilection towards nicknames, however basic they might be. 'A private investigator is exactly what Eugenia is looking for. It's a long story but basically she's helping me track down my birth family and she needs to hire someone. Are you interested?'

Bob 'Bobby' cracked his gum. 'I would be but I can't. Conflict of interest.'

Ricki wrinkled her brow, confused. 'I don't understand.'

The PI lifted his index finger a centimeter. Ricki followed his gaze across the street. She sucked in a breath, then whipped her head around to face Grimes. 'Are you telling me the new owners of Duncan-Sejour hired you to spy on *us*? At *Bon Vee*?'

'Like they'd say during criminal investigations at my old precinct, I can neither confirm nor deny that. But . . .' The PI winked at Ricki, then cracked his gum.

'That's it,' Ricki muttered, fuming. 'That is *it*.'

She stormed across the street and threw open the filigreed cast iron gate fronting Duncan-Sejour and stalked up the front path to the mansion's carved double doors which sat dead center between its half-dozen fat white fluted columns. She banged on one door and then the other, determined to continue until someone answered. 'Stop or I'll call the police!' a woman yelled from inside.

'Go ahead!' Ricki yelled back. 'This is Miracle James-Diaz from Bon Vee Culinary House Museum and I have friends on the NOPD force, so make that call and see where it gets you!'

Calling detectives Nina Rodriguez and Sam Girard her friends was a reach considering she'd mostly annoyed them by insinuating herself into a couple of their murder investigations, but the person on the other side of the door didn't need to know that.

'Ricki?' One of the heavy double doors suddenly swung open. A young woman in the ballpark of Ricki's twenty-eight years stood in front of her, clad in an oversized gray sweater over black leggings and Van's sneakers. She wore her auburn hair long and loose, and a diamond stud decorated each nostril. The tattoo of a shooting star jutted out above the sweater neckline.

'Do I know you?' Ricki asked, thrown by the friendly greeting.

'No, but I've been wanting to meet you.'

'Oh.' This was starting to make sense. 'You're a Chris-Cross,' she said, referencing the name her late husband's fans gave themselves.

'Not really.'

'Oh-kay.' Ricki went back to being puzzled.

'Sorry, I should introduce myself. *Duh*.' The girl fake-slapped her forehead. 'I'm Miranda. Miranda Fine. My boss knew your husband. He's the one who told me about you. This is his house. I'm his personal assistant.'

'And your boss is . . .' the mystified Ricki prompted.

'Blaine Taggart. The actor. The *movie star*.' Miranda delivered this with a smug smile. 'Maybe you've heard of him?'

A sick feeling roiled Ricki's stomach. She knew exactly who Blaine Taggart was. To the world, an A-list film star action hero. To her . . .

Blaine Taggart was the 'friend' who encouraged Chris's increasingly perilous stunts and filmed the one that killed him.

THREE

Blaine Taggart was Bon Vee's new next-door neighbor.
Ricki fought back nausea as she processed this development. Luckily, Miranda was too busy extolling her own virtues to notice Ricki's less-than-enthusiastic reaction. 'I'm actually way more than an assistant. I'm what I like to call a lifestyle manager. I make sure every aspect of Blaine's life is running smoothly while he's challenging himself to set the bar higher on his fab film stunts.' She giggled. 'He's extreme off the set too. Right now, he's free-soloing in Yosemite. That's when you climb without ropes. At least I think he is. He may have finished that and gone motorcycling in Mongolia. Whatevs. Anyhoo, nice to meet you. We need to get together sometime. There's tons to talk about. We have a lot in common.'

Miranda winked, which Ricki found odd, then went to close the door. Ricki stuffed down her emotions about the news the man she held responsible for Chris's death had moved in next door and thrust out an arm to block Blaine's 'lifestyle manager' from retreating inside. 'I need to talk to you *now*. I met the private eye you hired to spy on us at Bon Vee and look for problems you can try to blow up into issues.' She waved a hand at Duncan-Sejour and then to Bon Vee. 'Neither of these houses is going anywhere, so we need to find a way to peacefully co-exist.'

Miranda wrinkled her nose. Sunlight bounced off the diamond stud in her left nostril. 'Yeah . . . that's gonna be hard. Aside from all the issues . . . you know, noise. Garbage.' She faltered searching for other imaginary problems. 'And general other stuff, the bigger concern is a star of Blaine's magnitude living in the *second* largest house in the District.'

All the pieces puzzling Ricki about why Duncan-Sejour's new owner would harass Bon Vee suddenly locked into place. What better way to put the house museum out of business than barrage it with nuisance complaints, then make a low-ball offer to buy it, trading up from the *second*-largest house in the neighborhood to the largest?

'Bon Vee isn't for sale and won't be for sale,' Ricki said through tight lips, 'so your boss will either have to live with his decision, add on to Duncan-Sejour to make it the biggest home in the District if it's so important to him, or sell. I know for a fact Blaine has houses all over the place. LA, New York, London, and who knows where else. I don't understand why he bought this house to begin with.'

'I know, right?' Miranda sniffed with distaste. 'New Orleans is so nowhere. Nice meeting you! Bye.'

Miranda moved too fast for Ricki to intercede. The oak door slammed shut.

Ricki returned to Miss Vee's in a daze. She tended to a couple of customers who wandered in, selling them spiral-bound community cookbooks dating back to the 1960s that contained recipes culled from local church groups. But her mind was on her exchange with Miranda. The revelation about Blaine felt surreal. After Chris's death, she assumed she'd never see him again. Now he was the guy you borrowed sugar from next door. On top of that, Miranda hadn't seemed remotely interested in ending her campaign of harassment aimed at Bon Vee. *That was the world's worst conversation on every level*, Ricki thought glumly.

Her phone pinged a text. Her spirits lifted when she saw the sender was the amusingly named Lady Foucault, the manager of her favorite thrift store who'd become a friend. **I got goodies for you**, Ricki read. **Come on down**! Ricki checked to see if the twins had sold any tickets for the last tour of the day. Finding none, she decided to close up and drop by Lady's place of business, Good Neighbor Thrift Store.

Before locking the mullioned glass French doors enclosing Miss Vee's, Ricki took a moment to drink in the shop's beauty: the sunny location at the front of the home; the cheerful interior of pale green damasked-covered walls and white, ornately carved crown molding; the wingback chairs in front of the bay's window seat, all newly upholstered in a soft peach velvet; the rows of bookcases hosting a colorful array of vintage cookbooks, some over a hundred years old; the antique desk that served as a pay station; the round formal dining table in the room's center where a display of Halloween-themed books and gadgets sat ready to entice shoppers. This was *her* place. *Her* business. 'And no egotistical actor who needs a big house to make up for other inadequacies is gonna put me out of business,' Ricki said out loud to the air . . . and hopefully the universe.

Late afternoon traffic was its usual horrific self, especially at the clog where Carrollton Avenue slid under the I-10 overpass. It took twenty minutes but Ricki finally got through it. She made a left when she reached Tulane Avenue, passing blocks of nondescript storefronts and thrift stores until she reached Good Neighbor.

She exchanged cheerful greetings with the cashier working the register when she entered the store. Ricki had gotten to know the employees through her frequent vintage treasure-hunting trips there. She wound her way through racks of used clothing to the shop's back corner, where she poked her head into the stockroom.

Lady was cleaning a donated toaster-oven with a hand vacuum. She sensed Ricki's presence and turned off the vacuum. She greeted Ricki with a wide grin. 'Well, hey there, girl.'

Finding Lady's good humor infectious, Ricki grinned back. 'Hey yourself. What happened to the braids?'

'Too much work. And they were *heavy*. The headaches I'd have by day's end, I cannot tell you.' Lady patted her soft cloud of black hair. 'Natural works way better for me.' She put down the vacuum and picked up a medium-sized cardboard box from a shelf. 'I got old decorative items in there, pumpkins and such, that'll work with the holiday. Halloween-themed cookbooks were hard to come by. I checked in with managers from other stores. No one had anything earlier than the 1990s.' Lady handed the box over.

'I've found the same thing,' Ricki said. 'Specific holiday cookbooks weren't a thing in the past. Even for Christmas.' She examined the box's contents. 'I like the orange tablecloth. I can use that under my display.' She extracted a magazine-style cookbook whose cover featured cupcakes decorated to resemble black cats and checked the publication date. 'This is from 2000. The whole Y2K thing was pretty creepy. That kind of works with the theme. What do you think?'

Lady gave her a thumbs-up. 'I vote yes. Now, tell me what's bothering you.'

Ricki gaped at her. 'You really do have the sense, don't you?'

'Me and every other woman in my family. So?'

Feeling her emotions well up yet again, Ricki took a beat. Then she detailed her run-in with Miranda that culminated in the traumatic reveal of Duncan-Sejour's new owner. 'The strange thing is, the more I think about it, the more it feels like Blaine destroying Bon Vee so he can eventually buy it and own the biggest mansion in the Garden District doesn't feel like something he'd do. I mean, he's got a lot of bad traits. A *lot*. He's selfish, arrogant, conceited, competitive, at least in his career. He's definitely into things like crazy-expensive sports cars and motorcycles. But I never got that he cared much about where he lived. His LA house isn't even very big. Same with his New York apartment. I can't figure why he bought a place here. And a big one too, even if it's only the "*second* largest."' She mimicked Miranda to perfection.

'Hmmm.' Lady pondered this as she and Ricki walked from the stockroom to the checkout counter. 'You know, there is one thing Bon Vee has that the other Garden District mansions don't.'

Ricki placed the box on the counter. 'What?'

'A smart, pretty, sensitive gift shop proprietor.' Lady pointed both index fingers at Ricki. 'You.'

Ricki often joked that Thor and Princess were as much support animals as beloved pets, but even nestled between them, she wrestled with sleep that night. She found Lady's inference disturbing.

Like so many attractive, charismatic actors who'd come before him and those who would come after, Blaine was a giant flirt. 'But after what happened with Chris, he has to know better than to flirt with me,' she said to Princess. The shepherd mix responded by passing gas. Ricki made a face. 'Ugh. We need to change your food.' Ricki decided to dismiss Lady's theory and went to bed, negotiating a safe distance between her and the flatulent canine.

In the morning, after tending to the dogs, she slipped into jeans and a T-shirt emblazoned with the word 'Batitude' and set off for work. New Orleanians never met a holiday they didn't celebrate wholeheartedly, and Ricki drove by homes decorated with a variety of pumpkins, skeletons, witches, ghosts and vampires. One historic home boasted a ghost-pumpkin mashup, with ghoulish white pumpkins embedded on every finial of the iron fence surrounding the property.

The entertaining ride put Ricki in a good mood. But she came to a screeching halt in front of Bon Vee, stunned by what she saw. 'What the actual . . .' she muttered.

The city had allowed her to designate a parking spot on the street for customers visiting her shop. Now the 'Miss Vee's Vintage Cookbook and Kitchenware Shop' sign she'd had made was gone, replaced by a 'No Parking' sign. The length of the curb in front of Bon Vee still glistened with red paint.

Ricki let out a stream of profanity, then zipped into her regular parking spot by the staff offices. She slammed the door of her Prius shut and stormed up the stairs to the small staff lounge.

Cookie and Theo were already there, Cookie practically jumping out of her skin with excitement. 'Ricki, OMG, you won't believe who our new neighbor is. Blaine Taggart! It's all over OhNo!La.'

She held up her phone to show the city's gossip app. Ricki ignored it. 'I know all about it. For the record, Blaine Taggart was my husband Chris's best friend. He felt guilty that his career took off and Chris's didn't, so he encouraged Chris's whole Chriz-*azy!* act because it made Chris his own kind of famous. Blaine's the one who filmed Chris's last video, the marshmallow stunt that killed him.'

'Oh,' Cookie said, deflated. 'I'm sorry.'

'I went over to Duncan-Sejour yesterday,' Ricki continued, 'and met Blaine's personal assistant, who's a piece of work. Obviously nothing I said to her got through *because have you seen the curb outside Bon Vee*?' Infuriated, she gestured with both hands towards the windows facing the street.

'No,' Theo said, going to the window. 'I came in off the alley.'

'Me too.'

Cookie followed him and the two gazed down at the street below. 'Sonuva . . .' Theo murmured.

Ricki grabbed each of their arms. 'It's time for a come-to-Jesus with this personal assistant. I need you both for backup.'

She half-dragged Cookie and Theo with her out of the offices to the street, where they marched next door to Duncan-Sejour. Ricki pounded on one of the mansion's front doors. 'It's Ricki! Open up, Miranda! *Now*.'

The door opened. Miranda leaned against the other door, her stance casual. 'Hey. What's up?'

'You know exactly what's up,' Ricki said, steaming. 'Who do you think you are, painting the curb red? It's illegal and we will fight you on it. On everything you're doing to make Bon Vee and our lives miserable. Right, you guys?'

'Right,' Theo said with a vigorous nod.

Cookie said nothing. She stared at Miranda, open-mouthed. 'M-m-miranda? Miranda Fine?'

'Yeah.' Miranda looked back at her, confused. 'Do I know . . .' Her face cleared as something dawned on her. 'Oh, wow. It's not . . . Effie? Effie Mae Yanover? Is that you?' Cookie clapped her mouth shut and gave a mute nod. Miranda smirked. 'I didn't recognize you at first. I forgot that this . . .' She mimed a hook nose. 'Became this . . .' She pressed a finger to the tip of her nose and pushed it up. 'No more "Wicked Witch of Westwego."'

Cookie gulped. Then she suddenly let out a roar and lunged for Blaine Taggart's personal assistant.

FOUR

Miranda screamed. Then she reciprocated, throwing her own punches. Ricki tried to separate the women while Theo stood frozen in place. 'Theo, help!'

Theo snapped out of it. Galvanized into action, he managed to yank Cookie away and hold back Miranda, who kept swinging. 'Get Cookie back to Bon Vee,' he said, struggling to control Miranda. 'I'll handle this one.'

Ricki pulled a weeping Cookie down the mansion's limestone front steps and out the front yard back towards Bon Vee. She draped a comforting arm around her friend's shoulder as she led her into Miss Vee's, which was not yet open for business.

She sat Cookie down on one of the wingback chairs and fetched a water from the mini fridge under her desk. 'Here.' Ricki opened the bottle and handed it to Cookie. 'You could also use tissues.'

Cookie took a few from a box on the small table that sat between the chairs. 'Thanks,' she said, her voice thick with tears. She wiped her eyes with one tissue and blew her nose with another.

Ricki sat down in the wing chair opposite Cookie. 'Do you want to talk about it?'

Cookie took a big gulp of water. She drew in a breath, then said, 'If you didn't figure it out from what Miranda did back there . . .' Cookie copied Miranda's taunting illustration of a hook nose, 'I was born with a really ugly nose. Miranda was a couple of years behind me in high school but that didn't stop her from being the queen bee of all queen bees of the high school. The first time she saw me in the hallway, she went, "Oh no! It's the Wicked Witch of Westwego!" Her exact words. I've never forgotten them.'

Ricki felt terrible for her friend. 'That's why you didn't want to dress like a witch for our haunted house.'

Cookie gave a slight nod. 'The nickname stuck all through the rest of high school. I never dated. I barely had friends.' She looked down at the floor. 'I shouldn't have cared. I shouldn't have let her and the others get to me. But I did. I got part-time jobs like babysitting and working at the local dollar store, saved up my money, and got a nose job before college.'

Ricki got up and went to hug her friend. 'So? It's not like you're the only person on earth who ever got one. Nature isn't always right. I think this is the nose you were meant to have.'

Cookie shrugged. 'Maybe.'

Ricki put her hands on Cookie's shoulders and looked her in the eye. 'And let's be very clear about something. If there's any witch around here, it's that beeyotch Miranda.'

Cookie had to laugh at this. 'Oh, she is *such* a beeyotch. Hasn't changed at all.' She gave Ricki a tremulous smile. 'Thanks.'

'Of course.' Ricki returned to her chair. 'So . . . Effie Mae, huh?'

Cookie groaned. 'I know. My mother insisted I be named after one of her way-back ancestors who was apparently the very first Miss Sugar Cane Queen in some parish. Her beat-up old tiara is mom's most treasured possession. Dad hated the name and called me Cookie from birth.' She took a sip of water. 'I was much closer to my dad.'

Theo sauntered into the shop. 'Handled it.' Preening, he ran a hand over his sandy, rapidly thinning hair. 'I apologized on your behalf,' he said, oblivious to Cookie's glower, 'and offered to take Miranda to dinner. I've never seen two women go at it before like y'all did.' Proud of himself, he folded his arms in front of his chest and leaned back against the shop desk.

'If either the word sexy or catfight comes out of your mouth,' Cookie said through clenched teeth, 'I will remove your liver and sell it on the dark web.'

'I never would have guessed Miranda was from here,' Ricki mused. 'She seems so LA. I knew a lot of people like her there.'

'Nope,' Cookie said. 'She's Westwego born and bred.'

'That's such a weird name for a place.'

Theo reached into Ricki's mini fridge and helped himself to one of her waters. 'When they built a railroad in the 1800s heading west from there, supposedly the conductor would yell, "West, we go!"'

'I guess Miranda took the name to heart because West she

went.' Ricki stood up. 'The first tour starts soon. I need to get ready for customers.'

Cookie also rose. 'We have to meet with Lyla and Eugenia and go over our haunted house duties. You know what, if they want me to dress like a witch, I'll do it. I'll just make sure to stay out of Miranda's eye line.'

'You don't have to.' Ricki reached under her desk and retrieved the bag where she'd stored Miss Vee's female vampire costume. She handed it to Cookie. 'You be Vampira. I'll be a witch. It'll be easier for me. Black leggings, tunic, and a cheapo witch's hat.'

Cookie gave her a grateful hug. 'You are the best.' She raised an arm in a salute. 'East we go, to our meeting.' She dropped her arm. 'At least I think it's east. I've lived in New Orleans my whole life and I couldn't tell you the direction of anything.'

'It's this city,' Theo said. 'You gotta go east to get to the West Bank. New Orleans is all kinds of crazy.'

He and Cookie left, crossing paths with the day's first tour group, who happily proved to be vintage cookbook enthusiasts. As Ricki waited on them, she thought about Theo's comment. She'd define New Orleans' 'all kind of crazy' as much more endearing and affable than the crazy Miranda seemed to have imported from Hollywood. Ricki knew from growing up in LaLaLand that there was a high turnover among celebrity home-owners. Along with the financial ups and downs that mirrored their level of popularity, they tended to quickly bore of their residences. She hoped the same would be true of Blaine Taggart. *Maybe we'll get lucky and he'll move out before he ever moves in*, Ricki thought hopefully.

By the last tour of the day, Ricki had sold almost two dozen cookbooks, including the Halloween-themed remnant of the Y2K era, along with a vintage flour sifter and set of salt and pepper shakers shaped like a male and female zombies. She was closing up when she got a text from Eugenia summoning her to the conference room. The curt tone of the text made Ricki nervous.

She hurried to the conference room, where she found Eugenia, Cookie, and Theo already there, the latter two appearing perplexed. That's when Ricki noticed an unexpected fourth meeting attendee.

Detective Nina Rodriguez lounged in one of the chairs, her long, slim legs stretched out in front of her. She wore her usual outfit of jeans, white T-shirt, and navy-blue blazer, with her thick black hair bundled into a tight bun at the back of her head. 'Hello there.'

Nina issued the greeting with the sardonic edge Ricki had come to expect from her. Owing to recent murders that involved Bon Vee, Ricki had spent more time with the detective than she ever expected to spend with a law enforcement official. If she didn't find Nina so intimidating, she'd almost call them friends.

'Hey! Hi there, Nina. Detective. Detective Nina.' Ricki stumbled through her response.

'Oh, we're way beyond all that,' the detective said with a languid wave of her hand. 'Nina is fine. At least for now.'

'So, why exactly are you here?' Cookie asked.

Leave it to Cookie to get right to the point, Ricki thought as she took a seat, appreciating that she'd asked what they were all thinking.

'Nobody's been killed here lately,' Cookie continued.

'That we know of,' Theo added. 'We haven't checked the dumpster today.' He laughed at his own joke. Eugenia stared him down and he shut up.

Nina drew in her legs and sat up straight, her demeanor change indicating it was time to get down to business. 'A Miranda Fine has filed a harassment order against you . . .' She indicated Theo.

'What?!' Theo, outraged, jumped to his feet.

Nina ignored him. 'And has requested a restraining order against all of you. Not you, ma'am.' She hastily directed the last statement to Eugenia.

'I would think not,' Eugenia replied, affronted.

Cookie balled up her fists. 'Oooh, that . . . that . . . I could just—'

Ricki cleared her throat loudly and made a cutting gesture with her hand to her neck. Cookie got the message. She unclenched her fists and affected a more casual attitude. 'You were saying, Detective?'

'I'm here because I'm required to pay a visit to the instigators.'

Now Ricki was outraged. 'We haven't instigated anything. It's all her. Miranda. She's the problem.' Ricki whirled around to face Eugenia. 'We need to file counter charges for harassment on her.'

'*Yes*,' Cookie seconded this with intensity. 'Let's take Miranda *down*.'

'I wasn't harassing her, I was flirting.' Theo sounded more hurt than hostile. 'I know the difference. I'm no hashtag-me-too. Well, not anymore.'

Eugenia held up her hand. 'We're not taking anyone down, whatever that means. We'll take a more subtle approach. We'll socially ostracize this woman and her immediate family.'

'Her people aren't from Upscale, I mean Uptown,' Cookie said. 'They're from Westwego.'

'Oh,' Eugenia responded, disappointed. 'Then that won't work at all. Detective Rodriguez, tell me more about those harassment charges.'

'Look, I don't know what's going on between you dueling mansion dwellers,' Nina said. 'But do not gum up the already gummed-up NOPD with more nuisance charges. We're shedding NOPD officers like clothes on a Bourbon Street stripper. Figure this one out for yourselves.' She rose. 'Personally, I've found a dead rat in the mailbox works wonders in getting people to back off.'

They waited until Nina had cleared the building, then Ricki, Theo, and Cookie all began venting at once. Eugenia raised a single eyebrow and the three immediately fell silent. 'Enough of this. We have a haunted house to get up and running. I'll have our lawyer talk to Duncan-Sejour's and see if they can negotiate a truce.'

'And if they can't?' Ricki asked, pessimistic.

'If they can't . . .' Eugenia's eyes narrowed. 'We go with the rat.'

FIVE

Unfortunately, as Ricki predicted, the lawyers failed to strike a deal. She managed to talk Eugenia out of having her gardener secure a dead rat and instead file a restraining order against the residents of Duncan-Sejour, with a court date thankfully set after Halloween and not before.

At least the dueling restraining orders forced Miranda and whoever was aiding and abetting her to put the brakes on. The Bon Vee staff used the lull in complaints to complete their haunted house.

Zellah's boyfriend Mordant had been called into service to help create the Bon Vee haunted house attractions, his skills as an electronics aficionado complementing Zellah's craftsy bent. She delivered the props while he employed a variety of projections that could be illuminated for evening tours. Together they turned Bon Vee's front parlor into a dark and creepy nineteenth-century mortuary, replete with the requisite bowls of grape 'eyeballs' and spaghetti 'brains.' Since he already had the costume for it, Mordant cast himself as the morgue undertaker, albeit one who was also a zombie. Zellah agreed to play his zombie wife.

The estate's dining room featured a repast of gray food created from papier-mâché by Zellah for the ghostly wedding reception of a nineteenth century bride left at the altar. Eugenia had suggested the setting, inspired by her love of Dickens' classic novel, *Great Expectations*. The Bon Vee conservatory became a simulated crime scene complete with the tape outline of a body and the library was cast as a home to a literary-minded family of vampires.

Mordant turned off the lights and flipped a switch in Ricki's shop-turned-witches lair. Images of gnarled trees flashed on the darkened bookcases, transforming the room into the dark recesses of a forest. A cauldron replaced the display table in the middle of the room, emitting bubbling sounds while a light mist simulating smoke issued from it.

'What do you think?' Mordant asked Ricki.

'It's amazing,' she said, surveying the scene. 'I hope my witching can do justice to it.'

'I'm pretty excited about it myself.' Mordant's long, preternaturally mournful face and solemn tone belied this, but Ricki knew him well enough to know he meant it. 'Everything in Bon Vee is designed for two levels of scary. You can tone it down for kids or pump it up for adults.'

'Perfect.'

'Wait until you see the tomb. I outdid myself.' Mordant delivered this in his usual monotone.

Ricki followed him to the side yard bordering Duncan-Sejour, where Mordant and Zellah had created a true haunted house masterpiece using a derelict shed Eugenia sweet-talked one of her upper crust pals into donating. Zellah's painting skills had transformed the shed into a facsimile of one of New Orleans' legendary above-ground tombs, replete with trompe l'oeil moss and the illusion of decaying bricks.

'Zellah, you're a genius,' Ricki said to the artist, who stood outside the ersatz tomb. 'I could swear this is one of the real tombs from Lafayette Cemetery.'

Zellah waved off the compliment. 'You think what I did is cool? Wait until you see what Mordant pulled off inside.' She gazed at her boyfriend with an expression full of pride, then pulled open the tomb entrance, which came complete with eerie squeak. She gestured for Ricki to step into the tomb, which she did.

'This is awesome,' Ricki said, voice laced with wonder. Cobwebs covered the tomb's dark walls. Bats were projected against the ceiling with the accompanying sound effects. A marble bench that usually sat in the center of Bon Vee's parterre garden now served as the final resting place for the crash test dummy unearthed in the estate's attic, which had been costumed like a nineteenth-century robber baron with a handlebar mustache and ridiculously large mutton chop sideburns.

'Everything is so wonderfully creepy except him,' Ricki noted of the dummy. 'Is that to tone it down for the kids?'

'Yup. This is Chauncey. Eugenia named him. He's the guy who stood up her character at the altar and she got revenge by poisoning him with foxglove or something else old-fashioned. Eugenia was going on and on about her character's backstory and I kinda drifted.'

'She's really getting into this,' Ricki said, relieved that Bon Vee's reserved, occasionally imperial capo di tutti capi had embraced the haunted house so fully.

Zellah chuckled. 'Apparently, she did some acting in high school and this is scratching that itch. But wait until you see what Mordant pulled off for the grownups. He's a dang genius.'

Zellah removed a small remote from the pocket of her artist's smock and pressed a button. The dummy slowly rose sitting. 'Help!' a male voice cried out. 'I'm not dead, I am alive! Get me out of here! Ring the bell! *Ring the bell!*'

Ricki listened, transfixed. Zellah gave her a slight nudge. '*I'm* supposed to ring . . .?'

'Yeah, that's why they put bells in the tombs in the olden days,' Zellah explained. 'In case someone wasn't really dead, they were just in a coma or something. The bell let people know whoever was inside the tomb was still alive and needed to be let out.'

Ricki pulled the string on an old bell dangling from the roof over the dummy. It rang. Then an evil laugh erupted from the speakers hidden in corners of the tomb. Startled, Ricki shrieked. 'I will never let you go,' a deep, threatening voice boomed. 'You're mine now. *Buh whaa ha ha!*'

The laugh grew louder, accompanied by moans and shrieks. White lights strobed, then turned bright orange as flames were projected onto all four walls of the tomb.

'This is terrifying.' Ricki clapped enthusiastically. 'Bravo.'

'People gonna scream their brains out,' Zellah said with satisfaction.

'Good. I hope they drive our neighbor Miranda crazy.' Ricki delivered this with vindictive pleasure. She opened the tomb door to leave, then felt the sudden sensation of something brushing up against her ankles and jumped back. 'Mordant even created a sense of touch? He really is a genius. What was that supposed to be? A low-flying bat?'

Zellah looked confused. 'I have no idea what you're talking about. If you felt something, that wasn't on Mordant.'

Ricki's eyes widened. 'No? Uh oh. I think Eugenia might have to put in a call to an exterminator.'

'It's either that,' Zellah said, 'or a ghost.'

She wasn't kidding.

SIX

Anticipation for the launch of Bon Vee's haunted house built – at least among the staff. Potential attendees seemed more interested in catching a glimpse of Blaine Taggart. This became apparent to Ricki after a day spent telling disappointed customers that no one at Bon Vee had laid eyes on him and they had no idea when he'd put in an appearance at the latest addition to his portfolio of homes.

Not that she was complaining. Manners still mattered in New Orleans, even among the tourists who visited Bon Vee, and curiosity seekers felt obligated to add a purchase to their queries. Sales at Miss Vee's Vintage Cookbook and Kitchenware Shop had never been better, necessitating a run on local thrift shops and estate sales to drum up more inventory.

The day before the official kickoff of Bon V*eeevil*, Ricki mapped out a shopping route and left Miss Vee's in the hands of college intern Olivia Felice for a few hours. Olivia also happened to be Eugenia's granddaughter and yet another of Ricki's recently acquired cousins.

It was almost closing time when Ricki returned to Bon Vee carrying bags laden with items she'd picked up combing through everything from resale shops to yard sales to a dumpster outside a home in Algiers that was being remodeled – the latter defining the old saying that one person's trash was another person's treasure.

She stopped to say to Zellah, who was painting headstones with scary images on one side and silly ones on the other to service both haunted house age groups. The artist/café owner stood up and lifted a corner of her smock to wipe off a streak of gray paint on her cheek. She gestured to Ricki's bags. 'Whatcha got there?'

'*Such* a cool haul,' Ricki enthused.

'It's cool but is it *awesome*? Or *epic*?' Zellah, like everyone at the house museum, liked to tease Ricki about her frequent use of California slang.

'Both,' Ricki responded playfully. She put the bags on the ground and showed off her haul. 'A couple of fall-themed cookbooks from the 1970s, a set of Halloween-shaped cookie cutters, and my favorite . . .' She held up a tea towel decorated with five appliqued bats hanging upside down. 'See what it says? "This family is a little batty."' She reached into a bag and took out a small, hand-painted tray in the shape of a bat. 'I can display these together with the cookie cutters and a cookbook.'

'Can I see that?' Ricki handed Zellah the tray and she examined it. 'Some critter got hold of one of the bats in the tomb and turned it into a chew toy. You mind if I buy this and use it as a replacement? It looks pretty indestructible.'

'Of course. And you're not buying anything. Consider it my small artistic donation to the tomb.'

'Much appreciated.' Zellah made the tray swoop like the bat was flying, abetted by appropriate bat flutter sounds. 'This little guy's got some serious *battitude* himself.'

Ricki struck a disco pose, one hand holding a bag facing up, the other facing down. 'He's where it's "bat."'

Zellah groaned. 'Hi yourself and your seventies puns to your shop, girl.'

Ricki laughed and obeyed the facetious order. She walked past flattened inflatable decorations that by tomorrow evening would fill the yard with ghosts, pumpkins, and spooky trees. After entering the mansion, she made an immediate left into her shop, where she found Olivia ensconced in the shop's bay window seat and staring out the window at Duncan-Sejour.

'Blaine Taggart isn't there,' Ricki said, depositing her bags under the shop desk.

Olivia released an exasperated grunt. 'Is he ever gonna show up? This is *so* annoying.'

Ricki began removing items from the bags. 'You have nine thousand apps on your phone. Isn't one of them the kind where you can track private jets? Use it to locate Blaine.'

She shelved several cookbooks and draped the bat tea towel over an errant tree branch recovered from the detritus deposited all over the Bon Vee grounds by a recent hurricane. Ricki had spray-painted the branch black and given it a second life as part of her Halloween display.

Olivia tore herself away from the window and turned to Ricki. 'You know Blaine Taggart. Can't you text him? Welcome him to the neighborhood or something. Isn't that what people who own houses do when someone buys a house near them?'

'I wouldn't know. I've never owned a house.' Ricki played with the branch's location, then placed it on the desk next to the vintage cash register that had become purely decorative since she'd transitioned to fully managing sales through a laptop and occasionally her phone. 'And as opposed to the rest of the city, I have zero desire to ever run into Blaine.'

'You get to call him by his first name. I'm *so* jealous.' Olivia twirled a thick strand of long golden hair, currently sporting highlights in her sorority colors of light blue and dark blue, around a finger as she pondered the situation. 'I did check an app. His plane route isn't on Flight Bite. Maybe he already landed and he's on his way here.' Grasping this ray of hope, she resumed staring out the window.

Ricki opened the mini fridge under her desk. 'You want something to eat? I never had a chance to grab lunch and I'm starving.' She took out a meal from the fridge's small freezer. 'I don't remember opening this. Weird.' She reached in but instead of a meal, pulled out a small jewelry box. 'What the . . .' She held the box up to Olivia. 'Hello. *Hello. Olivia* . . .' Having gotten her young cousin's attention, she held up the jewelry box. 'This isn't reduced-guilt macaroni and cheese.'

'Oh, right. My mom's gold earrings. I saw this really popular video about where to hide valuable stuff and that was one of the places. I wore them during a Rush event and then came straight here, so I stuck them there for safekeeping. Totally forgot about them.'

Ricki held up the empty macaroni and cheese box. 'What happened to the meal?'

'Um . . . I think I just threw it out. Sorry.' The twenty-year-old had the decency to look slightly ashamed.

Ricki strode over to Olivia and handed her the box. 'Bring the earrings home. And don't do that again without telling me. I'm closing up now. I'm tired and hungry. All I can think about is food.'

Olivia jumped off the bay window seat. 'You're in the right city for that.'

'True,' Ricki acknowledged.

An oyster po'boy from Domilise's bought on the way home slated Ricki's hunger. She also indulged in a bottle of her favorite Abita's Purple Haze. 'It's not exactly reduced guilt,' she told her pups as they scrounged the floor beneath her kitchen table for bits of fallen food. 'More like excessive guilt. I'll bike to work tomorrow and burn it off.' She yawned and rubbed her eyes. 'I feel like I'm forgetting something. Oh, well. It'll come to me.'

Which it did. In the middle of the night, Ricki woke up, rolled over, and cursed. 'Bon Vee front door,' she muttered. Whoever was the last person out of the museum was tasked with locking both the top and bottom lock. Ricki had done the latter but forgotten to throw the deadbolt.

She quickly dressed. After promising Thor and Princess she'd be quick, made the short drive from the Irish Channel to the Garden District. She drove down dark, silent streets, past shotguns and bungalows silhouetted against the night sky. The homes grew larger as she reached the Garden District with its magnificent mix of nineteenth and early twentieth century edifices gently illuminated by the flickering glow from gas lamps framing almost every front door. It occurred to Ricki she'd never been on the road in New Orleans at this late hour and while it was discomfiting, especially as a woman alone, it also enabled her to see her adopted city from a new and unique beautiful angle.

She parked in front of Bon Vee and scurried up the front walk. Like Duncan-Sejour and many mansions in the neighborhood, the culinary house museum boasted imposing carved oak front double doors. Ricki tried the heavy brass knobs of each and they held but jiggled. As she thought, she'd forgotten to throw the deadbolts. She took a key to both locks and tried the doors again. They held firm.

She started for her car. Suddenly, a loud crash came from next door. Ricki gasped and jumped. She stood frozen for a minute. Then her innate curiosity took over. She tiptoed to the edge of the Duncan-Sejour property and peeked through an open knot in the wooden fence.

A man lay splayed out on the cement path next to the estate's garbage cans, one of which lay on its side, its contents strewn over a wide area. Some of the garbage had fallen on the man's black leather jacket, the back of which was decorated with what looked like an orange ombre graphic symbolizing infinity. He didn't move and for a heart-stopping moment Ricki feared he was dead. Then he moaned and moved slightly.

Ricki retreated, running to her car. She yanked the door shut and dialed 911. 'I need to report a prowler. At Duncan-Sejour House. 219 Persephone Street.'

'Duncan-Sejour,' the emergency operator repeated. 'That's Blaine Taggart's new home, ain't it?'

'Yes.' *Is every single person in this city obsessed with the guy?* Ricki thought, irked.

'Is he in town?' The operator couldn't keep the fangirl out of her voice.

'I have no idea,' Ricki said through gritted teeth. 'Can you get someone here fast? Because if you don't and he is home and the prowler breaks in and kills him, New Orleans will always be known as the city where legendary movie star Blaine Taggart was murdered!' Ricki stopped to take a breath.

'A patrol car's on the way. I got one on St Charles. It'll be there in a minute.'

'*Thank* you.'

Ricki slunk down in her seat. If the burglar changed his mind and decided to beat it, she didn't want to risk him noticing her. The sound of a police siren grew louder until a patrol car careened around the corner. It stopped in front of Duncan-Sejour and two officers exited the patrol car. They took turns carefully peering over the fence, hands on their weapons. Then they seemed to relax. They left the side yard for the flagstone path that led to the estate's entrance, disappearing from view. After a few minutes, they reappeared, exiting the estate property for their patrol car. They got in and drove off.

Ricki waited until they were gone. She got out of her car and snuck back to the fence. She squinted to peer through the peephole.

The garbage can stood upright, the side yard was clean, and the man she'd seen lying prostrate on the cement was gone.

The next morning dawned so sunny, cool – and miracle of miracles for New Orleans, dry – that Ricki wondered for a fleeting moment if she'd dreamt the sighting. Then she decided the vagrant or burglar or whatever he was must have escaped while she was calling the police and didn't have an eye on the house.

The day marked the debut of Bon V*eeevil*. Both tours, kids and adults, were sold out. Employees had been instructed to arrive an hour early and in costume for a brief run-through courtesy of Cookie, who'd appointed herself the haunted house director. Ricki filed away the mysterious man in her mind's recesses and focused on outfitting herself in full witch's attire of black leggings, tunic top, and peaked hat, along with spiked black suede boots that added three inches to her petite five-three height.

Ricki loved the palpable sense of excitement she felt the minute she stepped onto the mansion's property. Benny and Jenny waved to her from where they were draping last-minute fake cobwebs over the estate's hedges fronting the sidewalk. The twin seniors were dressed as the twins from the iconic horror movie, *The Shining*. Ricki waved back, thinking to herself, *why am I not surprised?*

'You look bewitching,' said the twin Ricki assumed but wasn't positive was Benny.

Ricki affected a curtsy. 'Thank you. I promise I won't cast a spell on you.' She winked at him . . . or her.

The shriek of a whistle blasted through the air, making all three of them jump. 'Library! Now!' Cookie issued this order through a bullhorn.

'We're gonna be hearing about that from their lawyers,' the other twin said, rubbing his/her ear and gesturing to Duncan-Sejour with their thumb.

Ricki and the twins trooped inside to the library. They found the others already there. Everyone was in costume from volunteers to Eugenia, who'd scrounged up an old wedding dress and had her dressmaker transform it into the sad, soiled gown of betrayed bride Philodendron Legrande.

Cookie, wearing the female vampire costume Ricki unearthed in the attic, lifted the whistle to her lips. Eugenia held up a warning hand, artfully torn lace hanging from her bridal sleeve. 'Do *not* blow that thing again.'

'Noted.' Cookie dropped the whistle and instead clapped to get the staff's attention. 'We're gonna run through both versions, kids and adults, in each room and then outside. I expect full moans, groans, and whatever else you wanna throw in. This is our one and only dress rehearsal, people, so commit to the bit.'

'Can I record it for a vid?' Olivia held up her phone. She'd made her own costume, which featured scary makeup, a mini skirt with a belt made of dangling knives, and a T-shirt that read 'Killer Fashionista.'

'No recording dress rehearsal,' Cookie barked at her.

'OK. Fine. Whatevs.' Olivia accompanied this with an eye roll. She lowered her phone.

'We're going to move through this quickly, right?' Lyla adjusted her bride of Frankenstein's monster wig, which was threatening to topple off her head. 'Kaitlyn has a lunchtime practice against another team and I promised I'd be there. It's going to take me all morning to get this white greasepaint off my face.'

'The rehearsal will be as long as it needs to be,' Cookie said, in a tone that sounded vaguely ominous.

The group made their way to Miss Vee's, where Ricki cackled and pretended to stir her cauldron. They moved on to the parlor, where Zellah and Mordant played their parts as zombie undertakers to perfection. Everyone made their way through the other rooms, finishing in the dining room with its repast of gray fake food. Cookie had laid out the tour so the story behind Eugenia's jilted bride character could start there and finish outside at the tomb.

'Woe is me!' Eugenia cried out, clutching her head with both hands and circling her body as she moaned.

'She is *good*,' the twin Ricki chose to ID as Jenny whispered. Ricki, equally impressed by Eugenia's unexpected talent, nodded agreement.

'My wedding is no more.' Eugenia hung her head with a sob, then lifted it. 'I am betrayed by my fiancé Chauncey, who has told me he's in love with another. But I have enacted my revenge!' She followed this pronouncement with an evil laugh.

She gestured dramatically to the mansion's back door and led the group outside. They wended their way through the inflated forest of spooky trees and ghosts to the tomb. 'Here lies

Chauncey, dead by my own hand from a brew of poisonous plants.'

'Agh!' Ricki shooed away something brushing up against her leg yet again. She glanced down and found herself staring into the peridot eyes of a beautiful red tortoise-shell kitten.

'That cat almost looks real,' Benny said.

'It is real.' Ricki bent down to get closer to the kitty, who emitted a tiny meow. 'Well, you're our ghost. Hello, sweetie.' Ricki reached for the kitten but it darted off, disappearing into the foliage behind Bon Vee. 'Darn.'

'*Excuse me.*' Eugenia issued this in her stentorian 'I mean business' voice.

'Sorry.' Ricki quickly stood up.

Eugenia furrowed her brow. 'Where was I? Brew of poisonous plants, dead by my own hand, blah blah blah . . . Ah, got it.' She shook a fist at the heavens. 'Chauncey Chauncemeister, you have paid the ultimate price for betraying me!'

Eugenia flung open the tomb door wide, triggering the effects Mordant had rigged up. Ricki saw him surreptitiously press the small remote that controlled the crash test dummy now cast as Chauncey. 'Help!' a male voice cried out. 'I'm alive! Get me out of here! Ring the bell! *Ring the bell!*'

But Chauncey didn't rise to sitting.

Mordant frowned. He pressed the remote again. Still nothing.

'What's the problem?' Cookie asked, irritated. 'Why isn't Chauncey sitting up?'

'Don't know.'

Mordant stepped into the tomb. Curious, the others followed. He bent down over Chauncey, then quickly straightened. His face paled. 'He didn't sit up because he's not Chauncey. He's not even a he.'

'What?' Cookie pushed everyone out of the way. She reached the marble bench and took in the body lying on it. She let out a scream and swayed, Mordant catching her before she hit the ground.

Ricki ran to them. Then she saw who lay on the bench and clapped a hand over her mouth. She closed her eyes for a minute, forcing herself to fight the urge to collapse like Cookie. She opened her eyes and dropped her hand.

'It's not a dummy. It's a person.' She sucked in a breath. 'Miranda Fine.'

Eugenia instantly dropped character. 'Is she . . .?'

Ricki nodded. 'Yes.' She swallowed, then said, 'She's far from fine. She's dead.'

SEVEN

'I never thought watching a crime unit investigate a murder at Bon Vee would become routine,' Eugenia said to Ricki as they sat with the others at a patio café table watching exactly that scene unfold yet again in the culinary house museum's backyard. 'And yet here we are again. Will this never end?'

'You know what they say. Third time's the charm.' Zellah delivered this in a tone dry as the Mojave Desert.

'Why here?' Eugenia asked for what must have been the tenth time. She'd reached the point where she sounded plaintive. 'How on earth did that poor girl end up in our backyard?'

No one responded. No one knew the answer.

'I had Olivia send out an alert canceling tonight's tours,' Ricki said. 'Then I sent her to Langenstein's to pick up cat food. Anything to keep her from turning this into one of her videos.'

The only positive of the horrific morning's events is that the stray kitten had reappeared, emerging from the hedges when the investigators searched them for the crash test dummy. They found Chauncey where someone – presumably the killer – had tossed him. The kitty now nestled in Ricki's lap, having enjoyed a few appropriate snacks and a dish of milk.

'I know we wanted to go dark on Sundays but we can't now.' Eugenia grimaced, watching a crime scene technician trudge over a deflated blow-up ghost. 'We can't afford it. We need every possible time slot.'

'I gave everyone the option of a refund or rescheduling,' Ricki said. 'No one took it. In fact, the whole haunted house run is sold out.'

'No surprise there.' Theo held up his phone. '"Movie Star's Assistant Murdered" is all over the news. National and local. Bad for Miranda. But good for business.'

Cookie jumped up from her chair. 'How can you say that? How can you be so rude and callous? A friend of mine was murdered. You're *horrible*.' She stormed off.

'Friends? I thought they were mortal enemies.' A confused Theo scratched under the fake beard he'd donned as Mephistopheles.

'Revisionist history,' Zellah said. 'Besides, what else is she gonna say? The girl I hated who made my life a living hell and traumatized me for life, just happened to be my next-door neighbor and gets herself murdered? Doesn't make Cookie look too good to the cops.'

'It sure doesn't,' Nina Rodriguez said.

'Ah!' The detective's sudden appearance threw off the preternaturally unfazed Zellah, who let out a startled exclamation.

'We didn't hear you,' Ricki said.

'Stealth approaches are part of my skill set.' Nina took an empty chair next to Ricki. She stroked the kitten. 'Hello there. You're a cutie. Does she have a name?'

'We're just calling her Red until we find her owner,' Ricki said. She found the casual conversation discomfiting considering the circumstances. 'I'm guessing you and Detective Girard want to talk to us.' She motioned to her witch's outfit. 'We're all still in costume. Weirdest interview ever, huh?'

'This is New Orleans, so not even close to the weirdest. But yes, Sam and I want to talk to each of you individually.' She called to her partner. 'Say hi, Sam.'

Sam, a large genial man who Ricki knew was counting down to retirement – the alarm he set to count off the days made it hard to ignore – gave them a mock salute. 'Hey.'

'Sam's lost a lot of weight since the last murder,' Ricki commented.

'Yeah, he went on one of those diabetes drugs. Unlike celebrities like your friend Blaine next door, he actually needs it for his health.'

'I doubt Blaine would ever take the drug. He's a workout fanatic.'

Nina eyed her. 'You knew him pretty well, huh? I'm looking forward to hearing more about that. Especially in relation to his deceased assistant.'

Ricki groaned and dropped her head in her hands. 'Why do I always forget how good you are at your job?'

'Yeah, you need to stop making that mistake.'

Eugenia emitted a sound that was half gasp and half moan and drew everyone's attention. Alarmed to see the woman had gone pale, Ricki clutched her arm to hold on in case she fainted. 'Detective . . .' The word came out of Eugenia in a strangled whisper. 'Is there a chance this killing was some kind of . . .' she gulped, then summoned the courage to continue, 'satanic ritual?'

'It's Halloween in New Orleans, so sure.'

The detective's casual response elicited another weird sound from Eugenia. Ricki clutched her arm tighter.

'But so far, no signs point in that direction,' Nina continued. 'Too bad. It'd be a break from the same old, same old.' She stood up and stretched. 'Okie dokie, we need two private rooms, one for me, one for Sam. You know the drill.'

'Sadly, we do.' Eugenia composed herself and also stood up, albeit with more effort. 'Benny and Jenny, if you would help me prepare the conference room and my office for our law enforcement guests.'

'Yes ma'am,' the twins said in unison, jumping up. They hurried after Eugenia.

'It's great having all of my prime suspects in one location,' Nina said. 'Thanks for making my job easier for a change.' Lyla's hand shot up. 'Oh, we're doing the hand-raising thing now? OK. I'll play along. Calling on you, Ms Brandt. Or should I say Mrs Frankenstein?'

Lyla lowered her hand, knocking into her tall wig and sending it askew. 'For the record, I never interacted with this Miranda person. I'd never even laid eyes on her until we went into the tomb. So I can't be a suspect this time.' Having been the prime suspect in another murder at Bon Vee, Lyla made sure to stress this. 'Oh, and small thing. I'm not Mrs Frankenstein, I'm married to the monster he created. But maybe this isn't the time to bring that up.'

The stress of the situation made Ricki cranky and defensive. 'Come on, Nina. You know none of us killed Miranda.'

Nina sighed. She shook a scold-y finger at her. 'Miracle James-Diaz, you know I can't rule anything out until I have alibis and evidence. What are the three immutables of murder?'

'Means, motive, and opportunity.'

The others chorused this with Ricki. She looked at them, surprised. 'We all know it by now,' Theo said.

'Alrighty.' Nina got up from her chair. She gave her long, lanky body a stretch. 'Enough chit-chat. Time for interviews. One of our officers will keep an eye out to make sure there's no collusion here. No lining up stories, my friends. Sam and I will speed things up by conducting the interviews simultaneously.'

'Can I request you?' Theo, who'd been crushing on the detective ever since he laid eyes on her during the first murder at Bon Vee, asked this, ever hopeful.

'That's a hella no. Ricki, you first.'

Nina crooked a finger at her. Ricki handed the kitten off to Zellah and followed the detective. She glanced back at the tomb-turned-crime scene. Everyone at Bon Vee wanted Miranda to back off and leave them alone. But no one wanted the contentious situation to end this way.

Or did they? Could a Bon Vee employee or volunteer be a murderer? Ricki refused to believe this. Then again, as Nina said, at this point no one could be ruled out.

Including me, thought a nervous Ricki. She closed her eyes and silently ran her favorite mantra a few times. *I am having a safe, uneventful journey. I am having a safe uneventful journey.* She blinked her eyes open and checked her emotional state. On a scale of one to ten, her nerves were still hovering near eleven, which led to a revision on her mantra: *Why is it so flipping hard to have a safe, uneventful journey?!*

Once inside the carriage house conference room, Ricki dropped down into an office chair across the table from Nina, who frowned. 'That's too far away. Makes this feel like a job interview. Roll closer.'

Ricki did so. It wasn't easy on carpet and she broke a small sweat, which she acknowledged to herself was more from being terrified than over-exertion.

'Better.' Nina leaned back in her chair. 'So . . . tell me about your relationship with Blaine Taggart.'

'I didn't have one. I mean, I did but it was peripheral. Through my husband Chris. They met at an audition at the beginning of their careers. The two of them started talking and found they had a lot in common. You know, dysfunctional childhoods, moving from small towns to LA with dreams of becoming movie stars.

Blaine got the job they both auditioned for, Chris didn't. That became their routine. Auditions for the same role. Blaine would get it, Chris wouldn't. Blaine became a star. Chris didn't.'

Ricki's throat felt dry. So did her lips. She licked them. Nina noticed and pushed a bottle of water on the table her way. 'Here.'

'Thanks.' Ricki opened the bottle and took a sip, as much to corral her emotions, which were threatening to get away from her, as to slake her thirst. Then she continued. 'Blaine always felt guilty about their different trajectories, so when Chris started getting attention as Chriz-*azy!* for his stupid online stunts, Blaine really encouraged it. He supported Chris emotionally and even financially sometimes. He boosted and amplified the videos. He even filmed some of them himself. Like the one where Chris did the Marshmallow dare, choked on one, and died.'

'That must have been hard for you.'

'It was. I mean, Chris and I were done by then. We'd started divorce proceedings. But I never stopped caring about him.'

Nina studied Ricki. 'I'm still trying to figure out how you wound up dating an actor. I don't see them as your type.'

Ricki, embarrassed, twisted the tissue. 'To be honest, I hadn't dated too much. I was kind of naïve. Chris was good-looking and charming. I couldn't believe he was interested in a book nerd like me instead of a hot actress or model. He said that's what he liked about me. I was "real."' Ricki added a touch of sarcasm to the air quotes. 'Actors can be incredibly charming and seductive. Then you get in a relationship with them and realize . . . they're actors.'

She wiped a tear that had escaped and rolled down her cheek. Nina pushed a box of tissues her way. 'Here.'

Ricki, sniffling, took one. 'Are you a therapist or a detective?' she asked, attempting to lighten the moment.

'L'il bit of both.' Nina smiled. 'So, tell me about your relationship with Miranda Fine.'

The tears stopped. '*And* there's the detective.'

Nina held up her hands. 'Guilty as charged.' She dropped her hands and leaned forward. So . . . Miranda.'

Ricki went with the opposite approach. She leaned back in her chair, resting her arm on an arm of it, affecting a casual attitude. Unfortunately, the chair had a loose wheel and Ricki lost her balance. 'Whoa!' She tumbled off, onto the floor.

Nina helped a mortified Ricki back into the chair. 'I'd say that's a lame way to try and get out of answering my question, but I know you well enough by now to know it was an accident.'

Ricki brushed herself off and did her best to regain a semblance of dignity. 'On the subject of Miranda, I think I speak for everyone at Bon Vee when I say she was a giant pain who loved to throw her weight around and create problems for us. But nothing she did was bad enough to drive a single one of us to kill her.'

'Uh huh. Walk me through your whereabouts from when you left Bon Vee yesterday to when you returned this morning.'

'After work, I stopped at Domilise's for an oyster po'boy and an Abita Purple Haze.'

'Both stellar choices.'

'Agreed. I went home, ate, walked the dogs, and went to—' Ricki gasped. 'OMG, I almost forgot the most important thing of all. I woke up in the middle of the night and realized I'd forgotten to throw the front door deadbolt, so I drove back here. I heard a crash next door, looked into the Duncan-Sejour side yard, and saw a guy lying there and a knocked-over garbage can. He probably did it climbing back over the wall that separates us from them after leaving Miranda in our tomb. I called the police and they didn't seem too interested. But there's your killer.'

Quite satisfied with herself, Ricki sat back and rested her elbow on the arm's chair, much more carefully this time.

'We checked him out and he appears to be a resident of the house. But we'll of course be chatting with the Duncan-Sejour folk as well as y'all.'

'A resident?' Ricki repeated, puzzled. 'I didn't know anyone else was staying there. It wasn't Blaine. I'd recognize him, even from the back.'

Nina drummed her fingers on the tabletop. 'Ever since we got the call about another homicide here, I've been thinking about something. You have an incredibly annoying tendency to stick your nose into our investigations.'

'Sorry,' Ricki said, abashed.

'But your clumsy efforts and jaw-dropping, farfetched theories haven't been completely useless. If you run across anything you think might be helpful in this case, feel free to drop me a text.'

What Nina was implying dawned on Ricki. 'Hold on. Are you saying it's OK if I do some amateur sleuthing?' Nina responded with a minute shrug. 'Doesn't that break the NOPD rules?'

Nina lifted a corner of her mouth in a half-smile. 'We know what we say: In Louisiana, we only follow the rules we like.'

Bon Vee remained closed the next day, which made it the perfect place for Ricki to meet with her snooping assistants Cookie and Theo in the private confines of Miss Vee's. Like her, they'd had dustups with Miranda, so like her, they fell under the NOPD category of suspects.

'Nina really gave you permission to investigate?' Cookie asked, skeptical.

'Yes. Which of course she'll completely deny if she's ever called out on it.'

'She's like a detective *and* spy.' Theo could not have sounded more besotted.

A meow came from inside the cauldron. Ricki reached in and scooped up Red. 'I'll have to put a cover on this thing at night.'

Theo helped himself to a piece of candy from a bowl meant for shop visitors. 'Aren't you going to bring her home?'

'No. I don't want her to get used to me. We need to find her owners. I put info on her up on OhNo!La and I'm going to have Olivia make a flyer so we can paper the neighborhood.'

'Glad you've locked down the kitty sitch,' Cookie said, oozing sarcasm. 'Now let's focus on how to keep me from being accused of murder and spending the rest of my life in jail.'

'You're not the only one who's in NOPD's crosshairs,' Theo said. 'She accused me of sexual harassment. It was a lie but that doesn't mean it couldn't ruin me. Talk about motivation for murder.'

'Really?' Cookie crossed her arms in front of her chest and gave Theo the stink eye. 'You think your motivation stacks up against the fact Miranda made my high school life a living hell, scarring me for life, and was about to start the bullying all over again? And that I attacked her, which was probably caught on the Duncan-Sejour security system, but even if it wasn't, you both saw me and would have to admit it or be charged with obstructing an investigation?'

'Hello.' Ricki waved her hands in the air to get their attention. 'You've both done a terrific job of convincing me you're prime suspects in Miranda's murder. I can either turn you over to Nina and let her take it from there or we can go with the original goal of getting everyone at Bon Vee off the hook.'

'That,' Cookie said, chastened. Theo, equally chastened, nodded.

'OK then.' Ricki removed Red from her lap, placing the kitten on a makeshift bed of tea towels. She paced the room as she talked. 'I thought we could divide the investigation into three categories: past, present, and future. Cookie, you would take the past. I'm sure you're not the only person Miranda bullied. Mean girls generally have more than one target. At least they did at my high school. Now that Miranda was back in town, who knew and was it someone who had a grudge against her?'

'Got it,' Cookie said, not looking up from her phone where she'd been taking notes.

'Moving on to the present.' Ricki directed this at Theo. 'Who else has Miranda offended or ticked off since she came back to town? Had she made enemies besides you? I'm guessing she had because she was that kind of person. Work your connections.'

'As the one person here *with* connections, you got it.'

Cookie fixed a look on him. 'Be a jerk much?'

Ricki said a silent prayer for patience. Then she continued. 'I'll take the future. What Miranda was aiming for, career-wise. I'll reach out to people back in LA. Chris and Blaine knew a lot of the same people. Miranda was ambitious in a way that means she might have made enemies in her climb up the entertainment ladder. I'll tap into the gossip machine and see if I can dig up anything or anyone. Are we good with this plan?'

'Definitely,' Cookie said. 'Nice job, Ricki.'

'Thanks,' Ricki said, pleased with herself. 'When we all have our lists of suspects, we'll lay out the next steps. I was thinking we'd—'

A knock at the shop door interrupted her. 'Huh. I wonder who that is. Everyone's off today.'

'Please tell me it's not the po po,' Theo said.

Cookie shook her head, horrified. 'No. No, no, no. You are not a man who can get away with saying "po po." Do the universe a favor and never say it again.'

There was another knock. Ricki exchanged a quizzical look with the others, then went to open the door.

A rangy, handsome man with windswept, sun-bleached hair stood in the doorway. He removed his sunglasses to reveal sparkling aqua eyes. Cookie squealed and clutched Theo's arm. Theo didn't notice. He was too enthralled by this vision of perfect manhood himself.

The gorgeous stranger smiled at Ricki, revealing naturally perfect teeth and dimpled cheeks that complimented the cleft in his chin. 'Hey, Rickster,' he said in the sultry baritone that had seduced moviegoers of every gender to the tune of billions in profit for his action-adventure movies. 'It's me. Blaine.'

EIGHT

Seeing Blaine, so many questions ran through Ricki's mind. *Why are you here? What were you thinking egging on Chris to endanger his life? Why was your assistant such a nightmare? Why is she dead? Did you kill her? If not, who did? Do you know? What do you want from us? Is your ego so humongous or your self-esteem so tiny that you'd do anything to own the biggest house in New Orleans? What is your problem?! And again . . . why are you here?!*

Instead of asking any of them, she went with a simple and chilly 'Hello.'

'Sorry, I didn't know you were with other people.' Blaine extended a hand to Cookie and Theo. 'I'm Blaine Taggart.'

Cookie gave him her hand and he gave it a gentle shake. Having lost the ability to form words, she responded with giggles.

'Hey,' Theo said. The single word came out as a roller coaster from a squeak to a forced basso profundo that aped Blaine's natural vocal tone.

Blaine shook hands with Theo. Then his smile faded, replaced by a more serious expression. 'Ric, I know it's been a while. And I know you have a lot of questions.'

Ya think?! Ricki managed not to scream at him.

'I was hoping we could—'

Eugenia, back to being clad in one of her classic Chanel suits, suddenly appeared behind him. 'If you don't mind.' She issued this as an order, not a request.

'Oh. Sorry.'

Blaine stepped out of the way to allow a path for the dowager. Ricki silently thanked Eugenia for the pleasure of seeing the movie star thrown off balance, even if it was for a split second.

'There's a chauffeur idling in a ridiculously large black SUV outside Bon Vee,' Eugenia announced in a tone indicating it was everyone's fault. 'He is both taking up valuable curb space and blocking all the Bon V*eeevil* signage we've attached to the fence.'

'Apologies. That's my car.' Blaine favored Eugenia with his trademark smile. She glared at him.

'Eugenia, this is our new neighbor,' Ricki said. 'Blaine Taggart.'

Eugenia continued to glare.

'*Blaine Taggart.*' Cookie repeated the name with more emphasis.

'Yes,' Eugenia said, unmoved. 'The actor.' She faced him. 'Mr Taggart, I would appreciate it if you would have your driver move your vehicle. And make sure it's not parked there again.'

With that, Eugenia strode out of the room.

Blaine stared after her. 'Gotta say, no one's put such a negative spin on the word "actor" since the olden days when they thought it was another way to say sex worker.'

'She's in a mood,' Theo said, hastening to add, 'Don't take it personally. It's not your fault.'

'It kinda is,' Ricki felt compelled to point out. 'You can bet that Miranda's murder put Eugenia in her bad mood, and the victim is – was – Blaine's assistant.'

Blaine grimaced and pinched the bridge of his nose. 'Man, I still can't believe that happened. Seriously bad stuff.' He gazed at Ricki with an expression she couldn't place at first. Then she recalled it as the one he used onscreen to convey concern. 'I really, *really* need to talk to you,' Blaine said. 'I don't want to interrupt your business day. Can you come by my place after work? Please?'

'I'm not working today. The shop is closed due to the recent homicide.' Ricki kept her tone even, but cold. 'Not that it matters because I don't think we have anything to say to each other.'

'Ricki, are you out of your mind?!' Cookie practically screeched this. 'Of course you have something to say to him. He's *Blaine Taggart.*'

'Argh!' Ricki's patience ran out. 'I am so tired of hearing that name.' She glowered at Cookie. 'If it will shut you up, I'll go meet Blaine. After work.'

'But the shop is closed,' Cookie said.

'I've changed my mind and now I'm working again, OK?!' Ricki yelled this.

'Geez. OK.' Cookie backed off.

'Thanks.' Blaine delivered this to Cookie with a warm smile flavored with a hint of self-effacement. Then he turned to Ricki. 'I'll see you later.'

As Blaine walked away, Cookie scurried to the door, reluctant to take her eyes off him until he'd fully disappeared. 'I've heard of people who make you feel like you're the only person in the room. But I've never experienced it until now.'

Ricki, her last nerve worked, could only respond with a growl.

'We should probably go,' Theo said, sensing Ricki's vile mood. He gave Cookie a gentle push out the door.

With the shop closed and inventory replenished, Ricki didn't have much to do but she was determined not to set foot in Duncan-Sejour until the end of the business day. Knowing Blaine was used to having his every need immediately tended to, she was determined to give off the impression of being way too busy to upend her life for him.

Bon Vee's quiet soon proved to be a welcome respite. After placing bids on a handful of cookbooks being sold via an online auction, Ricki went through every bookshelf to confirm each cookbook was in its proper place. She organized them first by decade, then type, followed by theme. She found a couple of 1960s community cookbooks on the 1950s hardcover shelf. One featured appetizer recipes, the other was all about fondues. She moved them to their proper locations. 'I have more cookbooks from the 1960s than any other decade,' she said to Red, the only other shop occupant. 'That's my new go-to destination if anyone ever invents a time tunnel.'

As the hours passed, practicality began to outweigh Ricki's emotions. Hostility to Blaine aside, a visit to Duncan-Sejour would allow her to suss out the house and meet other potential suspects in Miranda's murder, which is what was needed to deflect Nina's attention away from the Bon Vee crew.

Her phone pinged a text alerting her to a delivery. *I didn't order anything*, she thought, puzzled.

She left the shop for the front landing where a large box sat, adorned with a logo indicating it was from a local pet store. Too large to carry, Ricki dragged the box back to Miss Vee's. She used a box cutter to open it, revealing a state-of-the-art litter box with a note taped to the top. Ricki un-taped the note and read it: **A 'litter' welcome to Bon Vee's newest addition! Love and meows, Benny and Jenny.**

'Awww.' Ricki showed the note to Red, who was busy grooming. 'You have friends here. And these two are super loyal.' Ricki realized what she'd just said. She remembered the twins, equally infuriated, venting their hatred of Miranda. Could one of them have killed her and the other assisted in the coverup? Or more likely, could they have colluded in the murder?

Ricki knew the detectives had interviewed the twins but she wondered if Benny and Jenny had been upfront about how much they hated Miranda and the danger she posed to the future of Bon Vee Culinary House Museum. In case they hadn't been forthcoming, she shot off a text to Nina, detailing specifics about the times one or both of the twins had complained to her about Miranda.

Excited about delivering her first potential clues to the detective, she eagerly awaited Nina's reply. It came in the form of one word: **Alibis.** Disappointed, Ricki pocketed the phone and returned to shelving.

By six p.m., Miss Vee's Vintage Cookbook and Kitchenware Shop had never looked better. After organizing the cookbooks by decade, type, and theme, Ricki had arranged them by color, creating bookshelves that resembled rainbows. She'd created additional displays of vintage cookware throughout the shop. She'd dusted, vacuumed, and set up Red's litter box, along with the kitten's kibble and water. It was time to face the harsh fact that there was nothing to stop Ricki from paying Duncan-Sejour and Blaine Taggart a visit.

She locked up Bon Vee – making sure to throw the deadbolt – and traipsed next door, where she rang the doorbell, which let off a sonorous bong. As she waited outside on the estate's landing, it occurred to Ricki that the last time she stood there was also the last time she saw Miranda alive. She shivered and shook off the memory.

A moment later, Blaine opened the front door. 'You're here. Awesome. I wasn't sure you'd show. Come in.'

He moved aside to let Ricki pass and she stepped into Duncan-Sejour.

Once inside, Ricki took in the home's interior. The layout was similar to Bon Vee: a wide front hall running the length of the mansion, with expansive rooms lining accessible on both sides. The décor, however, was wildly different. Where the Charbonnet ancestral home was a study in dignified, muted elegance, Duncan-Sejour could have passed for a Storyville bordello. The hall's walls were covered in bright red flocked wallpaper and decorated with nineteenth-century paintings of buxom, scantily-clad women. Garish Oriental carpet ran under Ricki's feet down the hallway and up a staircase of dark walnut carved within an inch of its life. The mystery of why Blaine bought the garish estate increased tenfold.

Blaine noticed the expression on Ricki's face. 'Before you say anything, I hired a decorator.'

'Smart move,' Ricki couldn't help commenting.

'Let's go into the living room. Oops, I forgot. I'm supposed to call it *the parlor*.'

He said this with a perfect English accent. It was hard, but Ricki managed not to reward him with a chuckle. She pressed her lips together and followed him into a room whose over-the-top Victorian furniture and flocked wallpaper – pink this time – matched the hallway in garishness.

Blaine guided Ricki into the room. 'I'll get us drinks. You're Chardonnay, right?'

'Good memory.'

'I always remember a beautiful woman's drink order,' Blaine said with a wink.

'Oh, please.' This time Ricki couldn't control her reaction. His flirtation galled her, especially given the circumstances.

A tiny older woman wearing a long, gauzy dark-blue dress appeared in the doorway. Layers of silver necklaces sporting crystal charms hung from her neck. A crystal shaped like a teardrop dangled from a headpiece over her forehead and her forearms were covered with crystal-enhanced bracelets. 'Will you need me tonight?' she asked Blaine.

'Not sure. I'll text you later.'

She placed her hands together as if in prayer and made a slight bow to him, then repeated the same gesture to Ricki. She turned to go, revealing a mass of dreadlocks so long it dusted the floor as she walked.

'That's Lakshmi,' Blaine said. 'My spiritual advisor and masseuse.'

'Of course she is.'

Blaine either didn't hear or chose not to respond to the snarky comment. 'Take a seat.' He gestured to a chair sparkling with gold gilt.

'I see the place came with a throne,' she remarked, sitting. The chair was every bit as uncomfortable as she expected it to be.

'Ha. That chair'll be the first thing to go. Not my style.'

Or was it?

Blaine held up a bottle chilling in a wine bucket to show Ricki the label. She recognized the California Central Coast vineyard as uber-high end and nodded. As the actor poured her a glass, she studied him. He wore jeans, black boots, and a simple white T-shirt, all of which Ricki knew cost more than a small fortune. Music played softly in the background. The tune sounded familiar but Ricki couldn't place it right away, then recognized it as the theme from Blaine's latest film. She hadn't seen the movie and never would but the trailer was ubiquitous. Blaine might claim to have a minimalist esthetic. But his self-confidence and latent arrogance were definitely maximalist.

Blaine handed her the Chardonnay. She inhaled its scent and took a sip that proved the wine to be worthy of what she knew was a high price tag.

He took a beer chilling in another bucket and deposited himself across from her on a Victorian settee that looked less comfortable than her current seat, if that was even possible. 'So . . .'

'So . . .'

'I bet you're wondering what I'm doing in New Orleans.'

'A little.' *A lot!*

Blaine pulled the tab on his fake beer and took a chug. 'I've always loved the city. And the way you talked about when we were all hanging out in LA only made me love it more. I've had my real estate broker on the hunt for a place here for a while. Also . . . you're here.'

Ricki stiffened. She took a big gulp of wine.

'When my broker Jameel found a house right next to where

you worked, I was like, "Thank you, universe," Blaine clasped his hands, miming prayer. He dropped them and leaned forward. 'I want to make amends to you for Chris's death.'

Ricki took another gulp of wine. 'Buying the second biggest house in the city is an extreme way of doing that. And by the way, if you wanted to make amends, having your assistant bully us relentlessly and insinuate you wouldn't stop until you owned the *biggest* house in the city, which happens to be where I work, is a nasty, sneaky way of doing it.'

'Oh, man. You have to believe me when I tell you I had no idea Miranda was doing that. None. Zip, zero, zilch, nada. I don't know what she was thinking, I swear to God. Since she listed you as a reference on her job application, I assumed she'd go the opposite way. You know, make a point of reaching out, getting to know you, maybe going out for—'

'*Stop.*' Ricki stared at Blaine, dumbfounded. 'What are you talking about? What do you mean, Miranda listed me as a reference?'

'Yeah.' Blaine appeared equally dumbfounded. 'You didn't know?'

'*No.*' Ricki tried to process the bizarre turn of events. 'Blaine . . . Until I came over to Duncan-Sejour to complain about Miranda painting the curb in front of my customer spot red, I'd never seen her before in my life.'

NINE

There was silence. Then Blaine said, 'You mean . . . you hadn't met her?'

'I mean that until she showed up in New Orleans and started harassing us, *I'd never heard of her.* She didn't exist for me.' Ricki downed her wine and got up to refill the glass. She didn't care if she emptied Blaine's entire pricey bottle. 'I don't understand. You've got security up the wazoo. How could you not get in touch with me to vet her?'

'The timing was bad. It was right after Chris's death. I couldn't bring myself to call you and say, "Hey, sorry about my bestie your husband, but can you vet this girl I'm thinking of hiring as my new assistant?" It just felt, I don't know, too self-serving.'

'That's a shock. I've never seen you be anything but self-serving.' The wine superseded Ricki's internal editor and made her blunt.

'Ouch. But I get it. You're upset.'

Ricki controlled her urge to punch him. 'An extremely ambitious woman lied on her resume and somehow ended up working for you. And wound up *dead.* None of that should ever have happened. You need to fire your entire team.'

'The other references checked out. I assumed hers would too.'

'But why me?' Ricki wondered. 'How did Miranda pull my name out of a hat of lies?'

'Poetic. Nice.' Blaine finished his nonalcoholic beer, crumpled the can, and took a rebound shot off the back of the wall behind a small, filigreed trash receptacle. The can landed inside. 'It's not that hard to track. Chris's death was all over the news and internet, and you got mentioned a lot.'

'Tell me about it,' Ricki said, unpleasant memories of bumping up against Chriz-*azy!* fans still fresh.

'Miranda knew how badly I took his death. We talked about it at her interview. I know I brought up your name and how you moved to New Orleans and how cool I thought it was that you were getting a fresh start, especially after that whole deal with Lachlan Barnes.'

'Ugh,' Ricki groaned. 'One nightmare at a time, please.' Her former boss, multi-millionaire Lachlan Barnes, now called a federal prison home after perpetrating one of the largest Ponzi schemes in American history. He took his whole staff down with him, including Ricki, who'd managed his massive collection of first editions, all purchased with other people's money as it turned out. Having to accept that she was unemployable in her chosen field had motivated Ricki to launch her own business at Bon Vee. But she didn't know if she'd ever completely recover from the double whammy of Chris's death and Lachlan's thieving betrayal.

Ricki's phone pinged an alert from Eugenia: **NOPD cleared us to open tomorrow. Bon Vee and Bon V***eeevil* **are on. Staff meeting 8 a.m.** 'I need to go. I have an early start tomorrow. We're reopening and I know from past experience with these kinds of situations—'

'Murders?'

Hearing the word mentioned so baldly made Ricki wince. 'Yes. Those. They tend to draw a crowd. But I have to know why Miranda did what she did. I may have more questions for you.'

Blaine held out his arms to indicate the house. 'I'm here. Not going anywhere. Well, at least for a week. I'm supposed to shoot an ad video for a male fragrance I endorsed but my agent can always push it back.'

Ricki handed him her empty wine glass. 'Don't do it on my account. Don't do anything on my account.'

Blaine took the glass, his hand lingering on hers. 'I want to help you find out what Miranda was up to. Please. Let me.'

Ricki pulled her hand away. 'If I need help, I'll let you know,' she lied. The last thing Ricki wanted to do was give Blaine an excuse to spend time with her. She was still convinced his home purchase was prompted by an ulterior motive she'd yet to uncover. Plus, there was the fact no one interacted with Miranda more than her boss, which made Blaine a prime suspect in his assistant's death.

'Detective Rodriguez has given me permission to share a few updates on the investigation with you.' Eugenia addressed this to Ricki, Cookie, Theo, Lyla, Zellah, and Mordant, the select group of employees she'd included in the morning meeting.

'Any chance one of those updates is that we're all off the hook?' Theo asked.

'You can file that under the category of wishful thinking,' Eugenia responded with a rare hint of acerbity in her voice. 'Forensics was unable to access any useful prints from Chauncey. Whoever moved him tried to wipe off any evidence of the act. They did match partials to Zellah and Mordant but since neither of you had any record of conflict with the victim, you're relatively off the hook.'

'I'd prefer "totally," but I can live with "relatively,"' Zellah said.

'Lucky,' Theo muttered.

'Anyone else off the hook?' Lyla asked, tugging at her gray cardigan, which had slipped off her shoulder.

'My security footage will prove I never left the house during the relevant time period.'

'So will mine. *Yes.*' Lyla fist-pumped, then issued a sheepish 'Sorry.'

Cookie's faced creased with worry. 'My landlord hasn't gotten around to installing cameras.'

'Neither has mine.' Theo's face darkened. 'Cheap son of a bi—' he caught his aunt's warning expression and pivoted. 'Gun.'

'So Nina shared a time-of-death estimate?' Ricki asked. 'And how much do I hate that I know to ask that question.'

'To answer it, Nina said the medical examiner estimates Miranda met her demise somewhere between the hours of three a.m. and five a.m. And oh, how I hate that I'm on a first-name basis with an NOPD detective.'

'My landlady's footage will show I was right here at Bon Vee during that time period,' Ricki said, not happy about it. She pondered the timeline. 'Between three and five. That means Miranda might have already been—' She took a moment to find a more delicate way to phrase the obvious. 'Deceased by the time I came here to throw the deadbolt.' The thought sent a chill through her and she rubbed her arms. Then another thought occurred to her. 'It also means that whoever I saw splayed out on the Duncan-Sejour side yard was there during the time frame of the murder. What about security footage? With a star like Blaine, that's the first thing his team would have installed.'

'According to my NOPD "friend,"' Eugenia said, 'someone disabled the Duncan-Sejour security cameras around midnight. Our own system is no help because it faces the street, the goal being to deter burglars. It doesn't capture any other approaches to the house and NOPD suspects the suspect, along with Miranda, accessed our backyard through one of our neighbors, not the street. I take small comfort from the fact NOPD truly can't find any indications that the poor woman's demise taking place in our makeshift tomb was any kind of cult killing. Near as they can figure, the location was chosen purely because it offered privacy. And now you know everything that I and apparently NOPD knows. They have yet to commit to a cause of death.'

'She looked like someone you might see in an actual tomb,' Cookie said.

'Not too ghoulish,' Zellah said with a heavy dose of side-eye.

'I know what she means,' Ricki said. 'None of us stayed in the tomb for long, but I know I didn't see blood or . . .' she pivoted to a more delicate description, '. . .Visible signs of trauma.'

Eugenia took a sip of coffee from a cup she'd held with a firm grip since starting the meeting. Considering the stress the board president was under, Ricki wouldn't have been surprised if she'd doctored it with a shot of bourbon, despite the early hour.

After a second, much longer sip, Eugenia continued. 'If anyone from the press tries to talk to you, which I'm sure they will, considering Mr Taggart's high profile, say nothing. Do not discuss anything I've shared this morning with anyone outside of this core group.' She rose from her chair at the head of the conference table. 'Gird your loins for what I'm assuming will be an absolute madhouse. On the upside, as my granddaughter would say, Bon Vee will be making serious bank.'

'Madhouse' proved to be a spot-on projection. A crowd had already gathered outside Bon Vee's gates an hour prior to opening and descended on the house museum the minute the antique grandfather clock in the hallway bonged ten a.m. Eugenia was also right about the shocking event being a) a payday for Bon Vee and b) a potential gossip minefield. As she sold tickets and gift shop items, Ricki deflected nosy inquiries so often she felt like a PR flack. She did appreciate the dueling voodoo priestesses who were determined to use their talents to solve the case *and* cleanse Bon Vee of its murderous mojo. Considering the killer crime wave bedeviling the site, Ricki sincerely wished them both luck.

Late afternoon brought a welcome lull in activity. Ricki retrieved a sweet tea from her mini fridge, then locked the shop and stepped outside to catch her breath. She found a shady spot at a café table under the cast iron gallery on the side of the house and watched Red tease Gumbo and Jambalaya. The peacocks shrieked at the kitten. They spread their spectacular feathers, a gesture meant to ward off predators. Instead, Red entertained herself batting around a feather shed by an enraged Gumbo.

Cookie approached with a diet soda she'd bought from Zellah's café. 'I can't believe how many visitors showed up. It's been so insane today that Eugenia drafted me to give tours.'

Ricki gestured to Cookie's skintight navy mini-dress and spike heels. 'Of where, a casino nightclub?'

'Ha ha.' Cookie made a face at her. She yanked down her dress, which was riding up perilously high on her thighs. 'Not gonna lie, I spent a little extra tour time in the side yard between us and Blaine's place.'

'I know.' Ricki grinned at her friend. 'Whenever I got the chance to look out the shop window, I saw you there.'

Cookie patted her short blonde hair. 'You just never know when a gorgeous movie star might feel the need to toss somethin' into his recycle bin,' she drawled, going full Southern belle.

Ricki raised an eyebrow. 'Simmer down, Blanche Dubois. Have you dug up anything about Miranda's past that might be helpful?'

'Not yet. But . . .' Cookie plopped down in a café chair across from Ricki and spoke in a conspiratorial whisper. 'I did find out Blaine hasn't been in a serious relationship since he broke up with a German supermodel last year and according to multiple online sources, he's recovered from the heartbreak and eager to fall in love again.'

Ricki shook a scolding finger at her. 'Cookie Yanover, stop obsessing about Blaine. It's a waste of valuable time.'

Cookie fiddled with the hem of her dress. 'To be honest, it's a way of procrastinating.' She glanced up at Ricki. Her expression telegraphed a rare insecurity. 'Thinking about going back to the past . . . to the people from that time . . . it pushes buttons for me. I feel like the Wicked Witch of Westwego all over again.'

'I get it,' Ricki said, softening. 'But you have to remember, you are not that. And you never were. You were victim of cruel bullying. I bet anyone who teased you then would be blown away by who you are now: a strong, successful, beautiful woman.'

Cookie teared up. 'Thank you.'

Ricki heard a guttural grunt and glanced in the direction it came from. Theo came towards them, walking with a limp. 'Good, it's Theo. Hopefully he's got something useful to share.' She waved him over.

'Hey,' he said, making a face as he slowly eased himself onto a café chair.

'Are you all right?' Ricki said, watching the enormous effort it seemed to take.

'Yeah. Totally.' The groan Theo let out as he settled into the chair belied this. 'Blaine inspired me to up my game at the gym.'

'For "inspired," read "Oh man, I'm jealous, I wanna look that cut,"' Ricki said, calling him out on this.

'OK, fine,' he grumbled. 'I did feel a little competitive. But the universe punished me for being petty. I feel like I didn't pull something, I pulled everything.'

'It'll pass. Now, what about your investigation into Miranda's present? Did you discover anything from your connections? Enemies she made, someone who had a grudge against her . . .'

Theo shook his head. 'Haven't had time.' He winced. 'Ow. Even that hurt.'

'You guys, here's the deal,' Ricki said, her voice firm, 'We need intel on Miranda, or her case will keep dropping as an NOPD priority and we'll all always be under suspicion for her death. On the other hand, if it's some deranged Halloween killer targeting haunted house tours, we could all be in danger.' She pointed at Cookie. 'You can do this.' She pointed at Theo. 'So can you. If you don't seriously injure yourself at the gym.' She wiggled a finger back and forth at them. 'Past and present.'

'Yes, boss.' Cookie gave her short, tight dress another tug

down. 'You're totally right. What about you? Find out anything about Miranda's future?'

'Not specifically about the future. But I talked to Blaine last night and found out something pretty disturbing.'

She shared the revelation that Miranda had listed her as a reference on her application for the job as Blaine's assistant. Cookie and Theo reacted with shock. 'That's terrible,' Cookie said. 'It's . . . I don't know. Creepy.'

'Creepy is definitely the word for it.' Theo agreed. 'And risky.' He stroked the trendy stubble he was attempting to grow, much like the one Blaine successfully sported. 'It makes you wonder . . . If Miranda was willing to take a chance on a lie that dicey, what else did she lie about?'

'And,' Ricki said, 'could a lie be what got her killed?'

TEN

R icki came home to a box of homemade pralines and a note from her landlady Kitty explaining she'd be spending at least the next few days at the bedside of a patient in the final days of his life and asking if Ricki would keep an eye on her place.

After texting a 'Thank-you' and 'Of course' to Kitty, Ricki leashed up Thor and Princess for a leisurely stroll around the neighborhood that picked up speed when black clouds overhead began dispensing fat raindrops. Once back home, she fed her brood, along with herself. 'I think you made out better than I did,' she said to the dogs, who were woofing down the homemade fresh dog food her co-pet parent Virgil insisted on paying for. She peered into the carton of half-eaten shrimp etouffee she'd retrieved from the back of her refrigerator. 'I'm not sure this is even good anymore.' She took a sniff of the rancid scent and wrinkled her nose. 'It's not.'

After a makeshift dinner of crackers, carrots, and hummus buttressed by a couple of pecan pralines, Ricki fired up her laptop. Assuming Miranda worked her way up a ladder of small lies to the whopper on her resume, Ricki emailed a smattering of friends she had left in the entertainment industry to see if they'd ever heard any dirt about Blaine Taggart's late assistant. Most of the people 'in the business' had written her off, fearful of being tainted by association after the scandals of Chris's death and Lachlan Barnes' arrest. But a few friends in various studio positions had stuck with her and could be counted on to share whatever gossip churned in the pipeline.

With LA two hours behind New Orleans, Ricki figured her friends might get back to her that evening. Which they did. Except that Ricki, exhausted by the strain of recent events, passed out the minute she lay down on the bed to wait for their responses. She woke up to the same general replies. From casting director Jenny to film executive Aaron to costume designer Marjorie, the only thing anyone knew about Miranda was that she worked for Blaine Taggart. All three plied Ricki for whatever insider info she had on Miranda's demise, putting her in the position of feeding gossip instead of tapping into it.

Disappointed to hit a dead end, Ricki went to bed hoping Cookie and Theo had better luck. They'd agreed to rendezvous and compare notes after work the next day at the Bayou Backyard, which would be kicking off its Halloweenie Bar Crawl Challenge. *I have to come up with a new game plan,* Ricki thought as she readied for work. *Which sounds great in theory but I have zero idea what it might actually be.*

When she got to Miss Vee's in the morning, she found Olivia already there. The intern was leaning out the window, her body twisted to an angle that allowed her to aim her phone's camera at Duncan-Sejour's second floor.

'Morning,' Ricki said, knowing full well she'd startle her cousin.

'Ah!' Olivia bumped her head as she tried to extricate herself from the bay window. She hopped down to the floor and tucked her orange V-neck T-shirt into her boyfriend jeans. The T-shirt was an homage to the season, as were the bold streaks of black and orange in her blonde hair. 'Why are you here so early?' She managed to make this sound like an accusation.

'It's nine thirty, only a half hour before opening. I'm usually here even earlier, and the question is, why are *you* here so early? Oh, and by the way, it's a hella no on sneaking pix of Duncan-Sejour.' Ricki placed her to-go cup of coffee on the shop desk.

'I wasn't,' Olivia protested. 'I was taking pictures of . . . of . . . the sunrise.'

Ricki mimed shock. 'That is so wild, because it came up around six a.m. at my place. Which is maybe about a mile away from here. Oh, and also . . . in the *east*.' She pointed in the opposite direction from Duncan-Sejour.

'Whatevs,' Olivia said with the requisite Gen Z eye roll. 'Just so you know, I've gotten tons of likes on my socials about Blaine and Bon V*eeev*il. People have told me my posts are why they came to the shop or bought tickets for the haunted house tour. If you don't want to thank me, you should at least give me double internship credit.'

'How's this? I'm going to show my gratitude by letting you be the baker-teacher for the children's cooking class.'

'*Noooo.*' Olivia delivered this as an elongated whine. 'Not kids. They're the *worst.*'

'Don't worry, the first class is easy. Just making popcorn balls. You get to take home any leftovers.'

'I guess that's something,' Olivia said with a lack of enthusiasm.

Ricki thrust a stack of flyers into Olivia's hands. 'The class is at three. Zellah's going to help. I ordered everything you need from Winn-Dixie. You can pick it up after you distribute these flyers to see if we can find Red's owner.'

'I kind of hope we don't.' Olivia gazed at the kitten, who was curled up under the desk. 'She's so adorbs.'

'She is.' Ricki bent down to pet Red.

'Excuse me.' A young man appeared in the shop doorway. He had curly black hair, dark brown eyes, and an aquiline nose. His jeans, clean white sneakers, and brand-new pale blue polo shirt gave him the look of a recent college grad, which Ricki assumed he was. 'Sorry if I'm interrupting but the door was open, so I thought the shop was too.' He said this with a shy but warm hint of a smile.

'We will be in a—'

'We're open,' Olivia declared, cutting off Ricki to the shop owner's amusement. The newcomer's glow of youth was only slightly marred by a couple of blooming zits and Olivia's interest was instantaneous.

'Awesome,' he said. 'I wanted to do some shopping.'

He stepped into the shop and Olivia descended upon him. 'I'm Olivia. I work here. Well, as an intern. But I know the store really well, so I can help you.'

'Cool. Oh, and I'm Jason.'

Ricki watched as Olivia led Jason around the shop, explaining how the cookbooks were shelved by decade, then category. He appeared to be half-listening, pulling books off the shelves until he had an armful. He deposited them on the desk.

'I should get some stuff too,' he said, gesturing to a display of vintage gadgets like a 1950s butter dish and coasters dating back to the 1940s.

'Sure,' Olivia said. 'We have more in the back of the shop.' She handed Jason a shopping basket, one of a dozen Lady had scored for Ricki from an old grocery store going through a remodel, and led him towards the back wall of the small shop.

As Ricki began adding up the cost of the books, Cookie poked her head into the shop. 'Hey, I'm clocking in for work but wanted to tell you I dug up good dirt on Miranda. Are we still on for the Bayou Boneyard tonight after the last tour?'

'Excellent. And yes. Can you do me a favor and confirm with the others?'

'No problem. See you then, if not before.'

Cookie left and Ricki continued adding the cost of the books. Slowly, her amusement turned to suspicion, which morphed into annoyance. The two twenty-somethings returned to the desk counter, Jason's basket loaded with kitchenware. 'Ricki, guess what?' Olivia asked, excited. 'Jason was an intern too. And it turned into a real job.'

'Uh huh.' Ricki placed a fist on her hip and stared Jason down. 'And does your boss have the initials B.T.?'

'Kind of,' Jason admitted reluctantly.

'And did he send you over here telling you to spend a ton of money?'

'Mmm . . . maybe.' A flush worked its way up Jason's neck to his face as he stammered this.

'What's going on?' Olivia asked, confused.

'Jason works for Blaine Taggart. Right, Jason?'

Jason opened his mouth to respond, then gave a small, embarrassed nod.

Olivia gaped at him. 'You do? That is so cool.'

'No,' Ricki said. She glared at Jason, who wilted a little. 'Not cool. When people come to this shop, sometimes it's to replace a special cookbook that was damaged or lost or belonged to a late parent. Maybe a late grandparent. They buy a cookbook or a gadget that brings back special memories. Browsers may not have a specific goal, but they love it when they find a community cookbook from a church they belonged to or an historical site they visited. There's almost always a personal connection to what they buy. But this . . .' She gestured to Jason's books. 'This isn't a collection. It's a stack. You just pulled a bunch of books and stuff because your boss told you to.'

Ricki faced Olivia. 'Reshelve everything.' She faced Jason. 'And tell your boss we don't need his pity shopping.'

'S—s—sorry.'

'Don't be.' Olivia glared at Ricki. 'You were doing something nice. We're the ones who should be saying we're sorry.' She waved a dismissive hand at Ricki. 'Ignore her. She's in a mood. I'll walk you out.' Olivia gave her high ponytail a flip in Ricki's direction and tossed a '*Rude!*' to her as she exited the shop with Jason.

Ricki steamed as she restocked all of Jason's attempted purchases. She debated texting Blaine an angry message to stay out of her life and her shop, but after an internal debate opted not to. *Better not to engage,* she thought. *Plus, much as I hate it, I may need him to help uncover what was going on with Miranda. What I* definitely *need is a new affirmation that will help me not want to give Blaine a swift kick in the butt.*

She finished restocking and returned to the shop desk. She opened the desk's single drawer and took out a small, worn book of affirmations. Ricki flipped through it until she found the chapter on anger management. She read through them before landing on one that felt appropriate: 'I choose now to release anger and reclaim my happiness.'

She said it out loud several times, then repeated it in her head. But the anger and frustration remained. She finally gave up.

While the affirmation might not have achieved its intended effect, it did send Ricki a clear message. The only way for her to reclaim happiness would be to solve the mysteries surrounding Miranda Fine and rob Blaine of any reason to insinuate himself into her life.

ELEVEN

The Bayou Backyard, affectionately known as the BB by regulars, was a popular hangout any night, but the kickoff of the Halloweenie Bar Crawl Challenge magnified the size of the crowd. Two burly bouncers were kept busy ushering the over served out of the establishment and checking for fake IDs at the indoor-outdoor bar's entrance. Ricki waved a cheery goodbye to twenty-year-old Olivia as she was turned away with a group of her sorority sisters. Olivia stuck out her tongue in response before heading off to find a bar more loosey-goosey about proof of age.

The Bon Vee gang had assembled at 'their table.' Their friendship with owner Ky Nguyen, along with Ricki's amorphous relationship with co-owner Virgil Morel, earned them special privileges, like laying claim to a prime spot by the main indoor bar. The location was generally quieter than the outdoor area, where raucous games of cornhole and old-fashioned horseshoes drew throngs of frat boys. If the weather was bad, rain on the indoor bar area's tin roof sounded like guns going off on a battlefield, drowning out conversation. But on this evening, the night sky was awash in stars, not clouds.

Zellah hurried over and slid into a spot across from Ricki on the bench. 'Sorry I'm late. I wanted to finish my new mural at the deli.'

'Did you manage to get any paint on the wall?' Cookie motioned to blotches of color on the artist's black overalls and the tips of her braids.

'Funny stuff,' Zellah said. 'Don't take it personally if I add a dorky white girl who can't dance to the mural.'

A waiter delivered the group's drinks and took Zellah's order. 'Where's Mordant?' Ricki asked after a welcome sip of her Pimm's Cup cocktail.

'Doing a side hustle. He won't tell me what it is yet. It's all very secretive. But he needs to bring in more money. He's been so happy since we started dating that his tour tips have shrunk.' Zellah preened a bit. Off their quizzical expressions, she explained, 'People don't want a haunted history tour guide who's happy.'

'How can they tell?' Cookie asked the question on Ricki's mind, who was thankful she didn't pose it and wind up on the receiving end of Zellah's glare.

Theo approached their table and took a seat next to Zellah. 'Hey.' He flagged a waiter and ordered a whiskey neat. 'What?' he said to the others, noticing they were staring at him.

'Your hair,' Ricki said, choking back a laugh. 'The highlights.'

'Yeah.' Theo ran a hand over his moussed 'do.' His light-brown hair now gleamed with blond highlights. 'Thought I'd mix it up a little.'

'Someone brought Blaine Taggart's latest magazine cover to their stylist,' Cookie teased.

'She already had it. Boy, do the ladies love the guy.' Theo didn't bother to hide the envy in his voice.

The waiter delivered Zellah's dirty martini and Theo's whiskey. With the drink orders complete, Ricki got down to business. 'I got a message from Nina before I came here tonight. The Crime Scene Unit found evidence of a struggle in the tomb. There were signs of defensive wounds on Miranda, indicating she fought back against whoever was with her. They also found a footprint on the bat tray that's a match for Miranda's sneaker. The footprint indicates that at one point Miranda stepped on the tray, slipped, and fell. She hit her head on the hard edge of the marble bench and the medical examiner determined the blow killed her. The police think whoever Miranda fought with put her on the bench to delay the discovery of her body. Visitors would assume she was part of the tour.'

Ricki took a breath to recover, followed by a drink of her cocktail. She'd never get used to verbalizing the details of a murder. 'Nina also said the police need to hold on to the tray as evidence, but they'll get it back to me eventually so I can wash and sell it. I don't see that happening.'

Theo shrugged. 'If you don't wash the footprint, it's what they call murderabilia. People spend a lot of money for that stuff. You could make a killing on it.' He heard himself and added apologetically, 'that came out wrong.'

Ricki shuddered. 'Ugh, ghoulish. Calling a forever ban on murderabilia. Back to Miranda. Lyla can't be here because Kaitlyn has an early volleyball practice in the morning, but she couldn't think of any new development to share. Cookie, you said you have an update.'

'Yup,' Cookie said with a nod. 'I worked up the courage to insinuate myself into the Westwego grapevine.'

'Awesome,' Ricki said with a supportive pat on the back. 'I'm proud of you.'

Cookie glowed from the praise. 'Living next door to Blaine Taggart was a big help with that, no surprise. Suddenly people I haven't spoken to in fifteen years wanted to hear from me. Anyhoo, Miranda dated this guy Chess Villeneuve all through high school. They were going to go to the West Bank campus of Delgado Community college together and had saved up for an apartment. But Miranda dumped him and then took off for California with their money. Word on the Westwego streets is that Chess is still furious about this. And he has an ugly temper.'

'Interesting. What did you say his name is?' Cookie repeated it and Ricki typed it into the Notes app on her phone. She turned her attention to Theo. 'Have you uncovered anything useful?'

'I believe I have,' Theo said, a touch smugly. 'I ran into Father Gabriel on the way to getting my hair cut—'

'Done.' Zellah said this with a sly wink to the others.

'Fine, getting my hair "done."' Theo directed air quotes at her. 'I know he'd had issues with Miranda, so I brought up her death. And lemme tell you, that's one priest who didn't sound too priestly talking about her. Long story short, she made his life the opposite of heaven. His words, not mine.'

'Also interesting. Except . . .' Ricki hesitated. 'He's such a nice man. And it's hard to imagine a priest as a killer.'

'Nice people have killed before,' Theo said. 'When they interview people after a murder, there's always a neighbor saying, "I had no idea. He always seemed like such a nice guy." I don't know about priests, though.' He typed on his phone. 'Whoa. When I write "Priests who have", the word "Murdered" comes up as the second search result. Right after "left the priesthood."'

'I guess we have to add Father Gabriel to the list of suspects.'
Ricki did so. 'You all had better luck than me. I got in touch
with the few LA entertainment industry friends I have left and
asked if they'd heard any stories about Miranda. All they know
is she is – was – Blaine's assistant. She may have been despised
in Westwego but she was low-pro in LA.'

'Low-pro?' Theo repeated, confused.

'Low profile.' Cookie patted Ricki on the shoulder. 'Spend
enough time with this one and you learn to speak Hollywood.'

'I didn't expect to add anything to this conversation,' Zellah
said, nibbling on a martini olive. 'But it turns out I can. My café
is closest to the wall dividing Bon Vee from Duncan-Sejour, so
I hear stuff going on over there. Nothing much until last night.
I stayed late to wash down the tables and I heard Blaine on the
phone with someone. I knew it was him because he was yelling
at one point.'

Galvanized by this new development, Ricki pushed aside her
Pimm's Cup and leaned in toward Zellah. 'Could you hear what
he was saying?'

'Only a little because the hedges and wall baffle the sound.
But I know he said something about not being scared and having
enough money for the best lawyer in the country. Then he must
have realized he was yelling because he stopped and started talking
much quieter. I couldn't make out anything else he was saying.'

Ricki sat back and thought for a moment. 'It could relate to
Miranda. But it could also have to do with a Hollywood thing,
like a deal. Either way, you should let Nina know.'

'I hope it's the Hollywood thing,' Cookie said. 'He's too hot
to go to jail.'

Zellah fixed a look on her. 'You did not just say that.'

Ky Nguyen, Virgil's affable business partner, came their way
carrying a huge platter of assorted appetizers. 'Nice highlights,
Theo. You look like an ex-boyfriend of mine who went blond in
order to join the Krewe of Dolly.'

'Krewe of Dolly is a marching dance troupe of Dolly Parton
enthusiasts,' Cookie explained to Ricki.

'I've been in New Orleans long enough to know what the Krewe
of Dolly is,' Ricki responded. 'Ky, is your friend a member?'

Ky shook his head. 'He never made it to an event. He was

practicing how to walk in high-heeled rhinestone cowboy boots and it did not go well. He spent months in a much more orthopedic boot.' He placed it in the middle of the table. 'A treat for y'all. Ricki, before I forget, Virgil and I were talking over business today and I told him you were stopping by. He said to tell you he's sorry he hasn't been in touch but he will be.'

'That's a whole lotta nothing,' Ricki muttered. 'At least he sent over apology snacks.' She helped herself to a crawfish hand pie.

'Oh, those aren't from Virgil. They're from our celebrity guest.'

Ky beamed as he indicated a mob near the BB entry. A slim but muscled man clad in a black jacket over a black T-shirt and jeans, parted the crowd, using his taut arms to move people aside, creating a path for none other than Blaine Taggart. Blaine's recently anointed assistant Jason tagged along behind him.

'Well, if it isn't the maybe murderer himself.' Theo smoothed down his hair, a gesture that was rapidly becoming a tic.

'Can you believe the coincidence?' Cookie gushed this as she watched the star work his way through a receiving line of admirers.

'No. I can't.' Ricki glowered at the actor, her level of besotted a zero to Cookie's eleven out of ten. 'I'm a thousand percent sure that coincidence has nothing to do with this.'

TWELVE

Blaine spotted Ricki and his face lit up. The actor's bulked-up bodyguard led him to the Bon Vee friends. His head swiveled back and forth as he kept an eye on the BB patrons, who didn't bother to hide their excitement at the sighting of the man who'd led the *Code Name: Blue Heron* franchise about a hacker-turned-CIA operative to billions in ticket sales.

'OK if I join you?' Blaine asked, to a resounding yes from everyone except Ricki. He took a seat next to her while his bodyguard nabbed a place next to Cookie, positioning himself so he could scan the crowd.

'You get Mister Handsome while I get a Bond villain,' Cookie said under her breath to Ricki.

'Trust me, I'd switch with you in a heartbeat,' Ricki whispered back. 'But it'd be too awkward.'

Blaine gestured vaguely to both men. 'This is my bodyguard Nat and my friend and assistant Jason.'

'It's not too hard to guess which one of us is which,' Jason, who'd squeezed in at the far end of the same picnic bench, delivered this to polite chuckles.

A waiter and waitress, in competition for Blaine's order, hovered over him. 'Can I get you something?' They asked this simultaneously, then glowered at each other.

'Sure.' Blaine landed this in the space between them, which didn't help the competition. 'I'll have a—'

Nat cleared his throat. He and Blaine exchanged a look before Blaine put in orders of a club soda for each of them. Nat responded with an almost imperceptible nod.

'Jason, whatcha having?' Blaine called across the table to his assistant.

'Whatever you are,' Jason called back, sounding insecure and eager to please.

'You got it.' Blaine added a third club soda to his order. 'Man, is Jason gonna be disappointed,' he said sotto voce to Ricki, who forced herself not to reward him with a laugh.

The waiter and waitress dashed off in a race to retrieve the sodas. Blaine glanced around the BB. 'Cool place.'

'Yes,' Ricki said. 'How did you find out I'd be here? Because I know it's not an accident.'

'I'm not claiming it is. When Jason was at your store, he heard you and your friend talking about getting together tonight to talk about Miranda's murder. Seeing how she was my assistant, I've got skin in this game. I wanted to be in on the conversation.'

'Sorry, you got here too late. We're done talking about it.'

Blaine frowned and uttered a gentle curse. 'Any updates?'

'None worth following up on,' Ricki lied. Her checkered history with Blaine made Ricki instinctively wary. The possibility that he was Miranda's killer cemented those instincts.

The actor placed his elbow on the old wooden table and rested his chin on his wrist, consumed with thought. *That's a great pose for his next cover shoot*, was Ricki's immediate thought. Having beaten the waiter to the serving finish line, the waitress delivered Blaine's order, making sure to save his drink for last and to brush up against him as she set it in front of him. The gesture went down in defeat as he ignored her, and she slunk off. 'I keep trying to understand why Miranda would put you down as a reference,' he said. 'She had to have known I'd catch on to the lie and fire her once we got to New Orleans.'

'Maybe she thought I'd feel bad for her and talk you out of it,' Ricki said, knowing she was a softy at heart and wondering if it was common knowledge back in Los Angeles. 'Plus, in Hollywood, there's a history of people being rewarded for telling out-there lies. I remember there was a low-level agent who had a problem with his cell phone and sent a letter pretending to be one of his boss's big-time producer clients to goose the cell company into giving him a new phone. The producer was so impressed with his ruse that he fired his big agent and hired the low-level guy to replace him.'

'I know exactly who you're talking about,' Blaine said. 'He co-owns the whole agency now.'

'I know, I heard.' Ricki had to admit it felt good to share stories with someone who could relate to them.

Blaine dropped his arm and picked up his club soda. 'The thing is, I did respect Miranda's drive. She made all of her own connections. She didn't have the advantage of nepotism, like so many up and comers in town have.' He gestured to Jason, who indeed looked disappointed to be nursing a club soda. 'He's a nepo baby. His father's a huge entertainment attorney. Mine, in fact. That's how Jason got the job.'

Cookie contorted her body to see around Ricki and zero in on Blaine. The fact that the position enhanced her cleavage was no accident. 'Blaine, is it true you do all your stunts?' She actually batted her eyelashes as she asked this.

'Not all of them,' Blaine answered, the picture of modesty. He cast a fond glance at Nat. 'This guy doesn't just keep an eye out for me in places like this. He's my stuntman. And my half-brother.' He gave Nat a gentle poke in the ribs. 'Means I got two nepo babies on staff, don't it?'

Nat gave an embarrassed shrug. 'Guilty as charged.'

As Cookie engaged both Taggarts in a conversation about the excitement and peril of Blaine's stunts, Ricki thought about the movie star's references to 'Nepo baby,' the overused term for Hollywood offspring whose successful parents gave them a career leg up that eluded outliers like Miranda. Connections meant everything in the brutally competitive industry.

Something clicked for Ricki. She recalled her brief conversation with Miranda when they first met. A couple of things the assistant had said puzzled Ricki at the time, but she'd shrugged them off as small talk. But were they so small? Miranda had emphasized wanting to specifically meet Ricki. She'd made odd references to the two of them, complete strangers, having tons to talk about and a lot in common, then followed this with a weird wink.

A morass of thoughts suddenly coalesced into one out-there, but not impossible, idea. 'Do you think Miranda was related to me?'

Ricki's blurt silenced the other conversations and earned her stunned looks from everyone. Blaine spoke for all when he uttered a bewildered, 'Huh?'

'I know it sounds crazy,' Ricki said, the words tumbling out of her. 'But it's not. Genealogy apps show the biological connections ranging from really close to really distant. But still there.

Since I'm trying to find my birth family, I shared my DNA results on two of the most popular apps. I haven't had much luck because no relatives except Olivia seem interested in finding their roots and she dropped out the minute she found out she wasn't related to French royalty.'

'That's the trouble with being born in Louisiana,' Zellah said. 'We all pretty much know where we came from.'

Ricki extracted her cell phone from the 1980s brightly-colored patchwork fanny pack she'd bought on a whim and had proved indispensable. She opened an app and searched it. 'Nothing here.'

'I gotta say, it's a reach.'

Ricki ignored Blaine's skepticism. She closed the app and opened another: yourroots.com. The others watched, intrigued. Ricki's brow creased as she searched the app. Then she held up the phone triumphantly. 'Yes!'

'What, what?' Cookie, impatient, bounced up and down on the bench. 'I swear, this is as exciting as one of Blaine's movies.'

'Thanks,' the star said, doing his best to sound humble.

'I haven't checked this app in months. I pretty much gave up on it. If I had, I would have seen that Miranda is . . .' Ricki squinted at the small screen. 'My third or fourth cousin.'

'Seriously?' Blaine stared at the phone over her shoulder. 'This is wild.'

'Let me see that.' Cookie took the phone from Ricki. 'This is huge. Aside from the whole murder thing, it might be a clue to your birth family.' She swiped through screens. 'Dang. She didn't link to a family tree. There's only the standard genealogy site disclaimer: "You and Miranda may share a set of great-great-grandparents. You could also be from different generations (removed cousins) or share only one ancestor (half cousins)."' She handed the phone back to Ricki. 'Another dead end for you. Sorry.'

'I don't think it's a dead end at all,' Zellah said. 'It's the first connection you've found to someone besides a Charbonnet. Miranda may have family in the area. You need to track them down.'

'Oh, you know it,' Ricki said, buzzing with excitement from the discovery.

Theo held up his drink and motioned to Ricki with it. 'But keep in mind, you may also be tracking down Miranda's murderer.'

'True,' Ricki acknowledged, her excitement taking a hit. She silently castigated herself for missing the possibility that in terms of local residents from Miranda's past, there might be a family member in addition to an ex-boyfriend who had a grudge against her. 'I haven't had a chance to go through the journal I found from Charbonnet's. I need to do that and see if someone named Fine is listed. There might be genealogical link.'

Ky appeared at their table. 'Blaine, the current high scorer in our Halloweenie darts challenge asked me to invite you to play against him. Loser earns the title of Halloweenie. Winner gets the tab picked up for them and their guests. Feel free to say no.'

'Are you kidding?' Blaine stood up. He threaded his fingers together and cracked his knuckles. 'It is *on!*'

The crowd whooped so loudly Ricki's ears rang. Blaine made his way to the dart board hanging on the other side of the bar's interior, followed by Nat, who made sure everyone gave him space. His challenger, a beefy kid wearing a T-shirt decorated with his fraternity logo, aimed at the board and threw a dart, barely missing the bullseye. He moved out of the way so Blaine could assume the position. The actor lined up shot and took it. 'Bullseye!' Ky, who was keeping score yelled. After a few similar rounds, Blaine was declared the winner and his competitor a Halloweenie.

'Thank you, thank you.' Blaine took a few satiric bows. 'I'm picking up the tab for everyone tonight.' Once again, Ricki's ears rang from the crowd's enthusiastic reaction.

'That's not how it works,' Ky said, laughing. 'I'm supposed to comp you.'

'Yeah, I know,' Blaine said. 'But I spent a month being trained by darts experts for the fifth *Code Name: Blue Heron* film, so it wasn't exactly a fair fight. But . . .' He held up a hand. 'First, join me in a toast to my friend Ricki James-Diaz.' Jason ran over to Blaine and handed him his club soda. 'If it weren't for her, I wouldn't be in New Orleans and at this awesome bar.'

The entire bar roared a toast to a mortified Ricki, who shrunk into herself. 'This is a painful reminder of something I learned about actors from Chris,' she said out of the side of her mouth to Cookie. 'It's incomprehensible to them that someone might actually not want to be the center of attention.'

'Blaine is kind of a showboater,' Cookie acknowledged. 'Nat's actually a really nice guy. He's not only Blaine's bodyguard and stunt double and half-brother. He's also his sober companion.'

'Ah.' The look the brothers exchanged that resulted in Blaine ordering a club soda made sense to Ricki now. 'He and Chris used to get wasted, but I didn't know he was in recovery. I'm glad he's getting help.'

'He needed it,' Cookie said. 'Nat didn't come out and say so but I got the impression Blaine could be mean when he was under the influence.'

'I never saw that myself, but I'll make a note of it on our suspect list.' Ricki craned her neck. She saw Blaine surrounded by adoring fans of both sexes. 'All I can think about right now is my genealogy connection to Miranda. I'm going to sneak out. Tell the others I'll see them tomorrow.'

Ricki left the bar, speed-walking the few blocks between the BB and her home. She was determined to delve into the book-keeping journal but first, she needed to place a call. After plying Thor and Princess with love and treats and taking them for jog around the block, she FaceTimed her parents, who had retired to Puerto Vallarta, Mexico, Luis's ancestral home and still home to his extended family.

After a few rings, Josepha's cheery face popped up on the screen, accompanied by the strains of a mariachi band. '*Hola, querida niña*,' Ricki's mother greeted her.

Half of Luis's face joined Josepha on the screen. 'What she said.' He added the blow of a kiss to this.

'*Hola*, you two crazy kids,' Ricki said, grinning. 'Where are you?'

'The Isla Del Rio Cuale River walk.' Josepha flipped the camera focus to show the scenic location. 'We're taking a stroll after our Zumba class.' She flipped the phone's focus back to her and Luis.

'Everything OK, Querida?' As always, Luis asked this with much concern. He lived ready to jump on a plane at the slightest indication things were *not* OK.

'Yes.' Ricki chose not to mention the most recent murder at Bon Vee. 'I just have a quick question for Mom. Does the last name "Fine" mean anything to you? I know it's common but

still . . . Did it ever come up in conjunction to me? My abandon-
ment, my adoption?'

The strains of a lovely mariachi song filled the time Josepha
took to run the name through her bank of memories. 'No. Doesn't
ring a bell. But you should talk to Kitty Kat.' Ricki's landlady
happened to be a dear friend of Josepha's from their days working
as nurses at Charity Hospital prior to Hurricane Katrina. Thanks
to the friendship, Ricki rented her charming home at way below
market value. 'Kitty was on call for your delivery. My shift didn't
start until the day after you were born. And remember, I was a
NICU nurse. My concern was making sure you were thriving.
And you have been ever since your tiny little self came into my
life.'

Ricki joined her mother and father in tearing up. 'I love you
both so much. And yes, I'll talk to Kitty when she gets home.
She's with an end-of-life patient.'

'How did the name "Fine" come up?' Josepha wondered.

'It's a long story. I'll fill you in when there's more to tell you.'

'You sure everything's *bien*?' Luis asked, doubt in his voice.
'I got the flight schedule on my phone. I can be in New Orleans
in six hours. Quicker if I take a nonstop flight on a different
airline and don't worry about getting the miles. You know I'd do
that for you, *querida*.'

'I know. Trust me, Dad, if I need you, I will make the call.'

'Do you need a new baseball bat?'

'No, the one you got me for my birthday is still in great shape.'

'I'll order you a new one as backup.'

Knowing there was no way she could talk her father out of
this, Ricki didn't argue. She spent a few minutes hearing the
latest from her parents' lives – a fellow senior wound up in the
hospital after trying a pole dancing class; an avocado shortage
had created a black market in avocados; Luis's four sisters had
stopped talking to each other, then started, then stopped again
even though no one remembered why they'd stopped talking to
each other in the first place. Finally, the three James-Diazes
signed off with much love and tears.

Ricki inhaled another of Kitty's delicious pralines – *For an
energy boost*, she lied to herself. She then opened the drawer
where she'd put the Charbonnet's bookkeeping journal for

safekeeping and settled onto the living room sofa, recently re-
upholstered by Kitty in a purple, green, and gold tweed. She
cracked open the journal.

Two hours later, she shut it.

She'd searched through the journal several times. She'd even
held pages up to the light to see if she could detect any faded
or secret writing.

In the entire book, which covered the time frame during which
Genevieve Charbonnet would have been pregnant, creating the
genealogical chain that led to Ricki, there was no mention of a
'Fine'. Even more mysterious, there was no mention of an Irish
busboy.

It was as if the man Genevieve claimed had fathered her child
never existed.

THIRTEEN

Ricki slept poorly, unable to turn off her brain as it contemplated all possible scenarios pertaining to the mythical Irishman. She couldn't stop running through them – in the shower, getting dressed, walking the dogs, driving to work.

'Good morning,' Lyla said in a sing-songy voice as Ricki arrived at Bon Vee and exited her car, which she'd parked next to Lyla's.

'Morning.' The two started towards the mansion. 'I thought you were supposed to be at a volleyball practice.'

'I was. But I fell asleep at the practice and started snoring, which disturbed Kaitlyn's ability to concentrate on the game. Could be a while before she welcomes me back to court.' Lyla released a fake sigh, then flashed a cheery smile. 'Great shirt.'

'Thanks.' Ricki had donned another Halloween-themed tee. This one read 'My other car is a broom' over the illustration of a witch. The shirt was only available in an extra-large size, so she wore it as a tunic over black leggings and black ballet flats. 'I'd love to run something by you. Do you have a minute?'

'Due to my deviated septum-induced snoring, I have a lot of them. Shoot.'

Ricki shared her discovery about the Irish busboy – or rather lack of one – with Lyla. 'What do you think?'

'Hmm . . .' Lyla said, as they passed Gumbo and Jambalaya, who seemed to be having a contest to see who could screech louder. 'Shh, you two, I can't concentrate,' Lyla scolded. 'There are a few ways to go here. Vee could have made up the busboy to protect the real father of her child. But if he did exist and was from another country, the restaurant could have paid him off the books, which is why there's no record of him in the journal.'

'Hmmm. I hadn't thought of that.'

'There's also the chance the Irish busboy existed but worked for another restaurant. Do you know if Vee specifically said he worked for Charbonnet's?'

'I don't remember. I have to ask Eugenia.'

'Good timing. She's right over there.' Lyla indicated the parterre garden, where Eugenia was directing groundskeeper Darius as he layered more fake cobwebs and giant spiders over parterre bushes. 'I'll see you later. Kaitlyn insisted I watch volleyball tutorials so I have a better understanding of the game's intricacies. I have to go figure out a way not to watch them but let her think I did.'

'You adore your daughter,' Ricki said, amused. 'You're gonna watch the videos.'

'I know,' Lyla said with a genuine sigh. 'Lordie, it's hard being a good mother.'

She peeled off for her office. Ricki called to Eugenia to get her attention. The board president acknowledged this and completed her conversation with Darius. The two women met up halfway between the garden and the house, and Ricki repeated what she'd shared with Lyla. 'Did Great-grandmother Vee – and it will never not be strange saying that – did Miss Vee make a point of saying the busboy worked at Charbonnet's?'

'Yes.' Eugenia frowned, barely creating a line on her porcelain skin, still dewy despite her age nearing seventy. *Please let me have inherited the Charbonnet skin*, Ricki thought in a sidebar to the current conversation. 'But now it seems we don't know what the truth is,' Eugenia continued. 'I'll make sure to share this with whatever new private investigator I hired. I'm afraid I haven't had much luck on that score so far. I've found it to be a rather sketchy profession, at least in New Orleans.' She studied the parterre with a critical eye. 'I know what we're missing. One of those funny witches crashing into the bushes. I'll send Theo out to pick one up as soon as he returns from breakfast with one of our donors.'

Eugenia strode off, missing Ricki's amusement at Theo, who fancied himself one of the city's prominent movers and shakers, being relegated to errand boy.

After a thankfully busy day of sales, Ricki changed into her witch costume for the kids' haunted house tour, the first of the evening. Visitors included a group from the nearby Boys & Girls Club, and Ricki got a kick out of how enthusiastically they embraced the library as a witches' lair, fighting for turns to stir the prop cauldron. All wanted to pet Red, who climbed to the top of a bookshelf to escape the sticky clutches of her adoring kid fans.

After the tour ended, Ricki cleaned up the candy wrappers and empty juice boxes left by the kids, then sat in the window seat to take a break before the tour for adults began. She glanced out the window and saw limousines pulling up to Duncan-Sejour. Valets scurried to empty the limos of passengers and drive across the street to the St Aquilinus lot, which appeared to be the designated parking location. Small clutches of people dressed in black trod a slow, solemn path from the sidewalk to the mansion's front door where Nat stood. He gave each of them a once-over, then allowed them to enter the home.

'Blaine must be hosting a memorial service for Miranda,' Ricki said to Red. It occurred to her that the memorial would be a great way to meet Miranda's relatives – who might be hers as well. She shed her witch's cape and fake nose, then texted Olivia, who was on deck to help out wherever she was needed on the tours.

The college student wandered in moments later, chomping down on a caramel apple. 'This was such an awesome idea for today's kids' crafts. How have I lived my life without caramel apples? I won't be making that mistake again.' The statement, issued through a mouthful of sticky caramel, came out in a sort of slow motion.

'I need you to cover for me. It looks like there's a memorial for Miranda next door and I'm going to crash it.'

Ricki handed Olivia the cape and nose. Olivia looked askance at them. 'Do I have to wear the nose? It's hella janky.'

'Janky or not, put it on. Now, let me hear your cackle. It'll be an adult tour, so go for it.'

Olivia threw back her head and let out a guffaw so screeching it set Red yowling and skittering to cower behind the vase where Ricki displayed loose peacock feathers she collected. Olivia plucked the kitten from its hiding spot and issued soothing murmurs to the tiny being.

Ricki grabbed her black cross purse. 'If I'm not back by the time the tour is over, lock up for me. And thanks.'

Ricki hurried out of Bon Vee towards Duncan-Sejour, taking

a right turn onto its entry walk. She slowed to a respectful gait behind a stream of mourners, meeting eyes with Nat at the top of the mansion steps. He did a double-take when he saw her. 'I noticed you're holding a memorial,' she said in the most somber tone she could muster up. 'If it's for Miranda, which I'm guessing it is, I'd like to pay my respects.'

'Uh huh.'

Ricki gave Nat credit for his skepticism as he confiscated her phone – which Ricki expected, knowing it was de rigeur at similar Hollywood events – and stepped aside to allow her entry.

The mansion was packed with a wide spectrum of guests. From blue to white collar, from twenty to seventy-somethings, all looked in awe of their majestic surroundings. As Blaine worked his way through the mourners, he left a trail of giggling women and fan-guys in his wake. 'They got Commander's Palace to cater this thing,' she heard a guy in the group standing near her say. 'Nice, huh?'

'Too bad we don't have our phones to take pix for our socials,' said a girl whose outfit screamed wannabe influencer.

'I'll let you borrow this for a small price.' A punk of a guy held up his wrist to show off a smart watch.

Nat materialized at his side as if by magic. He held out a hand. 'Watch.'

The punk's friends smirked as their sheepish friend turned over the watch to Nat.

Not wanting to engage with Blaine, Ricki dodged him, threading her way through the throng to the dining room where a spread from Commander's covered the massive and ornately carved walnut table. The scent wafting up from a chafing dish of pecan-crusted gulf fish reminded Ricki she'd skipped dinner. She searched the table for plates.

'They're on the sideboard, along with flatware.'

Ricki turned to see who spoke. An older woman dressed in a utilitarian outfit of black pants and button-down blouse stood next to the sideboard in question. At first Ricki wondered if she was there on behalf of Commander's, but the woman's weather-beaten skin and long, thick single gray braid didn't jive with the restaurant's storied elegance. 'Thanks,' Ricki said. She picked up an empty plate and began adding servings of the delicious offerings to it.

'Nice to finally meet you, Ricki.'

Ricki stopped mid-spoonful of braised asparagus and leeks. 'Hi . . .?'

Discomfited, she posed this as a question, hoping the woman would fill in the blank. Fortunately, she did so. 'I'm Mooni Benson, Blaine's aunt. His mom was my sister.'

'Oooh. Blaine's aunt Mooni. Of course. Nice to meet you too.'

Ricki mimed shaking with the hand holding the serving spoon. Chris had told her that Blaine's childhood was what she'd call American Dickensian. His parents were drug addicts who died when he was young. He was on his own for a brief period until his aunt – the said Mooni – was released from jail after serving time for an attempted bank robbery committed with fellow members of a cult she belonged to. It was the kind of origin story Hollywood adored, with the added touch of Mooni having spent five years living under an assumed name before she was caught, then doing a 180 after being released from prison to become a vegetarian chef and doting guardian to her nephew.

'Make sure to fill your plate,' Mooni said. 'I hate waste. If there are leftovers, I'll send them back to Bon Vee with you. You've got a lot more mouths to feed over there than we do here.'

Sensing an ally, Ricki took Mooni's advice, then sidled up to her. 'I've met Nat and Jason. And of course Blaine. Now you. Who am I missing?'

'There's Lakshmi.'

'Right, the spiritual advisor and masseuse,' Ricki said, recalling the minute, middle-aged woman who'd wafted into her meeting with Blaine.

'Yes. That's what she calls herself.' Ricki caught Mooni's hint of cynicism. 'I think the only person you don't know is Delia Frontenac, Blaine's interior designer. She's a recent addition to our band of merry pranksters but seems to have done a bang-up job of ingratiating herself with my nephew.'

Ricki followed Mooni's gaze, landing on a zaftig brunette in her late thirties impeccably decked out in black suit and gray silk blouse with a pussy bow. Her perfectly waved hair fell to her shoulders. She would have been tall without heels, but her stiletto pumps made her appear twice the size of Lakshmi, who was piling a plate with the pecan-crusted fish. Delia grimaced at the elaborate floral display in the middle of the table. She plucked an infinitesimally wilted flower from the arrangement with fingers sporting lacquered red nails and thrust it in the hands of a cater-waiter standing guard over the table, obviously scolding him as she did so.

'I know her type,' Ricki said. 'I'd keep an eye on her.'

She said this half-joking. But Mooni's response chilled her.

'When it comes to Blaine,' his ex-con aunt said in an ice-cold tone, 'I keep an eye on *everyone*.'

FOURTEEN

Ricki hurriedly finished filling her plate and escaped to the mansion's spacious library, unnerved by the threatening undertone of Mooni's comment. She couldn't shake the feeling there was something off about Blaine's posse, something that went beyond the usual cloying vibe of celebrity hangers-on and wannabes. Whatever it was, the sooner the police ID'd Miranda's killer, the better.

She wandered from room to room eavesdropping on conversations and jumping on opportunities to ingratiate herself into them with a calibrated blend of grief and gossipy. 'Such a loss,' she murmured to one older couple. Noting they were of an age where they might know something about her own genealogical connection to Blaine's late assistant, she added, 'I heard there was an interesting story about Miranda's great-great-grandparents on the Fine side. Have you ever heard anything about them? Anything at all?'

The husband gave her the wary look she deserved and pulled his wife a little closer to him. 'Nope. Honey, isn't that one of our neighbors?'

They beat a quick exit. The scene repeated itself, with Ricki earning blank or strange looks from everyone she tried to mine for clues. 'I don't know a single person here,' one guest confessed. 'The invitation came for my roommate and she's out of town. Don't tell anyone I'm not Paige Offner, 'kay?'

'Sure,' Ricki said, discouraged by her failed attempts to snoop.

The girl studied Ricki's face. 'My mother is a dermatologist. If she was here, she'd tell you to get that mole checked.'

She walked away. Puzzled, Ricki checked her reflection in the hallway's gilded rococo mirror and saw she'd forgotten to remove her witch's wart. Mortified, she scraped it off. The wart confirmed her suspicion that guests were going out of their way to avoid her. *People can be so judgy*, she thought, offended. It also explained Nat's double-take when she showed up on the Duncan-Sejour doorstep. She wondered if he hadn't mentioned the wart out of politeness or as payback for Ricki butting her way into the memorial. Instinct told her it was the latter.

Lakshmi appeared at the end of the hallway holding a small, antique-looking gong. She tapped it and the gong emitted a forlorn bass note. 'Blaine would like us all to assemble for the official memorial,' she said in a deep, affected voice.

She ushered the mourners to the backyard, where a surprisingly sleek lap pool with a hot tub at the far end stretched along the estate's back wall. Folding chairs were set up on the grassy yard facing the pool. Outdoor chandeliers dangled over the seating area, casting a gentle glow.

Lakshmi waved a lit sage smudge stick over the crowd as she murmured an indecipherable chant. Guests fanned away the smoke wafting off the sage stick, which was causing several of them to cough. A violinist sawed a dirge-like tune as Blaine positioned himself behind a podium placed at the pool's limestone edge. Interior designer Delia, who appeared to be directing the event, signaled to a man operating a portable lighting board. The chandeliers dimmed and a warm spotlight bathed the actor.

Blaine's simple attire of black jeans, T-shirt, and black blazer was a textbook example of curated understatement. But Ricki knew the sum total of its cost was the equivalent of the best sales month she'd ever have at Miss Vee's. He made eye contact with his audience, who responded with rapt silence, thrilled to be honored by his soulful gaze. Then he began.

'When a soul is lost to a senseless death, it is always a tragedy,' the actor intoned, 'but when that soul is as young . . . and vibrant . . . and dynamic . . . as Miranda Jordan Fine, the world weeps a communal tear.'

A loud moaning and keening interrupted Blaine. He placed a hand on his heart. 'I feel your pain.'

'That's coming from next door,' a guest called to him, motioning to Bon Vee, where the evening's second haunted house tour was in full swing. A loud scream came from within the adjoining mansion. 'So's that,' the guest added.

Miranda might have had a point about the noise coming from our place, Ricki thought to herself, feeling a touch of guilt on top of embarrassment.

Blaine closed his eyes and drew in a breath. Then he continued, delivering a speech/performance worthy of an award, even throwing in a dash of Shakespeare, ending with 'May flights of angels sing thee to thy rest' from *Hamlet*. Ricki, who was an ardent fan of the bard, grudgingly gave Blaine credit for quoting the exact line and not shortening it like so many did.

As Blaine delivered Horatio's classic sendoff to his dying friend Hamlet, he gazed upwards to the night sky. The mourners erupted in applause. A few half-rose as if to give him a standing ovation, then caught themselves and settled back down. Blaine accepted the accolades by bowing his head and pressing his hands together in the prayer position, his go-to, fake-humble gesture. 'And now, Miranda's brother Gordy Fine would like to say a few words about his late sister.'

Ricki's antennae sparked. If Miranda had a brother, it meant Ricki had another distant cousin – someone who might offer clues to both his sister's death and Ricki's familial connection to the Fines.

Gordy Fine stepped behind the podium. He appeared to be in his mid-thirties, making him at least half-dozen years older than Miranda. The most remarkable thing about him was how absolutely unremarkable he was. The man was the walking definition of average in every aspect. His features were bland, his hair a basic brown, his height was around five-ten, and his weight correlated to it. In Ricki's eyes, he looked like the kind of guy the police would bring in to complete a lineup, his indistinguishable appearance allowing a perp's more distinctive attributes to shine.

Out of his element, Gordy fiddled with the mic, lowering it to match his height. Ricki left her spot lurking in the back of the memorial and moved closer to the front. Much to her annoyance, Blaine sidled up next to her. 'I haven't done a live performance in a while,' he whispered. 'It felt good. I'm gonna have my agent see if I can fit a Broadway gig into my sked.'

Ricki shushed him and took a step towards Gordy Fine to

make sure she heard him clearly. Not being an actor, he lacked Blaine's ability to articulate and project – although he didn't seem to have any trouble conveying resentment. 'I'm here on behalf of myself and my mother. Don't ask about my father, he cut and ran a long time ago. Mom would be here but she's, um, unavailable. Man, you'd think they'd let you off with a warning if you only kite one check.'

'How much was it for?' someone called from the mourners.

'Five grand.'

'Nice,' came the appreciative response.

'So . . . about Miranda.' Gordy fiddled with the mic again. This time, Ricki chalked it up to nerves. 'It's hard to know what to say. To be honest, we weren't close. In fact . . . she made it pretty clear she was embarrassed by her family. I didn't even know she was in town until the police called to tell me she had died.'

Gordy paused. He looked down at the podium. Ricki found herself feeling sorry for him. His sister's rejection understandably hurt. He might have been too ordinary for his high-flying sibling, but so far signs pointed to him being a relatively decent guy. His suit might not be high-end but it was respectable, as was his general appearance.

Gordy cleared his throat and continued. 'My sister may have left her friends, family, and city in the rearview mirror, but she pursued a career and made a name for herself in a tough business. What kind of sick person would kill her? No one deserves to be murdered. No one.'

The crowd murmured agreement. Ricki stole a peek at Blaine's posse, searching for a reaction that might incriminate someone. The light cast by the ornamental chandeliers was dim for sleuthing, but from what Ricki could make out, Nat, Mooni, Lakshmi, Jason, Delia, and Blaine himself were nodding with the rest of the guests. Delia even wiped away a tear. *Of course,* Ricki thought, *that could just be for effect.*

'In conclusion . . .' Gordy's stiff delivery sent the message he wasn't used to public speaking. 'Here's to my sister, and to her killer getting caught and spending the rest of their sorry life in jail.' Gordy took a step away from the podium, then stopped. 'I almost forgot the most important thing of all. In honor of my late sister, I'm offering a ten percent discount to anyone who buys a pre-owned car from my lot, Westwego Mardi Gras Motorworks.'

As Gordy handed out flyers to the nonplussed attendees, Ricki's positive impression of him plummeted. But she took a flyer, intent on paying a visit to her distant relative's used car lot for the purpose of mining whatever information she could out of him.

The mourners began to disperse. Figuring there was nothing useful left to be learned, Ricki joined them. She almost collided with a small clutch of women who suddenly came to a halt. They alternated between checking out the front entrance and whispering in gossipy tones to each other. Ricki circled around them to see what had caused the logjam.

An exceptionally tall guy in his late twenties with the kind of shaved head men resorted to when counteracting baldness stood planted in the doorway. He wore work boots, jeans, and a bright-red polo shirt with a store logo embroidered on its upper left corner. His deeply tanned skin sent the message that he didn't care if sun exposure aged him and possibly endangered his life – sunblock was for wussies.

Ricki maneuvered herself close enough to hear Nat in full security alert mode demand evidence of an invitation from the latecomer, who responded with a shrug and a sneer, 'I don't need one. I only wanted to make sure she's really dead.'

His eyes landed on the women and bore into them until one of them cracked under the pressure. 'She's gone, Chess, OK?' the woman said, her voice quavering with emotion. 'Now you know. Are you happy?'

'You bet I am.' He turned and stomped down the steps.

Chess. This had to be the boyfriend Miranda ditched, absconding with his share of their savings. His behavior made it clear that the ensuing ten or so years hadn't lessened her ex's grudge. *Which means he may have killed her or if not, have extremely useful dirt to dish*, Ricki thought.

She hurried down the estate steps, on a mission to catch up with him. 'Chess,' she called. 'Chess!'

He turned around. Ricki took a step forward and was about to engage with him when someone grabbed her. Ricki let out a scream, eliciting another scream from Olivia, the culprit who'd grabbed her arm. 'You scared me,' the intern said, ticked off. She dropped Ricki's arm. 'I almost had a heart attack.'

'*You* scared *me*,' Ricki shot back, equally ticked off, especially since Chess had disappeared.

'Whatevs. The tours are over for tonight. I have a sorority event at The Boot. It's a very popular bar near—'

'I know what The Boot is, it's won Best College Bar in America more than once, which I consider a dubious distinction. Why is the sorority holding an event there? Most of you aren't legal yet.'

'It's a mixer with one of the frats and you get a wristband if you're legal so they know they're not breaking the law. Anyway, I have to go or I'll get charged a hundred dollars because we can't miss more than two meetings a quarter and I already missed two, one for work here and one because my roommate got the world's worst haircut and she needed me.' Olivia stopped to breathe. 'I wanted to tell you I'm leaving and didn't have time to clean up the shop. But sales were good. I locked up and turned over receipts and any cash to Grandmama.'

'Thank you. Go.' Ricki made a shooing gesture. 'Have fun. It would be a tragedy for you to have to pay for missing a chance to hang out with cute guys at a bar.'

'Funny. Not.' Olivia used both hands to make thumbs-down gestures, then grinned and hugged Ricki. 'Thanks.' She ran off.

Ricki stood in place for a moment, debating whether to clean up the shop now or in the morning. She heard chatter behind her and circled around to see the women from the Duncan-Sejour hallway loading themselves into one of the limos Blaine had rented to transport mourners, who were reluctantly being ushered out the door now that the service was over. Acting on impulse, she scooted over and hopped in with them, much to their surprise.

'Hello?' The woman who said this made it very clear through her tone that her real question was, 'Who in the world are you?'

'Hello, hi.' Ricki aimed for bland with a hint of slight dim. 'I took the streetcar to the memorial. I didn't know Blaine Taggart was hiring limos for us. How cool is that? Oh, sorry. I forgot to introduce myself. *Duh.*' She put her hands on her head and rolled her eyes, gestures she hoped would telegraph she was a ditz. 'I'm Ricki. I went to college with Miranda.' She realized she had no idea which Southern California university Miranda actually attended. Before anyone could press her about this, she barreled on. 'I can't believe Chess showed up. Miranda talked about him. A lot. I don't want to gossip,' she said, adding silently to herself, *although praying you want to!* 'But I can tell you she would *not* have been happy about him showing up at her memorial.'

Ricki settled back into the limo's black leather bench. Having a billionaire boss and reasonably famous spouse, she'd been in enough limos in Los Angeles to know where they kept the booze. She casually used the tip of her high-heeled black ankle boot to press a button across from where she was sitting. A horizontal cover slid up, revealing a full bar, with wine and champagne chilling. The other limo occupants were suitably impressed. 'Anyone want a drink?'

Five hands shot up. Ricki reached for five wine glasses, but one woman had held up both hands, so she distributed four. Fortunately, while the wine was high-end, it had a screw top, so Ricki wasn't forced to futz with a corkscrew. She filled all the glasses with enough wine to generate a small booze buzz but not so much that it sloshed out of the cup every time the limo driver tackled one of the city's notorious potholes.

The women enjoyed the wine and gossiped about the night as the limo headed for the bridge that would take them over the Mississippi to the Westbank. 'So,' Ricki asked, 'how did you all know Miranda? From high school? I remember she said that's when she and Chess started dating.'

All four women nodded in the affirmative. 'It was so weird seeing him,' the woman who'd held up both hands said. Her enthusiasm had led Ricki to peg her as the limo passenger most ready to spill the tea, and the hunch was quickly proven correct. 'Miranda would have killed him for coming to her memorial.' Her eyes widened and she placed a hand over her mouth. 'Oopsie. Dumb choice of words.'

'Don't feel bad,' one of her friends said. 'Chess is *such* an a-hole.'

This comment spurred much agreement among three of the

women. But a fourth known as Britni said, 'I don't blame him
for being mad at her.'

Ricki raised an eyebrow, her curiosity about the outlier aroused.
She refilled all the women's wine glasses, using the time to subtly
check out Britni. The four women weren't twinning, they were
quadrupling: all wore extremely tight little black dresses, had
brown hair streaked with plenty of blonde, and showed off the
latest nail polish trend on similarly manicured hands. Nothing
about Britni indicated someone who would deviate from the
group norm – except her support of Chess.

'Don't listen to her,' the wannabe quadruplet named Sarah
Jane said. 'She's had the hots for Chess since forever.'

'Not true,' Britni protested. 'I haven't even thought about him
in years.'

'*Liar!*' Toni, the two-fisted drinker, sent wine spraying with
her blurt. She giggled. 'I saw the way you looked at Chess tonight.
You still wanna get with him.'

She delivered this with a little musical riff and a mock sexual
grind, earning laughter and 'You go, girls' from all of the others
except Britni.

They egged on Toni and teased Britni until Chess's defender
exploded. 'Shut up! Just shut up!' She yelled this with enough
rage to silence the other women. The energy inside the limo
instantly transformed from jocular to tense. 'Miranda was a
beeyotch. She dumped all of us the second she left New Orleans.
And she basically stole from Chess. She's the one who's low-
rent, not him. He's got a good job at Home Supply Hardware
and a condo in Metairie. Y'all been talking trash about Miranda
for ten years and now you're acting like you lost your best friend.
You're a bunch of hypocrites.' Britni had started shedding tears
during her diatribe. She grabbed a cocktail napkin and took an
angry swipe at her cheeks.

'Your mascara isn't smearing at all.' Paige, the fourth mean
girl, was impressed enough by this to ignore her friend's outburst.
'Would this be a bad time to hit up for one of your Terra Beauty
coupons?'

Britni responded with a glower. Everyone was quiet during
the rest of the limo ride, issuing muted goodbyes as they departed
one by one, leaving Ricki the sole limo occupant. She hadn't

missed the glances they shot at each other when Britni wasn't looking and wondered if they were thinking the same thing she was.

For someone claiming she hadn't thought about Chess in years, Britni knew an awful lot about him.

FIFTEEN

The empty limo made Ricki realize she hadn't given the driver her home address. She tapped on the partition separating her from him and it lowered. 'Twenty-four Odile Street, please.'

'Yes, ma'am.'

The driver turned around. Ricki froze. The man behind the wheel of the limousine was none other than Blaine's shadow, Nat Luna. Ricki's mouth opened and shut as she tried to form a reaction, finally going with a simple 'Nat! Hi.'

'Hello.' Ricki could see Nat was amused by her discomfort. 'We had to fire one of the limo drivers for making a video in front of Blaine's house, so I stepped in. I have a chauffeur's license since I sometimes drive Blaine to events and then provide his security. So, you and Miranda were best buds from college, huh? Which one?'

'Um . . .' Caught, Ricki took a chance and went with her own alma mater. 'UCLA?' She cringed, realizing she'd posed this as a question, totally giving herself away.

'Ding ding ding, the lady guessed right.'

'It was that or USC,' Ricki admitted, 'and I doubted Miranda could swing the tuition cost at USC. At least with UCLA, she could establish residency after a year and get in-state tuition.'

'I'm impressed. You really thought out your lie.'

Ricki couldn't tell from Nat's tone if he was still amused or now annoyed. She decided to be honest with him. 'The truth is, I never heard of Miranda until you guys showed up next door. I'm sure you know she listed me as a reference. Did you hear me at the bar when I discovered she and I are distantly related?' Nat shook his head. 'And Blaine didn't mention it to you? It was kind of a big development.'

'No. He's a very busy guy. There's no time to fill me in on anything that's not a top priority.'

'You'd think a murdered assistant would make the list,' Ricki said, needled by Nat's dismissal. 'Maybe he doesn't care about being a murder suspect, but I do. And so do my friends.'

'Nobody considers Blaine a suspect except a certain nosy neighbor.' Nat accompanied this dig with a meaningful look at Ricki.

'I wouldn't write off NOPD's interest so quickly,' she shot back. 'Miranda was basically Blaine's work wife. And when a wife is murdered, the husband is always the prime suspect.'

Nat tightened his grip on the limo steering wheel so tightly his knuckles turned white. 'My brother is a stand-up guy. If anyone has an issue with him, they better see me about it first.'

Ricki softened. 'Blaine talked about you sometimes when he came over to our house in LA to film videos with Chris. But I didn't know you were this close. He's lucky to have a big brother who cares about him so much.'

Nat's grip tightened further. 'I'd do anything for my little bro. Anything.'

The passion with which he delivered this made Ricki nervous. Could 'anything' also include murder?

I am having a safe, uneventful journey. She repeated the affirmation to herself, adding a bit of embellishment. *I am having a safe, uneventful journey that hopefully won't end up with my body being left by the side of the road for poking my nose where it doesn't belong.*

She faked a yawn. 'It's been a long night for both of us. Let's get out of wherever we are and go home.'

The rest of the limo ride proved uneventful, to Ricki's relief. She pretended to sleep as a way of curtailing conversation and kept the tone light when she thanked Nat for dropping her off. She casually strolled up her front steps until she was sure he was gone, then she darted inside.

Thor and Princess were snuggled up next to each other on the living room sofa. They wagged their tails and yipped greetings but didn't bother to get up. Instead, Ricki dropped down next to them. She administered pets and smooches, then texted Nina: **I have intel! Call in the morning.** Seconds later, her phone rang.

'I'm on a stakeout for a carjacking suspect and I'm bored out of my mind,' the detective said. 'Talk to me.'

Ricki shared how Chess had shown up at the tail end of the memorial, only there to vindictively confirm Miranda's death, segueing into how he had one staunch support in Britni. 'I don't know her last name but her crush on Chess borders on obsession. What if she confronted Miranda about the money she stole from Chess, they got into a fight, and Britni killed her?'

'Then hefted her over her shoulder, carried her to the Bon Vee yard, and subbed her in for the dummy in the fake tomb. How sturdy is this woman?'

'More on the boney than muscle-y side,' Ricki had to confess. 'Maybe Chess was in on it with her. But if that's a dead-end, Nat's love for his little brother is intense. And scary, frankly. I could totally see him offing anyone who's a threat to Blaine.'

'So could I. Except he's got an alibi. He went to Delcambre to buy fresh shrimp right off one of the boats for his aunt Mooni, who wanted to make a special dish for Blaine. Nat spent the night there.'

'Oh,' Ricki said, disappointed none of her leads had panned out. 'Did Zellah tell you the phone conversation she overheard where Blaine told someone he wasn't scared and could afford the best lawyer in the country?'

'Yes. We confirmed he was talking with his agent about a project. He and another actor are fighting for the rights to a biography about Charlie Chaplin. Both want to play him and their battle over it is getting ugly.'

'Big mistake on Blaine's part,' Ricki muttered. 'He's terrible at comedy.'

'I'll check out this Britni person you mentioned.'

'Are you saying that because you think she's a genuine suspect or to make me feel better?'

'Little of both.'

'Thank you. I'll take it.' Ricki hesitated, then took the plunge on an unrelated topic. 'I kind of feel like we might have entered the friend zone. If we haven't, no worries. But if we have, I'll let you know when we all go out on our next Halloweenie Challenge pub crawl. If you're up for it, you can join us. But if you're not, that's OK too. But if you are—'

'I've been to Halloweenie Challenges before. I could use a night of tomfoolery. Besides, I used to work undercover and I know firsthand there's nothing better than a relaxed, liquored-up suspect. Which a few of y'all still are.'

'OK, making the night sound a lot less fun.'

'I'd be happy to show up when I can. October is a busy month for me.'

'I bet. I can see how Halloween would inspire extra criminal mischief out there.'

'Right.' Ricki picked up an unusually evasive tone in the detective's voice. A crackle of radio communication on Nina's end interrupted the call. 'All units, perp is leaving the house. Let's get the son of a—'

The call ended.

Ricki leashed up Thor and Princess for their evening walk. She replayed Nina's vague comment in her mind as she and dogs made their way past the charming shotguns and camelbacks – shotguns with a half-second story added to the home's back – lining the narrow Irish Channel streets.

Working as a buyer for her store had made Ricki adept at picking up people's 'tells' – she instinctually knew when they were lying about the value or origin of an item they were trying to sell her. The skill also turned out to come in handy for murder investigations. While her intuition hadn't set off any alarms that could reveal who killed Miranda – yet – it did send a message to Ricki that the detective was hiding something.

'Which is none of my business.' She said this out loud as a way of confirming it to herself. Using her skill set to help free innocent people – including herself – from suspicion in a murder case was one thing. Using it to poke around a detective's private life simply out of curiosity was a bad idea on every level.

She returned home and readied for bed, as tired as she'd pretended to be in the limo with Nat. Her last thought before passing out was *we need to know more about what's going on at Blaine's place. Because hinky stuff is definitely happening there.*

In the middle of the night, Ricki bolted up, wide awake. Excited, she grabbed her phone and typed a text to the Bon Vee group chat . . .

Meet me in my shop at eight thirty. I have a great idea!

SIXTEEN

'**A** dual haunted house. Ours here. And one at Duncan-Sejour.'

After plying her coworkers with their favorite coffees and pastries from Peli Deli and building up to her brainstorm, Ricki laid out her idea. She scanned their faces for resistance. Seeing none, she continued.

'Everyone in New Orleans is thrilled we have a movie star living here, so I don't think we'd get pushback from the city or our neighbors. It's only for another week and a half or so anyway, depending on how long it takes to set up. Blaine has been trying to get on my good side since he showed up in town, plus it gives him a chance to look like a hero by raising money for local charities, so I'm sure I can talk him into it. We'd offer to help his people set up their haunted house using what we've learned from creating one here. It would put us on the inside at Duncan-Sejour, which would be a big help in tracking down clues to who killed Miranda.' Ricki cast a beseeching look at her coworkers. 'I'm excited about this. But I can't do it without you. What do you think?'

'I love it,' Cookie declared. She jumped to her feet, giving Ricki a standing ovation by clapping one hand against the chocolate croissant she held in the other. 'I call any task that puts me on Blaine's radar and takes me off NOPD's.'

'Me too,' Theo said. 'I'm hoping I can talk Blaine into running through his exercise regime with me. He's got the look I'm aiming for. Cut, but not so jacked up it's a turnoff.'

'Kaitlyn was considering allowing me back to her practices and games,' Lyla said. 'This would be the perfect excuse to get me out of it.'

Three yesses. That left Zellah and Eugenia. 'Zellah?' Ricki asked. 'Are you up for applying your talents to another haunted house? And maybe doing some snooping through drawers while pretending you're looking for paintbrushes?'

'Hmmm.' Zellah rested her cheek on her hand, making sure not to smear the intricately painted mummy decorating it. 'On the fence about snooping. But I've traded hellos with Mooni and gotten a whiff of tasty smells coming from her kitchen. I wouldn't mind chatting her up for clues if I can also snag some recipes.'

'Excellent.' Ricki turned to Eugenia for the final and deciding vote. 'What do you think? I won't pursue this without your approval.' She clasped her hands together. 'Which I really, really hope we get.'

'Heavy is the head that wears the crown,' Eugenia said with a sigh. 'Or tiara, in my case, from when I was Queen of Carnival way back when. Ooh, that tiara would be a perfect addition to my costume as Philodendron. Or,' she added with a rare hint of mischief, 'I could loan it to whomever needs it for a character at Blaine's haunted house.'

'Yes!' Ricki impulsively hugged the board president, then quickly released her. 'But I'm sure we can pull this off without you having to part with a family heirloom. I'll text Blaine and tell him I have an idea I'd like to talk to him about. I'll let you know what he says.'

'A chance for an actor to call attention to himself in a good way?' Zellah chuckled. 'I'm putting my money on a big old yes from our friendly neighborhood A-lister.'

The Bon Vee crew rose. 'Eugenia, I'm feeling like I might be coming down with something,' Cookie said to the Bon Vee boss of all bosses. 'I better take a sick day.'

'If the medicine for your illness is a day shopping for slinky outfits to flaunt in front of Mister Taggart,' Eugenia said, 'I'll risk your germs. But wear a mask the rest of the day to be safe.'

Cookie groaned as Eugenia shot Ricki a sly grin.

Ricki threw away the empty coffee cups and used a mini vac to suck up pastry crumbs, then texted Blaine to tell him she had an idea she wanted to run by him as soon as possible. A moment later, her phone pinged a text: **Jason made a rez for us at Freret's. Pick you up at five forty-five.**

'Of course he'd pick the newest, trendiest restaurant, and get a reservation for the same day,' Ricki muttered as she typed a return text: **I'll meet you there at eight.** Blaine instantly texted back a thumbs-up.

With a light day in terms of customers and Olivia on deck to run the evening's adult haunted house tour, Ricki opted to run home after the kids' tour and change into a more on-point outfit for dining at a hip destination like Freret's. She applauded herself for the decision the minute she stepped into the restaurant.

The décor offered a tongue-in-cheek take on old New Orleans, with flooring of old-fashioned octagon tiles, a tin ceiling painted white, and an array of paintings covering almost every inch of the sunflower-yellow walls. Closer inspection revealed most of the paintings were portraits of Storyville's famed bordellos and the tin ceiling wasn't old but new, decorated with a variety of couples in suggestive positions. Ricki wondered if the winking interior design sailed over the heads of the stuffier patrons packing the tables. She knew the younger crowd got it from the amount of photos being taken for social media feeds.

The hostess showed Ricki to a discreet table in the back of restaurant. It and the table next to it were the only empty ones in the restaurant. Ricki took a seat and waited for Blaine to make an entrance, which he did right on schedule. Heads turned in unison as he loped through the restaurant to Ricki. She was so absorbed in people watching she almost missed Nat, who followed in Blaine's wake. He took the seat at the second empty table.

'Hey,' Blaine said to Ricki after thanking the hostess for the complimentary bottle of champagne she'd parked in a standing wine bucket next to him. 'You look great.'

Ricki motioned to her navy-blue silk wrap dress. 'I've had this forever. It was my go-to date dress in LA. I think it's a year away from being labeled vintage.'

The hostess reappeared. 'Mr Taggart, Chef Emil wanted me to tell you not to bother looking at the menu. He's making a special dinner for you and your guest.'

'Awesome,' Blaine said. 'And thanks for scoring me a couple of tables on short notice.'

'No, thank *you*. We were slow this week because of all the Halloween activities.' The hostess made a sweep of the room with her hand. 'Once word got out you were coming here tonight, we booked up the whole night. We had to turn people away. I'll be right back with your appetizer.'

'Make sure he eats too.' Blaine gave his half-brother a wave.

Nat, who was eyeing the crowd like a Secret Service agent, didn't notice. The actor turned back to Ricki, who glared at him. 'What?'

'You couldn't live without fans falling at your feet for one night? You had to "alert the media" to your presence?'

'Whoa.' Blaine held up his hands in a defensive gesture. 'That's not on me. All I did was make dinner plans for us, based on your text that you had an idea to run by me.'

'I'm sorry,' Ricki said, feeling contrite. 'Celebrity stuff pushes my buttons. It reminds me how much Chris loved attention and fawning fans. More than anything else in his life.'

'Yeah. I know. I feel kinda responsible for that.'

You're responsible for a lot of what happened with him, Ricki managed not to blurt out. She changed the subject. 'So anyway, my idea.'

'Hold that thought.' Blaine poured Ricki a glass of champagne. He picked up his water glass and offered it for a toast. Ricki clinked glasses with him. 'Now, pitch me.'

'Bon Vee and Duncan-Sejour are the two finest houses in the Garden District, which is saying something because the District is block after block of gorgeous homes. Rather than have an antagonistic relationship between us—'

The hostess gifted them with small plates, each holding a delicious-looking rectangular slab of alternating white, pink, and pale green stripes. 'Salmon, crab, and avocado mousse terrine,' she said. 'An amuse bouche.'

Ricki and Blaine thanked her, then Ricki resumed her spiel. 'Rather than have an antagonistic relationship,' she repeated, 'we should—'

'Excuse me, Mr Taggart . . .'

A middle-aged man appeared at the table's edge, along with a woman he introduced as his wife. 'We're both huge fans of the *Code Name: Blue Heron* movies. Our whole family is.' He struck a pose and delivered Blaine's catch phrase in the franchise. 'Blue Heron flies solo.'

'Isn't he good?' his wife said, utterly enthralled with her husband's imitation. 'If you ever need a new stand-in—'

'Never mind that.' Her husband, embarrassed, dropped the pose. 'We wondered if we might get a picture with you to send home to everyone in Omaha.'

Blaine flashed his dazzling smile. 'Sure thing.'

The woman handed Ricki her phone without taking her eyes off Blaine. Ricki gritted her teeth and snapped a few pictures. The couple gushed thanks – to Blaine, not her – and left. Blaine took a forkful of his terrine. 'You were saying,' he prompted.

'Yes. I'd like to see our two households work together. My idea is—'

'Blaine? *Hi!* What a surprise.'

Interior designer Delia flounced up to the table, wearing a white dress so snug it might as well have been spray-painted on to her. 'I've been working so hard on coming up with fabulous concepts for your remodel that I ran out of energy for cooking. So I took myself out to dinner.'

She pointedly ignored Ricki, who steamed. Instead, Delia eyed an empty space at the table with the obvious game plan of being invited to join them. 'Have a nice dinner,' Blaine said, either missing or ignoring her ploy. He lifted his fork. 'This terrine thing is awesome. Highly recommend it.'

'Oh.' Delia barely masked her disappointment. 'Well . . . See you tomorrow.'

She slunk off . . . almost bumping into Theo and Cookie, whose own minuscule tight dress could have given Delia's a run for her come-hither money. 'Well, hey—'

Ricki cut Cookie off. 'Don't you dare say this is a surprise.'

'Cookie made me do it,' Theo said, throwing his cohort under the bus without a second thought. 'I'd rather be at the gym.' He flexed a non-existent muscle.

'Tell me how you knew we'd be here,' Ricki demanded. 'I didn't say anything to anyone and Blaine says his people didn't spread the word.'

'It's so cool you have people,' Cookie delivered this to Blaine with a combination of awe and envy.

'To answer your question, it's all over OhNo!La,' Theo said. 'Someone posted it this morning.'

'And I bet I know who.'

An angry Ricki called up Olivia from her Favorites list. 'What's up?' The college student had to yell to be heard over the noise at the bar where she'd obviously gone post-Bon Vee tour. 'If it's about the smell of beer in the shop, I can explain.'

'It's not about that. But I will want an explanation. Anyway, why did you post about me having dinner with Blaine at Freret's? I can't get more than half a sentence out without someone wanting a picture or flirting with him.' Ricki aimed the last comment at Cookie, who was too busy basking in Blaine's presence to notice.

'I didn't! I swear. Let me see if I can find out who did.'

Olivia signed off. Ricki clapped her hands to get Cookie and Theo's attention. 'Hey. *Hey*.' The two reluctantly tore themselves away from admiring Blaine. 'Make yourselves useful and go sit with Nat. If anyone else tries to get to Blaine, don't let them. Otherwise I'll never get to pitch him my idea.'

Grumbling, they went to join Nat, who didn't look any happier to welcome them than they looked to be there. Ricki's phone pinged. She checked it and saw Olivia had texted a single word: **Jason.** 'Aha. We have our leak.'

She showed her phone to Blaine, who made a face. 'Hoo boy. Sorry about that.'

'You don't sound surprised.'

'I'm not. Feeding items to gossip sites is Side Hustle 101 for assistants. They make a few bucks and their bosses hardly ever complain, especially if it keeps them visible when they're between movies. Like me.' Cowed by the look Ricki gave him, Blaine added, 'But I'll talk to Jason. It won't happen again. At least not when any plans involve you. Speaking of which, let's get back to your idea.'

'A double haunted house. Ours and a new one at Duncan-Sejour.'

Blaine raised an eyebrow. 'I'm listening.'

'Since we've been through the planning and setup, we can work with your "people"' – Ricki couldn't resist putting a spin on the word – 'to set it up. Our tours are on the even hours, six and eight. Yours can be on the odd hours, seven and nine, so people can do one, then the other. Whatever money you raise can go to the charity of your choice. Of course, if you want to throw a little Bon Vee's way, we won't say no. It would earn you community goodwill too.'

'Bon Vee and the church on the corner. Place looks like it could use a dose of cash love.'

'St Aquilinus? Father Gabriel will bless you for it.'

Blaine rubbed his hands together. 'I'm loving this. We can keep it to the rooms downstairs and the backyard. That'll make it accessible. Oh, I know. A maze. A corn maze, right in my backyard.' His crystal blue orbs practically glowed with excitement.

'Not sure we can pull that off,' Ricki cautioned. 'But we can make everything else work. So, you're in?'

'I'm in. It's a terrific idea. And . . . a way of making amends to you.'

Blaine extended a hand and they shook on it. His hand lingered on hers briefly before they separated. *I'm sitting here with one of the Sexiest Men Alive,* Ricki thought to herself. *Literally. He's got the magazine cover to prove it. Blaine is charming, self-deprecating, and is genuinely apologetic about what happened with Chris. So why do I feel nothing?* With no other answer springing to mind, Ricki chalked it up to her brief marriage forever burning her out on relationships with actors.

Dinner went on for another two hours, with Chef Emil delivering complimentary dish after dish until Ricki and Blaine were the only patrons left in the restaurant. The chef himself delivered dessert, another terrine, this one of rich dark chocolate and utterly divine. Blaine and Ricki brainstormed throughout the meal, with Ricki taking notes on her cell phone.

As Blaine finished the evening by posing for photos with the Freret's staff, Ricki allowed herself to enjoy being credited with a great idea. In fact, the notion of a Duncan-Sejour haunted house had gone over so well, she almost forgot its original goal . . .

To ferret out a possible killer among Blaine's 'people.'

SEVENTEEN

In the morning, Ricki texted her friend Lady at Good Neighbor Thrift Store to see if she could scare up Halloween decorations for Duncan-Sejour. Lady texted back that the shop's stock was picked over but she'd have no problem hitting up friends and family, many of whom were, in her words, 'over-decorators.' **How many blowup ghosts does one front yard need?** Lady texted, followed by a row of eye roll emojis. **About five less than my Cousin Taneisha has on her lawn.**

The news from Lady generated concern on Ricki's part that at this late date in the decorating-happy city of New Orleans, it might be hard to track down everything Duncan-Sejour needed for their haunted house. *I'll put Olivia on it,* Ricki thought as she drove to Bon Vee. *And see if Blaine can spare Jason to help her score the necessary merch.*

She parked in the small space in front of the estate carriage house and opened her car door to an ear-shattering racket. 'What the . . .' She scurried along the path that snaked around the estate's grounds and traced the sound to the tall wall separating Duncan-Sejour from Bon Vee. She came to a dead stop when she saw what was going on.

A crew of workmen had blasted a large hole in the wall between the estates. A sturdy gate lay on the grass near it. 'What *happened*?' Ricki yelled this to be heard over a jackhammer breaking the wall's cement footing.

'Blaine had the best idea,' Benny yelled back. Today the senior twins were dressed in facsimiles of the dresses Rosemary Clooney and Vera-Ellen wore when they sang the iconic number 'Sisters' in the movie, *White Christmas*. The outfits flattered neither of them.

'He's putting in a gate between Bon Vee and Duncan,' Jenny yelled by way of explanation. 'It'll make it easier to go between the haunted houses.'

'Eugenia agreed to this?' Ricki asked, incredulous. 'What

happens when the haunted houses end? Blaine puts the wall back the way it was?'

'Probably not.' Zellah, who'd sidled up to Ricki, said this in a loud but relatively normal voice. 'It'll make it easier for Mooni to come by with a batch of the treats she makes and bottles of her homemade gin. Blaine doesn't touch it but Eugenia's become a fan.'

'Whatevs, as Olivia would say.' Ricki saw Cookie observing the action and beckoned to her. The programming director tore herself away from the wall's demolition and went to Ricki. 'Are you free?' Ricki asked. 'I need to run something by you.'

'If you have coffee, yes. I need the buzz. I'm meeting with Eugenia and Lyla in half an hour to sell them on a few adult programming ideas I have.'

The two women retreated to Miss Vee's where Ricki, who eschewed pods as an environmental debacle, made two cups of coffee via her very basic coffee maker. Once Cookie had sweetened her coffee with a couple of teaspoons of Steen's Cane Syrup, Ricki shared the details of her limo ride with the Westwego girl posse, ending with her latest investigative tack. 'Britni is a strong suspect. She's in love with Chess and seems to have hated Miranda. One of the women mentioned a store called Terra Beauty. I got the impression Britni works there.'

'Totally makes sense. It's the biggest beauty supply shop in Westwego. Britni started working there when we were in high school. She's probably a manager or *the* manager by now.'

'We need to know more about her and you're our in. You can go to the store, pretend it's a surprise to run into her, and make plans to get together.'

'No.' Pain etched Cookie's face. 'I can't.'

'You've already infiltrated the text thread,' Ricki said, surprised by Cookie's resistance. 'This is just the next step.'

'Texting is one thing. But seeing any of them in person . . . I don't think I can handle it.'

Ricki felt for her friend. She cursed the bullies who'd inflicted such emotional trauma on Cookie that a decade and a half later she still feared coming face to face with them. 'The thing is,' she said, her tone gentle, 'you may find Britni isn't too crazy about the other women either. That's the sense I got in the limo.'

'Were the other women Sarah Jane and Paige?'

Ricki nodded.

'Yeah, I can see how Britni might be going through the motions of friendship with them. They're both married and have kids. I'm sure their dream is to be "tradwife" influencers. You know, the women who post pictures of themselves vacuuming in dresses and pearls with captions like "Making the house pretty before the man of the house gets home."'

Cookie picked up a 1950s cookbook displayed on the shop desk. The cover features a woman wearing an apron over a party dress as she removed a casserole from a Mamie Eisenhower pink oven. 'Like this. Women like SJ and Paige think they're so superior to divorcees like me. And I don't think Britni ever married, so she's even lower on their snobby list.'

Sensing Cookie's resistance weakening, Ricki pressed further. 'And remember, none of us have been cleared as suspects in Miranda's murder. Spending a happy hour with Britni beats spending any time in a Louisiana prison. Cookie, I love you but the ugly truth is, you have more of a motive than any of us. Miranda caused trauma that still affects you. Like you pointed out, the two of you got into a physical altercation. We can't underestimate Nina. She cracks a lot of jokes but she's totally serious about catching killers. Or people she thinks are the killers based on whatever evidence she has, circumstantial or not.'

'Very true. And very scary.' Cookie closed her eyes. She drew in a breath, then blew it out. Her eyes popped open. 'I'll do it. I'm almost out of my favorite mask anyway and Terra is the only store in the city that carries it.'

'Perfect.' Ricki gave Cookie's shoulder a reassuring pat. 'As a shopkeeper, trust me when I tell you there's no better way to become friends with a salesperson than by racking up charges on your credit card.'

The day proved busy, courtesy of Bon Vee Culinary House Museum having recently been added to the agenda of several local tour operators. Benny and Jenny had a contest going to see who could generate the most tips, which seemed unnecessary, since they lived together and pooled their resources. But since this resulted in the twins being extra-helpful to Ricki's customers, she was all for it.

Mid-afternoon, Olivia showed up after leading the first session of a cookie-making workshop with local kids. The original theme for the day had been bats, but with the bat-shaped tray a clue in Miranda's murder, Ricki had quickly changed the decorating theme to pumpkins.

Olivia deposited a cookie frosted within an inch of its life on the desk for Ricki. 'A leftover. The kid already ate two of them and his mom said if he ate another, she'd still be peeling him off the walls by Christmas.' Olivia held up her fingers, which were stained orange. 'This coloring better be safe. I got so much of it on me I think it's been absorbed into my bloodstream.'

Ricki took a bite of the cookie. 'This is lunch. Thanks.'

Olivia leaned on the desk. 'I'm worried about Jason.'

'Really?' Ricki reacted with amusement, but also a touch of concern. 'I didn't know you two were at the worrying-about-each-other-stage.'

Olivia blushed. 'We're friends,' she said, adding sarcastically, 'Is that OK with you?' Her tone switched back to apprehension. 'Do you think he's going to get in trouble for leaking where you and Blaine had dinner last night?'

Ricki shook her head. 'Blaine wasn't upset. Hollywood assumes assistants feed the gossip mill. I bet plenty of celebrities actively encourage it.' She removed two feather dusters from under the desk and handed one to Olivia. 'The top shelves need some love. I heard a couple of customers sneeze and wave away dust when they removed books from them.'

Olivia took the feather duster. She pursed her lips as she dusted. 'Celebrities are so rude. Instead of giving their assistants a raise, they force them to do side hustles. People think that because Jason's a nepo baby he can coast, but it's the opposite. He has to work even harder to prove himself. All the assistants work really hard. Some even have to have their own assistants! You should hear his stories. One friend was fired because he accidentally looked his rich guy boss in the eye, which he wasn't allowed to do. Another got reamed because he missed a spot of bird doo when he washed his boss's Maserati but that's only because he was tired from being up all night guarding the guy's koi pond fish from a coyote who was wandering around the neighborhood.'

'You're reminding me of the reasons I don't miss LA.' Ricki sneezed and waved away dust herself. She made a mental note to stay more on top of overall shop maintenance.

'Jason told me some assistants are so overworked they have to take drugs like Adderall to keep going. You know, the drug for ADHD that makes people hyper focused and energized even if they don't have the condition. Jason used to do them himself but stopped because a couple of his closest friends took what they thought was Adderall but turned out to be a worse drug, and one died.' Olivia stopped dusting. 'Oooh, I have a theme for my internship paper: "Workplace Abuse of Assistants and Interns." She held up her feather duster as if she was making a gesture of solidarity. 'I may even start a union for us!'

'Yeah, not sure how starting a union will fly with the krewes picking Mardi Gras courts from next year's debutantes,' Ricki said, knowing the krewes leaned conservative and Olivia dreamed of following in her mother and grandmother's footsteps as Queen of Carnival, an honor bestowed by the Krewe of Rex.

Olivia dropped the feather duster to her side. 'OK, maybe I'll do the union thing after I debut. Besides, Jason does love his job. He says Blaine is an awesome boss and is giving him scripts to read. Jason thinks he's got a shot at being a junior exec when Blaine launches his own production company next year.'

Olivia nattered on, switching to one of her favorite subjects, who among her deb friends might be chosen for the Mardi Gras courts. Ricki pretended to listen but her focus was elsewhere. Miranda's murder had given Jason's career a jumpstart, instantly propelling him from lowly intern to valued assistant and now future development executive, a role that served as a stepping-stone to a vaunted title of producer.

People had killed for much, much less.

EIGHTEEN

Lady texted Ricki that Good Neighbor would be closing early for an inventory check, so Ricki left Miss Vee's in Olivia's hands and drove over to the thrift store.

Ricki's friend greeted her at the door and ushered her through the store to the stockroom, where she handed her a large, full black trash bag. 'I did the best I could. I couldn't get Taneisha to part with any of her ghosts, though. I swear, her front yard looks like Halloween threw up on it.'

Ricki chuckled. She sorted through the bag, which was filled an assortment of plastic pumpkins, foam faux-headstones, costume pieces, and whatever else Lady dug up. 'Thanks so much. This is a good start. What do I owe you?'

'Nothin'. Half of it's junk I was gonna toss or recycle.'

'Nuh uh. No freebies. I have to pay you something.'

'Fine. Ten bucks. Not a dime more.'

'If you say so.'

Ricki stood up and pulled the drawstring closure on the trash bag to secure it. She wiped perspiration from her forehead. Feeling logy from the room's heat, she gave her body a little shake to wake it up. Lady eyed her with concern. 'You OK? I been thinking about you since the latest murder.'

Ricki winced at Lady labeling Miranda's death the 'latest' murder. 'It's hard – no, it's impossible – not to have something as awful as that get to you. Especially since I found out I have a strange connection to Miranda, the victim.' Ricki shared their distant but existent DNA connection. 'Aside from my personal questions about this, there's always a chance NOPD could somehow use it to move me up on their list of suspects.'

'That's a lot,' Lady said when Ricki finished. 'I feel for you, girl.'

'Thanks.' Grateful for the support, Ricki added, 'I'm really glad we've become friends.'

'Me too.' Lady gave Ricki a hug. She stepped back and examined her. 'You know what you need?'

'An excellent but affordable lawyer?'

'Probably. But also . . .' Lady reached up to a shelf and took down a plastic box. She lifted the lid and took out an item in a small cellophane bag. 'A sweet potato praline. Made from an old family recipe. It's a side hustle for us. My cousin's kid Clinton from Pelican upriver is going to Loyola. We make and pack them together. He sells his at the dorm, I sell mine wherever I can.'

'My landlady makes these incredible pecan pralines but I've never had sweet potato before.' Ricki opened the cellophane bag, filling the air with the delicious scent of autumnal spices. She took a bite and swooned. 'OMG, this is amazing. Add another location to where you sell these: Miss Vee's Vintage Cookbook and Kitchenware Shop.'

Ricki left Good Neighbor with a handshake deal and the rest of Lady's pralines. As she entered Route 90 from Claiborne Avenue, she mused how her own side hustle of dealing in vintage cookbooks and kitchenware had become her main hustle. Distracted, she realized she'd missed the last exit prior to crossing the Mississippi River over the Crescent Connection Bridge. She let out a loud cuss word.

After crossing the river, she exited at the first opportunity and pulled over to call Olivia. 'I messed up and missed my exit off 90, so I won't be back in time to close the shop for the dinner break before the tours. Could you do it for me?'

'I would but I'm not there anymore.' Ricki heard the white noise of chatter in the background. 'Jason invited me to grab coffee with him on his break, so the twins are running the store. We're at Thanks a Latte. He's getting our drinks now. I tried texting you.'

Ricki checked her phone and saw she'd accidentally turned off the sound. She switched it back on. 'My bad. The twins have closed for me before, so they know what to do. I just hope those poufy dresses they're wearing don't knock anything over.'

'They're not wearing those anymore. They changed into pumpkin costumes.'

'Uh oh. That's worse.'

'No, they practiced walking around at home so they didn't

knock into any of the valuables on the tour. It looks like they have it down. They even choreographed a fake bump into each other that's hilarious. There's a third-grade class trip stopping by from Audubon Charter. I think the kids will love it.'

'Fingers crossed.' Ricki hesitated. 'You and Jason are only having coffee, right?'

'Yes, *Mom*. Why do you . . .' What Ricki was implying dawned on Olivia. 'Oh my *God*. You do *not* suspect him of murder.' Ricki started to speak. Olivia cut her off. 'No. I swear, you are losing your mind. Not everyone is a killer, Ricki. *Gah*.'

Olivia ended the call. Left unable to defend herself, Ricki obsessed about Olivia's accusation. Was she right? Had the deaths at Bon Vee so skewed Ricki's view of the world that everyone remotely associated with the victim was guilty until proven innocent? *That is the Napoleonic Code here in Louisiana*, she thought wryly.

This train of thought, coupled with her location, led Ricki to think of Miranda's brother, Gordy Fine. She entered Mardi Gras Motorworks into her GPS link. The pre-owned car dealership popped up on her car's screen as a mere two miles away from her current destination.

Ricki turned on her car engine and took off in the opposite direction of New Orleans. After a brief attempt to convince herself that her main goal in chatting up Gordy was to see if he could provide clues to their familial link, she gave up. *Olivia isn't wrong,* she thought as she drove off. *I do suspect pretty much everyone when there's a murder that affects Bon Vee. I might as well go all in on it.*

Ricki chided herself for expecting the Mardi Gras Motorworks lot to live up to the stereotype of a low-rent used car lot. Instead, a fleet of appealing pre-owned cars sparkled under the New Orleans sun. Reasonably priced newer car models from every manufacturer sat in neat rows. Several potential buyers wandered the lot with salespersons wearing plum blazers with the discreet but colorful logo of a Mardi Gras jester's hat.

She headed down the walkway leading to the lot's showroom, housed in a small, well-maintained single-story building painted the same plum shade as the logo. She walked inside and saw

Gordy Fine in conversation with a couple. He glanced at the door, his salesman instinct triggered by the slight whoosh of the door as Ricki opened it. A curious expression crossed his face, then passed. He lifted an eyebrow to signal he'd be with her shortly, then continued with his customers.

Ricki followed as he walked them outside, keeping enough distance to maintain a semblance of not spying on the conversation. They stopped at a white mini SUV that looked brand-new. 'My sister has the same car, only in black,' the woman, who was heavily pregnant, said. 'She loves it.'

'You will too,' Gordy said. 'It's a great car for a new family. Excellent mileage for its size, dependable, and got the highest safety score in its class.'

He handed her a set of keys. She released a small gasp and showed them to her husband. 'Ryan, look. There's a mini license plate with baby Lucy's name on it. Oooh.'

She teared up. Despite herself, so did Ricki. Ryan extended a hand to Gordy and said in a husky voice, 'Thanks, buddy.'

'It's a small thing,' Gordy said, sincerely modest. 'How many cars have you bought here over the years? You're like family.'

The three exchanged hugs, then the couple got into their new ride and negotiated their way off the lot. Ricki took advantage of their departure to introduce herself. 'I'm Ricki James-Diaz. I own the gift shop at Bon Vee, next to where your sister worked. I was at her memorial.'

'Yes, I recognized you,' the car salesman said. 'The mole on your cheek made you hard to miss that night. I'm glad you had it taken care of.'

'Right,' Ricki said, making a mental note to confirm she'd removed all distinguishing characteristics before any future snooping.

'I'm guessing you're here to talk about Miranda and not shop for a new car.'

'Afraid so.' Feeling self-conscious, Ricki added, 'But when I do need a new car, I know where to come.' She read the tagline on the brightly-lit sign advertising the lot. '"Mardi Gras Motorworks. We're in your court." A play on sports *and* Mardi Gras. Well done.'

This sparked the smallest glimmer of a smile. 'Let's go to my office. It's private.'

Ricki followed Gordy back inside the lot showroom through a side door to his spacious office. Two chairs faced his desk. A round white table with four matching chairs sat in the corner. A glass wall looked out over the showroom. Framed kids art, along with accolades from local business organizations, decorated two of the walls. A poster featuring Gordy's headshot under the title 'Purveyor of Pre-Owned Vehicles' graced the third wall next to an award from the local Rotary Club. Photographs of Gordy with a cheery woman about his own age and two young boys were grouped on his neat desk. The office theme was 'Family Man Who Also Happens to be a Respected Local Businessman.' Whether manipulative or sincere, the image it projected was effective.

Gordy sat down at the table. Ricki took the seat opposite him. 'First off, I'm so sorry about your sister.'

'Thank you.' Gordy sounded more aggrieved than grief-stricken. 'It's been a pretty unpleasant experience. First, her death, then finding out she was murdered, then going through a lot of questions from the police. Thank the Lord I had an alibi. My wife and I were on a spiritual retreat sponsored by our parish.'

'So you can thank the Lord literally,' Ricki quipped.

'Amen.'

Ricki appreciated the hint of humor in his response. Since he'd apparently been ruled out as a suspect in his sister's murder, she decided to bring up their shared DNA. 'Miranda listed me as a reference on the resume that she gave Blaine Taggart, which was bizarre because I'd never met or heard of her. I'm adopted. I was born at Charity Hospital and abandoned by my birth mother. I've been searching for my birth relatives and on one of the sites I joined, Miranda came up as a third or fourth cousin. Which means you are too.'

Gordy stared at her. 'Wow. I'm not sure what to say.'

'There's the usual list of ways we might be related on the site. The one that makes the most sense to me is that we may share a set of great-great-grandparents. Genevieve Charbonnet was my great-grandmother. It's not hard to trace her side of the family. In fact, it's so easy that none of them bother to join ancestry sites. All they have to do is check out the giant family tree Eugenia Charbonnet had painted as a mural in her foyer. Well, my cousin Olivia did join genealogyandme.com, that's how I found out I was half-Charbonnet, but she only did it to see if she was related to someone who owned a chateau in France. She's not. I mean, we're not.'

Gordy adjusted his position. Catching him sneak a glance at his smart watch, Ricki picked up the pace. 'So far, I haven't been able to find out anything from the Charbonnet side of the family about the baby Genevieve gave up, which means I have to track down a birth parent by finding the father of her baby. If I could drill down into *our* familial link,' she gestured back and forth between her and Gordy, 'It could help me identify him. Have you done any genealogy research? Did Miranda ever share what she learned from it with you?'

'I have two kids under six and I run a business,' the salesman said. 'I don't have time for hobbies. If Miranda was on an ancestry site, I can guarantee you it was transactional and not motivated by any interest in our family's history. She'd do anything to get ahead. The fake reference stunt she pulled makes you proof of that, doesn't it?'

Ricki had to agree.

'She was embarrassed by me.' Gordy's bitterness was in full swing. 'I can call myself a "purveyor of pre-owned vehicles" all I want but to my stuck-up sister, I was nothing but a used-car salesman. Like I told the police, I didn't love her or hate her. We didn't have enough of a relationship for either.'

There was an awkward pause as Gordy seemed to stew in unpleasant memories. 'I'm sorry you two were estranged,' Ricki said. 'It's sad.' She searched for another way to extract any leads from him. 'Are there other family members you're close to? You know, to fill this void? Your parents . . . other siblings . . . cousins . . .'

'You want to know if there's any other Fines you can hit up,' Gordy said, seeing through her ham-fisted attempt. 'Sorry, no. My parents divorced when we were kids. Like I said at the memorial, our dad took off. I found out he died when I got a bill for a credit card he took out using my name. No one was close on either side of my family, at least not to us.' Gordy took one of the photos off his desk and held it up to Ricki. 'My wife's family is mine now. And I'm grateful for them.'

He placed the photo back on the desk and stood up. Ricki got the hint and rose too. 'I wish I could be more help,' he said. 'Tell you what. Since you're technically family, I'll give you twenty percent off on one of our cars when you're ready to trade up. That's ten percent more than I offered the other mourners. I can put it in writing if you want.' He reached for a pad on his desk.

'It's OK. I'm sure we'll both remember.'

Gordy walked over to the door and held it open for her. 'Good luck.'

'If I learn anything interesting about our biological connection, I'll let you know.'

His shrug of a response telegraphed she'd be wasting her time.

NINETEEN

Feeling burned out on amateur sleuthing, Ricki put all her energy into witching it up on the Bon Vee tours that night. Her commitment to her cackling character inspired an excellent night of sales at the shop, which she allowed herself to feel good about when she crawled into bed, exhausted by her efforts.

In the morning, she dropped Thor and Princess off at the pet hotel up the street for baths and a playdate with a few pals, then cruised over to Bon Vee.

She hit the breaks in front of Duncan-Sejour.

Trucks were parked up and down the street. Men and women on headsets directed crews hauling props and equipment out of rental trucks. There was so much activity it was as if they were filming a movie at the estate. In fact, Ricki wondered if they *were* actually filming a movie there. Then she saw two men hauling a coffin behind a woman pulling a wagon loaded with pumpkins, and Ricki realized what was going on.

She parked in her usual spot by the carriage house, retrieved the trash bag of Halloween decorations she'd gathered up at Good Neighbor from the trunk of her car, and strode over to Duncan-Sejour. She saw Blaine leaning against one of the mansion portico columns, gleefully watching the chaos with Jason at his side. Ricki dashed around the obstacle course of props on front lawn to reach him. 'Tell me you didn't hire a film crew to set up your haunted house.'

'No. I hired a production designer and she hired the crew.' He gestured to a woman barking orders at crew members. 'My team is helping out too.'

Ricki scanned the beehive of activity and saw Delia being ignored by a lighting crew laying down cable while Mooni conferred with the man setting up a craft services breakfast station, and Nat stood watch over the perimeter.

Lakshmi stormed up to Blaine. 'Delia is trying to talk them out of putting up my fortuneteller tent.' The bangles covering her forearms collided with each other as she angrily indicated the interior designer.

'I'll handle it,' Jason said.

'That's my guy,' Blaine said, slapping his assistant on the shoulder. Jason blushed, then went off with Lakshmi.

'Blaine,' Ricki said, 'When I suggested you mount a haunted house here, I didn't mean for you to do all . . . this.'

'You know what they say, go big or go home. Of course, I am home, so that kind of doesn't make sense in this case.' The actor noticed the trash bag Ricki clutched. 'Whatcha got there?'

Ricki reached into the bag and took out a stuffed vampire missing an eye. 'Decorations for you. Which you definitely don't need now.'

'Who says? Hey, Marise!'

Blaine called to the woman he'd identified as the production designer. She grabbed the excuse to extricate herself from Delia and trod a quick path to Blaine. 'Jimmy asked if you want a spotlight on Dracula when he rises from the coffin,' she said to him, not bothering to introduce herself to Ricki.

Blaine gave her a thumbs-up. 'Sounds like a plan. Hey, this is my friend Ricki. She's donated decorations for the haunted house.'

'I really don't think—' Ricki began.

'It's good stuff, Rickster. Give her the bag.'

Ricki glumly handed the motley collection of decorations to the production designer, who reacted as if she'd been handed a large bag of dog poo. 'Thanks, I appreciate it,' Marise said, trying to cover up her distaste with a bald-faced lie. She took off with the bag, holding it at a distance.

'We should have the show ready to go in a couple of hours,' Blaine said to Ricki. 'Which is good news because Delia used her connections to set up a soft opening at five tonight for locals. We're trying to head off any complaints from them when we open to the public because things could get a *leeetle* nuts.' Blaine twirled his fingers around his ears in the universal sign for crazy.

Seeing her plan to embed the Bon Vee staff with Duncan-Sejour's slipping away, Ricki desperately searched for an alternative. 'A dry run,' she exclaimed. 'That's what you need. I'll close my shop early and bring my friends over at four. You can have your team do a run-through for them.'

'Awesome idea,' Blaine said, enthused. 'I'll let my director know.'

'Director?' Ricki squeaked.

Blaine went off to find whoever it was and Ricki rushed back to Bon Vee to share the new game plan with the others. As she passed a row of garbage cans, she saw her bag of Good Neighbor decorations stuffed into one of them. Ticked off by the production designer's snobbery, Ricki yanked the bag out of the can and handed it to a nonplussed crew member. 'Marise said to make sure to use everything in this bag as part of the haunted house,' she told him, flashing her most winning smile.

Back at Bon Vee, she updated her own crew on the change. 'The timing conflicts with one of Kaitlyn's matches,' Lyla said. 'So that's a big yes from me.'

'I'm not happy about this,' Cookie sulked. 'It deprives me of valuable flirting time with Blaine.'

'I'm good with it. Watching instead of doing is fine with me.' Theo rubbed his calf and grimaced. 'I pulled a couple of muscles at the gym. On the upside, the pain is giving me a cool monster walk.' He demonstrated a lumbering walk accompanied by pained grunts, to the amusement of the others.

Next, Ricki looped in Olivia, along with Benny and Jenny. The twins were happy to man the shop while Ricki and the others helped Blaine out. Olivia jumped in with an offer to be of assistance at Duncan-Sejour. Ricki guessed her cousin's enthusiastic response was prompted by a chance to spend time with Jason, but Olivia had proved herself clever in past amateur investigations, so Ricki welcomed her company.

Shortly before four, the Bon Vee gang trooped through the spanking-new gate between estates to Blaine's place. They came to a dead stop at the sight that greeted them.

A large portion of the Duncan-Sejour yard had been turned into a corn maze. Rows of stalks wafted gently in the breeze. Blaine emerged from between two of them. He wore a circus ringmaster's costume complete with top hat. He carried a whip and his face was made up with a gray pallor. 'Welcome, Bon Vee friends,' he greeted them in a booming, theatrical voice. He grinned and spoke like himself. 'Since this is my circus, I figured I should be the ringmaster. Well, the ghost of a ringmaster. More Halloween-y.'

'You did it,' Ricki said, taking in the impressive attraction taking center stage in the yard. 'You came up with a maze. I shouldn't be surprised. But I am.'

'It's not just any maze. Marise set up the corn in blocks on rolling platforms so we can move it around whenever we want to. You know, make it easier for the kids, tougher for the adults. What do you think?'

'I think it's amazing.' Ricki reluctantly gave Marise credit for a brilliant idea.

'A-*maze*-ing. I like it.' Blaine waved the group over. 'Come on, give it a try.'

'Get lost in a maze with Blaine Taggart?' Cookie said under her breath. 'Yes, please.'

She practically leapt in after Blaine. Theo and Lyla followed her into the maze. Olivia stuck with Ricki.

They entered Duncan-Sejour, which had been transformed into a palace of haunted horrors. Like Bon Vee, each room had a different theme. But unlike Bon Vee, the rooms could have served as film sets. Concoctions in the mad scientist's lair bubbled and foamed as lights sizzled and sparked above the actor who was playing the scientist. The library had been transformed into the replica of a room in a nineteenth-century insane asylum, complete with moaning, straight-jacketed performers.

A maid's room toward the back of house now replicated a little girl's bedroom but was lined with shelves of terrifying dolls. Ricki was glad she'd added a warning to the Bon Vee website that Duncan-Sejour's haunted house might not be suitable for young children. The minute Ricki and Olivia took a tentative step into the spooky room, a human-sized robotic doll with pupils that looked like flames sprung to life, almost giving Ricki a heart attack. 'Wanna play with me?' The 'doll' followed the question with a spine-chilling laugh.

'OMG!' Olivia exclaimed, elated. 'I don't believe it. Are you the real actress from the movie, *My Killer Dolly*?'

The actress broke character and nodded. 'Yup. Blaine flew me out for the haunted house run. I'm so psyched to be in New Orleans. Tell me a couple of places I should go while I'm here.'

Ricki left Olivia chatting with the killer dolly and went to check out the other rooms, which were equally elaborate. She reached the staircase leading to the upper floors. It was roped off with a velvet stanchion and a sign reading 'No Admittance.'

The main floor's elaborate conversion into a haunted house rendered searching for clues downstairs moot. Which left the forbidden upstairs. Duncan-Sejour only had a single-story carriage house, which didn't allow for living quarters on a second floor. Ricki surmised that Blaine most likely allotted the spacious second-floor bedrooms that were common to a nineteenth-century Garden District mansion to family members Nat and Mooni. That would leave employees like Miranda housed in the third floor servants' quarters.

Ricki pretended to be checking both ends of the hallway for easy access and egress as she contemplated how to sneak past the stanchions and snoop upstairs without getting caught. She was debating several plans when the lights suddenly dimmed. The first floor rooms had been outfitted with blackout curtains to block incoming light, so the result was almost total darkness.

She stuck out her hands to feel for obstacles as she made her way down the hall and was almost at the far end of it when she collided with someone. She shrieked – as did the other person.

'Ow!'

'Olivia?'

Ricki squinted and her eyes began adjusting to the lack of light. She made out her intern cousin's form. She was with someone.

'Sorry about that.'

'Jason?'

Just as suddenly as the lights went off, they came back on, their brightness almost blinding the three.

'We didn't have time to upgrade the electrical capacity of the house,' Jason explained. 'The indoor lights dim when we run the light show outside. We need a generator but they're hard to come by because there are too many other Halloween-themed events going on in the city.'

'Plus, everyone around here buys them for hurricane season,' Olivia added for Jason's benefit.

'Marise is on it, though.'

'I have no doubt she'll come through,' Ricki said, thinking of the almost obnoxiously-efficient production designer. She motioned to Jason's costume, an elegant tuxedo and cape that transformed him into a handsome vampire. 'You look dapper.'

'Oh. Thanks. It's kind of cool. I might try this out as a pick-up look when I get back to LA. Kidding, of course.'

A disappointed expression quickly passed across Olivia's face, confirming Ricki's suspicion she was attracted to Blaine's assistant. With everyone at Duncan-Sejour a murder suspect, Ricki would never have encouraged a relationship between the two. Still, she'd grown close to Olivia and felt for the girl.

Her phone pinged a text. So did Jason's. Both of them checked their phones. 'Blaine's called a final meeting before the soft opening,' Jason told Olivia.

'You two go ahead,' Ricki said. 'I'll catch up.'

She waved them off. As soon as they were gone, she eyed the stanchion again, trying to determine the best way to get around it and access the upper floors. *It's high enough for me to slip under*, she decided. *I just need to find the right time to do it.*

On her way out to the front lawn where everyone was assembling, Ricki found herself walking with Mooni. The older woman wore her straggly white hair loose and a shapeless black dress. 'Let me guess,' Ricki said. 'You're a witch.'

'I will be when I put on my costume.'

'I'm so sorry,' Ricki apologized, mortified by her mistake.

'Don't be. My general look is Modern Day Witch.' Mooni said this with a twinkle in her eye that made Ricki feel slightly better. 'I've been racing to put together "ghoulie bags" for our soft opening guests. "Ghoulie bags" not goody bags. Delia came up with that gem.' Mooni didn't bother to hide her dislike of the interior designer.

'It's not bad. It's actually pretty clever.'

'At least she put her mind to something besides hitting on my nephew. She's got a one-track mind on that score and good luck to anyone who gets in the way.'

Ricki eyed Mooni. 'I'm guessing there's one roadblock she won't be able to blast through.'

'Ya got that right, sweetie.' Mooni's malicious chortle made Ricki glad she wasn't interested in anything but the most superficial relationship with the over-protective woman's nephew.

They reached the expansive front yard where everyone had

clustered around Blaine, including Delia, whose slinky, form-fitting costume had turned her into a sexy ghost. Nat stood by Blaine's side. He'd eschewed a costume for his standard body-guard attire of all-black, which was scary enough on its own. Scattered around the yard were a half-dozen brawny men dressed the same as Nat, hired to augment security. An older man among them looked vaguely familiar. Ricki couldn't place him at first. Then she recognized him as Bobby Grimes, the PI hired by Blaine's team to spy on Bon Vee. Despite the détente between the two estates, he was still on the actor's payroll.

To get everyone's attention, Blaine cracked his whip. Being a well-trained actor, he did it with enough punch to send a few people scurrying. 'First off,' he said. 'I wanna thank every person here for their part in pulling off the best haunted house this city has ever seen in the fastest time it's ever been done. Whoo hoo!' Everyone joined him in the cheer. He cracked the whip again and they fell silent. 'My friend Ricki from Bon Vee very nicely offered to view the dry run we just went through, along with her co-workers. Rickster, you got any notes for us?'

'I don't.' She addressed her friends. 'Do you?' All shook their heads.

'We don't need notes.' Lakshmi declared this. 'We got this.' She raised a fist in the air, almost losing her balance.

'I think she got herself a dose of liquid courage,' Theo whispered to Ricki, subtly miming a liquor flask.

Blaine cracked his whip again. 'Awesome. Soft opening starts in fifteen. It's showtime, people!'

He raised the whip high above his head. The sky filled with a thrilling light display of flying ghosts and bats. The mansion lights dimmed to almost non-existent. 'Marise,' he said, irked, 'you gotta get me a generator.'

Under the guise of offering additional help if needed, Ricki stuck around for the soft opening. Secretly, she planned to use the distraction to sneak up to Miranda's room. She knew NOPD had done a thorough search. But her desire to crack at least one of the two mysteries haunting her – Miranda's death; her own birth – drove Ricki an almost obsessive need to check out the space for herself.

She picked a discreet location in the hallway to watch the estate's neighbors arrive. They swarmed the place. Ricki could tell they were there as much for a celebrity sighting of Blaine as for the haunted house. Delia, eager to reinforce her presence on his team, greeted guests with excessive enthusiasm. 'What a wonderful event,' exclaimed an attractive, hip woman she'd traded air kisses with. 'I didn't know you were still working for Blaine Taggart. I'd heard you'd been fired.'

'Fake news.' Delia's tight, tense smile made Ricki wonder if the news wasn't so fake. 'I had a difference of opinion with Blaine's previous assistant, who was difficult, to say the least. Sadly, she passed. But in better news, her replacement is a young man who wouldn't know the difference between Swiss Coffee and real coffee.'

'Swiss coffee is a paint color, honey,' the guest said to her husband to rid him of his blank stare. She favored Delia with a smile so condescending Ricki almost felt sorry for the grasping designer. 'Well, I'm glad you landed on your feet after the lawsuit.'

Ricki was too busy typing 'Delia – lawsuit' into her phone's Notes app to hear any fatuous pleasantries exchanged between the three after that.

The packed house gave Ricki a chance to sneak over to the staircase, aided by the lights dimming on and off. The patrons ate this up, assuming it was part of the haunted house experience. Ricki took advantage of a longer semi-blackout to run up the stairs to the second floor. Another semi-blackout covered her dash to the third floor.

Ricki adored historic homes and had toured many of them. The floor that housed servants was basically the same at all of them, even Bon Vee, which had third floor servants' quarters in addition to those in the carriage house: narrow halls, unadorned walls, and small bedrooms designed to discourage the household staff from spending time in them.

Ricki stood quietly, listening for any sound that would indicate someone else was on the floor. All she heard was ambient sound wafting up from the festivities below. She tiptoed past a couple of empty rooms. A door decorated with a USC pennant denoted Jason's room. Ricki tamped down her desire to poke her nose inside and moved on. She passed a few more empty rooms, finally stopping in front of one where remnants of police tape dangled from the doorjamb, marking it as Miranda's room. Ricki slipped inside.

With its utilitarian furnishings of a bed, a desk, a freestanding closet, and a dresser, the room resembled a college dorm room. There was even the kind of mini fridge and microwave combo Ricki recalled from her own college days. The bed had been stripped, most likely by NOPD for potential evidence.

Ricki examined every inch of the room, giving the police credit for a job well done. The room appeared devoid of clues or personality. If Miranda had bothered to hang a poster on the wall to add a little life to the place, there was no evidence of tape or Contact strips. The closet and chest drawers still held her clothes, the bathroom her toiletries. Several yogurts still sat in the refrigerator; the freezer contained a couple of low-calorie frozen meals.

Ricki got a catch in her throat at the items indicating a life was once lived in the room. But all told, the portrait painted was of someone with no patience for self-care or frills. Like many Millennials, the only way to take a deeper dive into Miranda's life was through her electronics, all of which were in police custody.

As she searched, something niggled at Ricki but she couldn't land on what. She was about to call it quits when it came to her. She'd scolded Olivia for dumping one of Ricki's own frozen meals and using the box to store valuables inside Ricki's mini fridge's freezer. Olivia had gotten the idea from the videos she watched endlessly. She'd said the video was popular. Might Miranda have seen it?

Ricki opened the freezer and took out a frozen meal. It showed no sign of ever being opened, so she put it aside. She took out the second box. The flap at one end was loose. Ricki studied it. The flap showed evidence of having been opened and resealed with a glue stick. She easily lifted it and emptied the box. A phone fell into her lap.

Ricki stuck the phone in the waistband of her leggings, pulling her tunic top over the band to hide it. Fueled by the adrenaline rush of her find, she raced from the room. The lights dimmed to almost-black once again, forcing her to feel her way along the wall of the hall. They brightened again and Ricki froze.

At the end of the hall stood Nat and Mooni.

TWENTY

Ricki's heart thumped with fear as Nat and Mooni glared at her. 'I told you I heard something,' Mooni said out of the side of her mouth to her nephew.

'Good catch.' Nat glowered at Ricki with an expression as terrifying as any on the face of the creepy dolls downstairs. 'What are you doing up here? You know you're trespassing.'

'I thought I heard something too,' Ricki said, borrowing Mooni's motivation and saying a prayer it would work. The looks on their faces told her it didn't. Seeing no other way out, she opted for honesty. 'I was looking for clues in Miranda's room. Anything the police might have missed. The sooner they catch Miranda's killer, the sooner we're all off their lists of suspects. And out of danger. You know this wasn't a random act of violence.' She added in a heavy-handed and foreboding tone, 'Which means the killer walks among us.'

The two didn't seem remotely placated. 'You don't think Blaine has his own people investigating?' Nat asked. He didn't add 'dummy!' but Ricki could tell he was thinking it.

'What happens at Duncan-Sejour is none of your business,' Mooni said. 'Stay in your lane. Snoop around your own coworkers at Bon Vee.'

Nat seconded this with a nod. 'Go back to playing detective with Miranda's low-rent friends, like you did in the car after the funeral.'

He indicated for Ricki to exit the area, making sure she walked in front of him and his aunt to rule out any possibility of sneaking back into Miranda's room. 'It's my security team's job to have eyes on everyone who enters or leaves this house,' he muttered to Mooni as they headed downstairs. 'Somebody's getting fired tonight.'

'Don't blame them,' Ricki said, feeling guilty. 'Blame the old wiring in the house for the blackouts.'

'Good point,' Mooni said. 'Warn your boys about the possibility of someone taking advantage when the lights go out. But I don't think we have to worry about this one anymore, do we?'

She gave Ricki a pat on the shoulder that wasn't remotely reassuring.

Shaken, Ricki sprinted back to the relative safety of Bon Vee, where she changed into her witch's costume and immersed herself in prepping for the evening's official dual opening of the Bon Vee and Duncan-Sejour haunted houses. Cars packed Persephone Street and a line of ticket holders had already formed, stretching from the Bon Vee front steps to the sidewalk. 'It's like a Hollywood movie premiere,' Ricki heard one visitor say as a valet whipped the car keys from their hand and zoomed away with their car.

Benny and Jenny, who were dressed as traffic lights, one red, the other green, helped Ricki scan tickets for admittance. While she scanned, Ricki debated what to do with the phone she'd discovered in Miranda's freezer. She'd offered NOPD detectives Nina and Sam free admission to the haunted houses. Nina had booked hers for that evening. This would be the perfect time to turn the phone over to the NOPD, but it would mean admitting Ricki acquired it illegally.

After a frantic twenty minutes of checking people in, there were only a handful of people left in line. Nina was one of them. She reached Ricki, who welcomed her without mentioning the phone. 'Hi. Welcome to the Bon V*eeevil* and Duncan-Sejour Festival of Fear. Prepare for the scariest night of your life. And don't forget to stop at Miss Vee's Vintage Cookbook and Kitchenware Shop on your way out. You must be Nina's niece and nephew.' She addressed this to the boy and girl Nina had in tow.

'This is my daughter Isabella and my son Ethan.'

Ricki's jaw dropped. She instantly clamped it shut, then said, 'Your *own* kids. Well, hey there.' She tried disguising her discomfort with excessive cheeriness. She didn't blame the kids, who appeared to be between ten and twelve, for responding with dour expressions as they stepped inside.

'I'm divorced. My ex and I have joint custody.' Nina eyed Ricki with amusement. 'Are you disturbed by my humanity?'

'To tell the truth, a little,' Ricki confessed. 'Only because it's unexpected. You didn't mention you were bringing them.'

'No,' Nina said with a mischievous grin. 'I thought it would be much more fun to see your reaction.'

She started to follow her kids inside. Ricki made a snap decision. She surreptitiously dropped Miranda's phone into the bushes. 'I can't believe it!' She declared this dramatically, making a big show of discovering the phone. 'This must be Miranda's. She thought she lost it when she came over here to complain one day but we never found it. Until now.'

Ricki picked the phone out of the bushes. She handed it to Nina, who let out a guffaw. 'That was the lamest attempt at lying I've seen since the guy I caught taking a sledgehammer to a jewelry store window tried to convince me the window broke because he tripped and fell into it. Two questions: did this phone belong to Miranda?'

'Yes.'

'Do I want to know how you ended up with it?'

'No.'

'Alrighty then.' Nina pocketed the phone.

'Also, I've learned through personal experience that Mooni and Nat are a united front against anyone who they perceive as a threat to Blaine. I also overheard something interesting about Blaine's interior designer Delia Frontenac.' Ricki detailed the conversation between Delia and the snobby couple. 'I don't know what kind of lawsuit Delia was involved in but Miranda was definitely a threat to her.'

'Congrats on a bout of successful amateur sleuthing. I'll be in touch.'

Nina went to join her kids, leaving Ricki off-kilter as usual, unsure if the detective was being sincere or sarcastic.

After closing, the Bon Vee crew decamped to an uptown bar in the Carrollton neighborhood to celebrate the Festival of Fear's popular and financial success. A local favorite for over sixty years, the Riverbend Bar and Grill's paneled wood walls emitted the scent of cigarettes and mildew, and the grill existed in name only, replaced by boiled hot dogs and bags of chips. Nobody cared. The place was crammed with people drinking while they waited to participate in the Riverbend's Halloweenie Challenge, a competitive game of Simon Says.

Ricki and her friends managed to score a table and cobble together enough rickety old metal chairs to seat everyone. Even Mordant was able to make it.

She shared what she'd told Nina with the group. 'I wonder if Nat and Mooni's hostility came from their fear I'd find something I wasn't supposed to. Like Miranda's phone.'

'It could also be legit annoyance about you trespassing,' Theo pointed out.

Cookie seconded this. 'Remember, Nat has an alibi.'

'I know,' Ricki said. 'But he could be protecting someone else. Like Blaine. Or Mooni.'

Zellah held up her phone. 'While y'all were talking, I did a search for the Delia lawsuit. She had a partner in a design and housewares business. He accused her of stealing his designs and marketing them under another name. Things got ugly. He took out a restraining order on her. He won the lawsuit, she lost, and basically had to start from scratch.'

'Hmmm.' Ricki considered this. 'One of the ironies of movie stars is that even though they've got money to burn, they've always been gifted with free goods and services. Businesses think it's worth it for the publicity. I bet Delia's working for Blaine for free. It's a hugely important gig for her. If Miranda was threatening to fire her, file that under motivation for murder.'

'What about Miranda's family members?' Cookie asked. 'Weren't you going to go down that road?'

Ricki played with the bag of cheese curls she'd yet to open. 'I did.' She relayed her conversation with Gordy. 'I get there are a lot of reasons people aren't on genealogy sites. They're expensive. There's also the danger of your DNA falling into criminals' hands if they're hacked. Some people don't care about their ancestry. Some people already know what they need to know. And some people just don't want to connect, period.' Ricki gave frustrated sigh. 'I need a PI, which I can't afford. Or a detective. Too bad Nina's too busy with the nine-thousand crimes in the city to take on a side hustle. Plus, she's a divorced mom with two kids.'

'What?!' Theo sounded horrified. '*No*.'

Ricki fixed a look on him. 'I told you she has kids, not a communicable disease.'

Zellah eyed him the same way. 'From the expression on his face they're one and the same.'

'No, it's great, good for her,' Theo protested. 'I do have "no kids" as a requirement on my dating profile but for her, I'd make an exception.'

Cookie clasped her hands over heart. 'Awww, that's so nice of you. You're the best catch ever!' She dropped her hands and matched the glare emanating from the other women.

'Hey, how about another round? On me.' Theo leaped up from his seat and escaped to the bar.

Ricki saw Olivia sweep into the bar and make a beeline to them, elbowing a couple of malingerers out of her way. 'I have *such* good dirt,' she announced, dropping into Theo's seat.

'Great but you shouldn't be in here,' Ricki said. 'You're not twenty-one.'

Olivia held up a license. 'I am on this driver's license.' She put the fake ID away in the purselet dangling from her wrist. 'So . . . I hung out with Jason at Duncan-Sejour tonight and he told me a *lot* about Miranda. She got into a super bad fight with Delia. Her relationship with Nat and Lakshmi wasn't too great either, although Jason said she was more of an irritant than a threat to them. The only person she was nice to was Mooni. Jason thinks it's because Miranda was scared of her.'

'I can relate,' Ricki said, having been on the receiving end of Mooni's implied threats.

Mordant, who'd been quiet up to this moment, joined in on the conversation. 'I tapped into a couple of law enforcement databases,' Mordant said, his serious tone accentuating his naturally hangdog features. 'Mooni's counter-culture activity was much more violent than the public ever knew because she struck a deal where she narc'ed on her co-conspirators for lesser charges and a shorter sentence.'

'How did you access those databases and could you do it again if we needed you to?' Ricki asked.

'I'd rather not talk about it,' Mordant said, pulling back. Zellah shot Ricki a warning look and she didn't press it.

Olivia dropped her voice to a stage whisper. 'I learned something even more critical.'

The others leaned in. Theo reappeared carrying a pitcher of

beer. 'I got our drinks. *Hello*.' He said this pointedly to Olivia sitting in what was formerly his seat.

'Shhh.' Ricki indicated for him to be quiet. She prompted Olivia. 'Go on.'

'Well . . .' The entire table leaned in to hear Olivia's juicy tidbit. Theo hovered over them with the pitcher. 'You know how Lakshmi does yoga with Blaine and gives him massages? Miranda found out she was selling Blaine's sweaty towels on the internet. She told Lakshmi that if she didn't cut her in on the profits, she'd report her to Blaine. Jason found out because he was in charge of washing the towels and noticed the count was off. He was going to report them both, but then Miranda died. I guess that scared off Lakshmi because she stopped selling the towels.'

'Another side hustle,' Ricki murmured. She spoke louder. 'An argument over sweaty towels doesn't seem like motive for murder on the surface but if it endangered Lakshmi's cushy position at chez Duncan-Sejour . . .'

'Oh, it would have,' Olivia said. 'Blaine pays everyone insane amounts of money to work for him. If he offered me a job, forget college. I'd take it in a sec.'

'No!' Ricki yelled this, knowing Eugenia and Olivia's parents would blame and possibly kill her.

'Jeez, chill. It's not like I'd do anything until after my debut. I'm not going to pass up all those parties.' She reached for Ricki's half-full mug of beer and made a grumpy face when Ricki pulled it away.

Theo helped himself to an empty chair from another table and began refilling everyone's mugs. 'Thanks,' Zellah said. She studied Ricki. 'You've got your thinking face on. The one that comes right before you say, "I have a plan." And . . . now it's your "I have a plan" face.'

Ricki shared a smile with her friend. 'You know me so well. I do have a plan. The one thing I missed at the Duncan-Sejour haunted house was paying a visit to the fortuneteller's tent. So, tomorrow night, I'm going to stop by Lakshmi's tent, get my "fortune told," and see if I can drill deeper into the towel-selling scam she had to cut Miranda into.'

TWENTY-ONE

T he next night, Ricki used the downtime between Bon Vee tours to pay Duncan-Sejour's haunted house a visit. She exchanged greetings with Jason, who was manning the front door. Or rather, lounging on the home's front porch since the tour had already begun. 'I missed visiting the fortuneteller's tent at the soft opening, and I thought it would be fun,' Ricki said. 'Would it be OK if I snuck around the back and went straight there?'

'Sure. From what I hear, Lakshmi does a pretty good job. At least it gives the rest of us a break from the sage stick she's always waving to "cleanse" the place of bad vibes. I'm over the smell of that thing.'

Having coughed through Lakshmi's 'cleansing' at Miranda's memorial, Ricki had to laugh at this. She glanced down the estate's front path. Confirming it was devoid of latecomers, she took advantage of her rare moment alone with Olivia's crush. 'Jason . . . I love Olivia. And I'm very protective of her. I know the two of you have been spending time together. Is it on a friend basis? Or more than that?'

'Friend,' he instantly responded to Ricki's relief. 'Please don't worry. I like her a lot but I'm keeping it casual. I don't expect to be in New Orleans much past Halloween. Where Blaine goes, I go.'

'Any idea where that might be?' Ricki asked, relieved Olivia would be spared heartbreak but knowing her cousin would still be sad nothing came of her obvious crush.

Jason shrugged. 'No idea. Could be back to LA. Could be reshoots for *Code Name: Blue Heron 5*. Blaine also said something about visiting countries without a US extradition treaty. But then he said he was joking.'

'Really.' Ricki filed the comment away to be shared later with Nina.

She left Jason and walked around the side of the mansion to

the backyard. Nat, who was patrolling the outdoor area, eyed her suspiciously as she headed for Lakshmi's tent. 'Nothing to see here,' she assured him as she passed. 'Just a girl going to get her fortune told.'

Ricki edged her way around the cornstalk maze. She could hear laughter coming from inside the maze as people searched for each other or a way out. Lakshmi's tent was in a far corner of the yard. Made from yards of rich red velvet, filmy gauze, and yards of dangling gold tassels, the tent's elaborate construction read like an apology for the afterthought of a location.

A couple of teenage girls emerged from the tent, giggling. Since no one else was in line, Ricki lifted the tent flap and entered.

Lakshmi, dressed in full fortuneteller regalia complete with silk turban, sat on a stack of large, ornate pillows behind a squat table holding a crystal ball. Two more pillows sat in front of the table. 'Please avail yourself of a pillow,' she intoned, wafting her hands over the crystal ball without glancing up at the new arrival.

'Thanks. Agh!' Ricki toppled over in her attempt to sink down onto a pillow that proved unevenly fluffy.

Lakshmi looked up from the crystal ball. 'Ugh,' she said, dropping the fortuneteller shtick. 'It's you. What do you want?'

'My fortune told. I have questions about my personal life.' Ricki had decided to ease into queries about Miranda's murder. Besides, if Lakshmi did have any genuine psychic abilities, Ricki figured she might as well take advantage of them and see if the woman could shed any light on her confusing relationship with Virgil.

'Oh, OK,' Lakshmi said, assuaged by this. 'What's your question?'

'There's a man. I thought we were on the verge of something. But he had to leave town on business and the only contact I've had with him since has been about the two dogs we co-parent. I'm wondering where we stand, if anywhere.'

'Do you have any item he's touched?'

Ricki took a folded-up piece of paper from the credit card holder attached to her phone and handed it to Lakshmi. 'He wrote down the name of a vet near us when we first adopted Thor and Princess.'

Lakshmi took the piece of paper. She held out her free hand. 'Give me your hand.' Ricki did so. Lakshmi closed her eyes, holding tight to both the paper and Ricki's hand. 'He is nearby. I feel it strongly.'

'He is?' If Lakshmi's instincts were correct, Virgil had some explaining to do about why he hadn't gotten in touch with Ricki.

'Yes. My sense of his presence was strong.' Lakshmi let go of Ricki's hand and returned the slip of paper to her. 'Any other questions?'

'Yes. I'm still haunted by Miranda's death.' Ricki added a shudder for effect. 'I have nightmares about it. I wondered if a psychic like you has a sense of who killed her.'

Lakshmi released an un-psychic-like snort. 'Took you long enough to get to the real reason you're here. The answer is no. Goodbye.'

'I know about your sweaty towel deal with Miranda.'

Ricki purposely dropped this on Lakshmi out of the blue to see the woman's reaction. The fortuneteller emitted a hostile grunt, then shoved her crystal ball aside and bent over the table towards Ricki. 'I don't need a crystal ball to see huge problems for you if you don't mind your own business.'

Her face was only inches from Ricki's and the warning came with a strong whiff of alcohol. Ricki recoiled. 'You're drunk.'

'How dare you,' Lakshmi hissed at Ricki. 'Blaine's in recovery and so's Nat, so we're not allowed to have booze in the house. Anyone caught with it would be fired and black-balled. Do me and yourself a favor and go. Take your nosy butt elsewhere. Trust me, you do not want to mess with Blaine World. It can be vicious. And dangerous.'

TWENTY-TWO

D isturbed by her confrontation with Lakshmi, Ricki left Duncan-Sejour for her car, parked next door at Bon Vee, where the tours had already ended. She climbed into the driver's seat and was about to head home when her phone pinged a text from Cookie announcing to the Bon Vee thread that she was heading to another bar, the Freret Jet on Freret Street. **Assemble the troops! Had a girls night with Britni etc. Deets tk!**

Ricki yawned and rubbed her eyes. *We were just at a bar last night,* she thought, weary. *I don't have the stamina to party like everyone else in New Orleans. I swear, sometimes I wonder how anything gets done in this city.*

Her debate about whether to go to the bar or not was short-lived. Cookie's text made it clear her friend had something to share. Instead of driving toward home, she headed away from it.

As Ricki drove, she had the sudden sense she was being followed. A black sedan with heavily tinted windows and a dent in the right front fender seemed to be taking the exact same route she was. To test her theory, she made a left on Prytania and a right on Third Street, then circled back to Prytania. The sedan stayed on her tail.

Heart thumping, Ricki stayed on Prytania until she made a left on Henry Clay. She made a sharp right onto St Charles Avenue, shooting between cars lined up to drive by one of the city's most iconic Halloween displays. Homeowners of an elegant mansion on the famed avenue had earned the nickname 'The Skeleton House' by turning their front yard into a collection of skeletons with tongue-in-cheek names like 'Boney Curtis,' 'Game of Bones,' and 'TromBONE Shorty.' Ricki ignored the amusing display, instead making sure cars piled onto the avenue behind her, blocking the sedan's view of her car. She passed the house and drove for a few more blocks until she made a sharp right onto Jefferson Avenue, cutting in front of a streetcar and earning the wrath of its driver. She checked her rearview mirror. To her relief, there was no sign of the sedan.

The Freret Jet Bar paid homage to the nickname of the bus that traversed the street out front from Uptown to the French Quarter, its kitschy interior mimicking an old bus's interior. Ricki found friends Zellah, Mordant, and Theo ensconced in a back booth where the seating consisted of vintage bus benches. Ricki slid into a bench next to Zellah and Mordant. 'I'm so glad you're here. I was followed.'

'What?!' The others joined Zellah in exclamations of concern.

'I noticed almost as soon as I left Bon Vee. A nondescript black sedan. Perfect car for following someone. I lost them in the traffic around the Skeleton House.'

'Are you OK?' Zellah asked, worried.

'Yes. Just a little shaken up after that on top of my not very pleasant meetup with Duncan-Sejour's fortuneteller. I'll fill you in on that in a minute. I need to calm down first.' She picked up a pitcher. 'Pimm's Cup. My favorite.' She filled a glass and took a sip, then looked around. 'No Lyla again?'

'Kaitlyn's team won the first round of a tournament,' Zellah said. 'Now it's going to go all weekend, so Lyla has to go join the fam in Baton Rouge. She was weeping when she gave me the news. And they were not tears of joy.'

Cookie approached the table taking tiny steps. She wore a form-fitting bright-red cocktail dress under a black leather jacket, and black pumps with four-inch heels. 'How-do, all.' She deposited herself next to Zellah and kicked off her shoes. 'Never break in a new pair of heels at a casino,' she said, rubbing her feet.

'Is that where you went tonight with Britni?' Ricki asked.

'With Britni, Sarah Jane, and Toni. We went to Harrah's and had a fantastic time. I won four hundred dollars. Next pitcher is on me. But only one. I have to use my winnings to pay down my credit card debt.'

'You texted you have deets,' Ricki prompted. 'Did you learn anything tonight that would help solve Miranda's murder?'

'Britni's absolutely got the hots for Chess and has way more hardware supplies than she needs because she's always making trips to the store where he works to connect with him. It took a while but it paid off because he invited her out for dinner. Most of all to dunk on Miranda together, but it's a start.'

'We already know she's into him,' Ricki said, nursing her drink. 'But the timing of him finally asking her out after all these years is an interesting development. Why now? Does it have anything to do with Miranda's murder? We need to know more about Chess. I thought anyone who showed up at a memorial to make sure the person was really dead probably didn't kill them. But you never know. That could be him covering or him owning it.'

Cookie flagged a waiter and ordered a dirty martini. 'Britni invited me to join her and the others for a spa day once Halloween is over, so I don't think she killed Miranda.'

Zellah gave Cookie the side eye. 'Seriously? The mean girls welcomed you into their coven and that makes them innocent?'

'Why would you plan a spa day if you killed someone?' Cookie protested. 'It makes no sense.'

'It does if you want to look your best for a mug shot,' Theo said.

'I can't even with this conversation,' Zellah said, shaking her head in disbelief. 'Ricki, what happened with you and the fortuneteller? You haven't told us.'

Ricki relayed her conversation with Lakshmi.

'Do you think she was exaggerating when she said Blaine World was dangerous?' Cookie asked, concerned.

'I thought she might be because I'm sure she'd been drinking even though she swore she hadn't been. But after being followed tonight—'

'You were followed?' The waiter handed Cookie a martini. She clutched it to her chest.

'Yes. I'm sure it was someone from Duncan-Sejour. Jason seemed fine with me and judging from her breath, I don't think Lakshmi was in any shape to follow anyone but a booze delivery van. I bet it was Mooni or Nat. They both scare me.' Rattled by reliving the experience, Ricki took a swig of her drink.

'Nat's not a bad person,' Cookie said. 'I've run into him a couple of times on my way into Bon Vee for work and we've had nice chats. I think he's sensitive and covers it up with a lot of bravado.'

Ricki raised a brow. 'If by sensitive, you mean thuggish, sure.'

'I found out more about Mooni,' Mordant said in his usual doleful voice. 'She wasn't only in on the bank robbery she went to jail for, she was the ringleader. But because she turned state's witness and identified her accomplices, *and* where they'd hidden the stolen money, she got a reduced sentence, even though she'd been on the run for five years. After meeting her parole requirements, she wound up as Blaine's guardian and her life has been about his ever since. Mooni didn't like or trust Miranda, who got Blaine's professional publicist fired and was manipulating her way into taking over every aspect of his life. Mooni thought she was harming, not helping, Blaine's image. She confronted Miranda . . . and stories suddenly began leaking about Mooni's past. Blaine was not happy.'

'Wow, Mordant, this is huge,' Ricki said, impressed. 'Nice job.'

He responded with a self-conscious shrug. 'Without as many tours on my schedule as before, I have time to do other things, like research.' He gazed at Zellah, moony-eyed. 'And day-dream.'

'Stop that.' Zellah gave Mordant a light swat. Mordant captured her hand in his. She didn't pull it away.

Ricki mulled over what Mordant had uncovered. 'So . . . Miranda was a threat to Mooni's relationship with Blaine, the most important thing in Mooni's life.'

'The only thing,' Theo added.

'An ex-con who stood to lose everything,' Cookie summed up. 'Sounds like motivation for murder to me.'

A commotion at the bar front door distracted the group. Blaine emerged from a throng of enthusiastic admirers. Ricki groaned in annoyance and let out an obscenity. Cookie looked at her, bemused. 'You have to be the only person on earth who curses at the sight of Blaine Taggart.'

Blaine scanned the room, his glance alighting on the Bon Vee team. He made a beeline for them, with Nat in tow as always. 'These chairs taken?' he asked the table next to theirs and was met by squeals and giggles from the college girls occupying it.

Nat moved the chairs to the Bon Vee table while Blaine posed for selfies with the girls, then both men sat down – Nat next to Cookie, Blaine next to Ricki. 'Stop following me,' she said with an icy stare.

'I didn't.'

'Then how did you know I was here? Lakshmi's crystal ball?'

'Ha. Good one.'

'A black sedan with tinted windows was on my tail, Blaine. It had to be you.'

'It couldn't be. Our fleet is black SUVs with tinted windows. So it was someone else or your imagination.'

'It was *you*,' Ricki insisted, thrown by the twist but stubbornly refusing to give up.

Blaine released an exaggerated sigh. 'Ricki. Ricki, Rick, Ricki. Why the hate? We're young, we're in New Orleans, it's almost Halloween. Give the past a rest. Focus on the present.'

Ricki squeezed her fists together, suppressing the urge to pummel the supercilious movie star. Rather than resort to violence, she turned her back on him. But his declaration that he and his team only drove black SUVs rang true. Ricki was positive she hadn't imagined it. *If Blaine or one of his minions wasn't following me . . . then who was?*

A voice boomed over the bar's sound system. 'Attention, Jet Setters. It's time for the Freret Jet Halloweenie Challenge! The first ten volunteers get to play Musical Chairs.'

'Me!'

Grabbing the chance to divest herself of Blaine's company, Ricki leapt up and hurried to claim a spot in the challenge, along with a throng of other eager players. The bar manager counted off and Ricki made the cut.

'We have our contestants. Everyone else can sit – wait a minute, we have a ringer. Blaine Taggart, do my eyes deceive me or did you just slip a guy a twenty to take his place?'

'No, I swear.' Blaine took a beat. 'I slipped him a fifty!'

The crowd roared. The manager blew a whistle to quiet them. 'Let's put it to a voice vote. All in favor of Blaine buying his way into the challenge say aye!' The affirmative response was deafening. 'All against!'

'Aye!' Ricki yelled alone. She glared at her friends. '*Et tu?*' None showed the least bit of remorse.

'Contestants, assume your positions,' the manager ordered. 'Let the games begin!'

The Chicken Dance, embraced by wedding partygoers everywhere, blasted from the speakers as Ricki, Blaine, and eight others circled nine chairs. Or attempted to, on the part of several unsteady contestants. Their ranks quickly dwindled until the only competitors left standing were Ricki and Blaine.

A drum roll played over the speakers. 'One of the two remaining players will go home a winner,' the manager declared into a mic in his best game show host voice, 'one will go home a Halloweenie? Which will it be?'

'The Monster Mash' boomed from the sound system. Ricki and Blaine, eyes locked on each other, circled the last remaining chair. 'Go Ricki, go Ricki,' her friends chanted.

'You better all be Team Ricki.' She said this without breaking eye contact.

'I'm not,' Cookie chirped.

'You just lost your discount at Miss Vee's.'

In what was almost a vertical Limbo contest, Ricki and Blaine hunched down to get closer to the chair. The music stopped and Ricki zoomed into the seat. She bumped into Blaine, who lost his balance and fell into her lap. The bar patrons hooted and whooped it up with a new chant of 'Halloweenie!' as Ricki pushed Blaine off.

'Yo! Everything OK there?'

'Now that he's off my lap,' Ricki said, straightening her T-shirt, 'I'm f—'

She glanced up at the man who issued the question and her jaw dropped.

Standing in front of her, looking perturbed, was the long-lost Virgil Morel.

TWENTY-THREE

Ricki's first thought on seeing Virgil was, *Wow, props to Lakshmi. I guess she really is psychic.* Her second was, *What the eff?! He practically goes MIA on me and then shows up out of nowhere with zero warning? I choose to feel calm, I choose to feel – oh, what the eff. I am NOT calm!*

A murmur of recognition buzzed through the crowd. Virgil might not be in the highest echelon of fame like Blaine but he could be labeled a TV star, in addition to being one of the city's most famous chefs. The fact his taut build, strong features, and pale blue eyes – a stunning contest to his rich brown skin – once got him anointed 'Sexiest Chef Alive' by a national magazine helped. It didn't escape Ricki's attention that the excited buzz in the bar was more female than male.

'I see you met my girlfriend,' Virgil said to Blaine, a challenge in his eyes.

'Girlfriend. Huh.'

Blaine sounded surprised. But not more surprised than Ricki. 'Are you high?!' she blurted. She was about to ream him but stopped herself. Blaine might perceive her dismissal of Virgil as encouraging news for him, the last message she wanted to send. Aggravated, she held her tongue.

'I'm Virgil Morel.' Virgil extended his hand, delivered his name in a way that dared Blaine not to know who he was.

Whether intentionally taking the dare or not, Blaine responded with a friendly but clueless greeting as they shook, which prompted Virgil to add, 'From the TV show. *America's Next Top Southern Chef.*'

'Sorry, man, I don't watch TV. But hey, nice gig.' Ricki got a modicum of satisfaction watching Virgil's reaction to the pity compliment.

The bar manager interceded. 'Halloweenie, rules of the game are you pick up your competition's check.'

'I don't play by the rules,' Blaine said in a gruff voice. The bar patrons roared. It was another signature line from the *Code Name: Blue Heron* franchise. Blaine threw an arm around the manager's shoulder. 'I'm picking up the tab for the whole bar tonight.'

The two headed off to chants of 'Blaine, Blaine, Blaine!' leaving Ricki to face off with Virgil.

In the past, Ricki would have been reticent about confronting him in any way. When he first seemed to show interest, she felt so out of his league that she thought she was imagining it. But she'd built her own business out of the ashes of her former career. She'd lived through the notoriety of Chris's death and Lachlan Barnes' arrest. And she'd helped NOPD identify more than one killer, saving the lives of people she cared about. All of this made Ricki stronger than she ever thought she'd be. And allowed her to light into Virgil with a fury that made him take a step back from her as she lambasted him for his thoughtless behavior, his ego, and his nerve.

'Whoa. OK. You're right,' Virgil said when she finally gave him a chance to speak. 'I deserve all of that. Even those words I've only heard coming from dockworkers.'

'You have no right strolling in here out of nowhere and going all "Me Tarzan" Neanderthal.'

'I know, I know. I'm sorry.'

'I deserve better.' As she said this, Ricki truly felt it for the first time in her life, giving her a heady sensation.

'You do.'

'I do! I don't know what's going on inside your head, but I am *not* your girlfriend. We are *not* in a relationship, Virgil. We haven't even kissed.'

'*That* I can fix.'

Virgil pulled Ricki into an embrace. He brought his face to hers and delivered the hands-down best kiss of her life. They separated. Ricki felt so woozy she feared she might pass out. She used every fiber of her being to bat back an overwhelming desire to repeat the moment. 'Fine. Now we kissed.' She made a vain attempt to fix her hair, much of which had strayed out of its ponytail during the amorous exchange. 'It doesn't mean we're in a relationship.'

'Noted.' Virgil appeared genuinely apologetic. 'And I get it.

I'll back off. But would it be OK if I spent extra time with Thor and Princess? I missed them too.'

'Yes. Of course. Spend as much time with them as you want.' Ignoring the ping in her heart as she registered the meaning behind 'I missed them *too*,' she added in a steely voice, 'Just not with me.'

Virgil sagged a bit. He gave a slight nod and departed. With him went Ricki's righteous energy, replaced by a whirlwind of conflicting emotions. She marched over to her friends. 'OK, 'fess up. Which one of you told Virgil where I'd be?'

Cookie's hand instantly shot up. 'Me. I knew we'd all be here, so I told him to come. He wanted to surprise you.'

'Mission accomplished on that score,' Ricki said with a snort.

Cookie faced her, defiant. 'I'm not going to say I'm sorry. I've never seen two people get in each other's way as much as you two. This whole, "Hey, let's co-parent the dogs" is such an obvious front for your attraction to each other. I get that you both have a lot of relationship baggage. But if you don't either work through it or stop giving it the power to hold you back, both of you will end up alone, staring across Odile Street at each other's houses, regretting that you let fear dictate your life choices.'

The others gaped at her. After they collected themselves, Zellah spoke. 'Going on record to say I'm jealous, Cookie. I'm usually the one coming up with stuff all thoughtful like that while you're in the bathroom adjusting your bra to make more cleavage.'

Cookie glanced down at the lowcut neckline of her slinky black spaghetti strap top. 'Now that you mention it, the girls could use an adjustment. When Nat wasn't worrying about Blaine, I could see him giving me the eye. I am not uninterested.'

'Everyone at Duncan-Sejour is a murder suspect,' Ricki pointed out.

'You say that like it's a deal breaker,' Cookie said, adjusting her top. 'And reminder, he's the only one of the suspects in Miranda's murder who's got a legit alibi.' She circled the table with her finger. 'Including all of us.'

Ricki didn't have to work hard to dodge Blaine on her way out. He was at the bar, so surrounded by fans she could only catch a glimpse of his head. She didn't have to worry about running into Virgil either. He'd left to retrieve Thor and Princess shortly after Ricki had called him out on his 'now you see him, now you don't' disappearing act.

The Uptown streets were close to empty at eleven p.m. Ricki made a right onto Napoleon and took it toward Tchoupitoulas. Centuries-old oak trees covered many of the road's streetlights, rendering the route dark. Fat raindrops from a shower earlier in the day dropped onto Ricki's windshield, slipping off the leaves where they'd landed. Coming from a city where weathercasters could go weeks without reporting anything but 'dry and sunny with high of eighty' Ricki loved the fat, bossy raindrops of a New Orleans storm. She couldn't articulate why but she found comfort in them. It was as if they had a confidence she sometimes lacked. And alone at night on a close to pitch-black road, Ricki felt the confidence emboldening her when she confronted Virgil slipping away.

She was about where she made a left towards home when her phone rang with an unexpected caller. Ricki pressed a button on her steering wheel to answer the call. 'Nina?'

'The one and only.'

'Why are you calling so late? What about the kids?' Ricki's heartbeat zoomed up to panic level. 'Was there another murder?'

'It's a big city, chere. There's always another murder. It's what gives me these wacky work hours. But that's not why I'm calling. We got an interesting tidbit left anonymously on the tip line we set up regarding Miranda Fine's murder. You never told me you were related to the victim.'

'I'm not, no, I mean I am . . .' Ricki's heartbeat went from ten to eleven on the panic scale. 'I'm not lying, ignore that. What I mean is we're very distantly related. It's the level on genealogy sites where it comes with a string of caveats. And . . .' A memory slightly lowered her level of panic. 'I didn't even find out we were related until after she was killed.'

Ricki quickly recapped the mysterious reference from Ricki listed on Miranda's job application and how it sent Ricki down a rabbit hole of searching for the reason why the ambitious assistant would take such a risk. 'I had no motive to kill Miranda. Yes, she was a troublemaking beeyotch, but that's not a motive for murder for any of us. I mean, I can't even kill a spider. I trap them and release them outside. I do kill roaches, but who doesn't. Never mind. You have to believe me.'

Whether it was the desperation or tears in Ricki's voice, something reached the detective. 'I do,' she said, without a hint of sarcasm or caustic attitude. Instead, there was a hint of an emotion Ricki had never heard before in the detective's voice: warmth. 'My job is to follow every lead, no matter how minuscule or farfetched. We've solved murders based on far less of a connection to the victim. I'll verify what you've told me. But I feel it's the truth.'

'Thank you. If you need me to come down to the station and repeat this or if you need any more details, let me know. I'm so sorry I didn't tell you sooner. I truly believed it had nothing to do with Miranda's murder.'

'Which was a judgment call on your part. When I said I'd look the other way if you did some snooping on your own, I meant you needed to tell me any possible lead you dug up. Even if it potentially implicated you. Got it?'

'Yes, ma'am,' Ricki said, chastised.

Nina released an aggrieved grunt. 'Ugh. Nothing worse than the day a woman transitions from "miss" to "ma'am". Even for tough birds like me. Now, go get some sleep. My highly trained detective instincts tell me you need it.'

Nina clicked off. Ricki pulled over to regain control over her emotions before finishing the short drive home. *I need one of those watches that checks your blood pressure because mine must be off the charts.* She closed her eyes and did deep breathing exercises to take her heart rate down from beating like a drum in a big parade to fairly normal levels. This time, repeating her *I choose to feel calm* mantra helped.

Feeling at least relaxed-adjacent, Ricki pulled back onto the road and finished the short drive home. She chastised herself for not cluing in NOPD about her DNA connection to Miranda. She'd meant to but was thrown off course by the development of the haunted house on steroids at Duncan-Sejour. She knew the call to the tipster line wasn't the work of a Good Samaritan. The fact the caller wanted to remain anonymous sent two possible messages: a) they wanted to put a light on Ricki as a suspect to stop her from sniffing around, or b) the caller was the killer hoping to frame someone else for the murder. She made a mental list of who might have left the tip. It included everyone on Blaine's team – plus Gordy Fine, or anyone he might have told about his newfound distant cousin, Ricki James-Diaz.

Ricki parked in front of her house. She heard muffled barking and glanced across the street to see Thor and Princess standing on a couch to peer outside the window of Virgil's shotgun abode, a more spacious version of Ricki's. It was the home where Virgil grew up and now lived when not traveling with this show, to be closer to his mother, who was housed in a nearby memory care facility.

Ricki waved and blew kisses to the pups, who responded with more barks and much tail wagging. She went inside and the barking faded. The quiet of her own home was oppressive. Exhausted, she washed up and got into bed. She reached for Thor, who usually burrowed under the sheets and stretched prone along her side, then remembered he wasn't there. Instead, she wrapped her arms around a pillow. *I'm an adult woman hugging a pillow for comfort,* she thought before drifting off. *Cookie's right. I have to figure out how to move on with my life or this will be my future.*

She'd barely fallen asleep when her phone alerted her to a text. Sleepy, Ricki turned off the sound. Seconds later, the phone vibrated with the alert of an incoming call. She snatched it off the nightstand. She was about to give the late-night caller an earful when she saw it was Olivia. Knowing using a phone to make an actual phone call was the equivalent of traveling by horse and carriage for a Gen Z-er, a worried Ricki answered. 'Olivia, what's going on? Are you OK?'

'I was on my way home from this bar in the Lower Garden—'

Ricki cursed her cousin's fake ID. NOPD was not forgiving when it came to underage drinking. 'Are you in jail? Do you need me to bail you out?'

'What? No. Of course not. I saw fire trucks in front of Bon Vee, so I made the rideshare driver stop.'

Ricki got a sick feeling in the pit of her stomach. 'Oh, God. No.'

'There was a fire but it wasn't at Bon Vee,' Olivia rushed to reassure her. 'It was at Blaine's place. In the backyard. The fortuneteller tent caught fire. And the lady playing the fortuneteller was inside.'

TWENTY-FOUR

Fire engines and police cars blocked Persephone Street, their flashing red lights casting an ominous glow. Worried neighbors in bathrobes or with coats flung over their nightwear watched the fire department do their job from the safety of their porches.

The Bon Vee friends huddled together on the sidewalk. Cookie and Theo, who had stuck around the Freret Jet, were still in their bar-hopping duds. The others had come from home. Nat's team formed their own huddle on the sidewalk in front of Duncan-Sejour, where plumes of smoke twirled upwards from the backyard. No one said a word. The only sounds came from the crackle of emergency responders contacting each other, the hum of their engines, and the stream of water gushing through the fire engine hoses. The acrid scent of burning matter filled the air.

'It's gray now,' Theo finally said. 'Gray smoke is good. It means the fire is almost out.'

'The water's slowed too,' Olivia said. 'It's not flowing as hard through the hoses.'

She shivered. Concerned that it was shock as much as the slight chill in the air, Ricki wrapped her arms around the girl in a protective hug. 'It's late. You should get back to the dorm.'

'No way,' the twenty-something said, adamant. 'I'm the one who called the fire department. I was here when the ambulance left with the fortuneteller. I'm not going anywhere until this is all over.'

Ricki glanced over to Blaine and the others, torn between avoiding contact and wanting to make sure they were OK. Blaine caught her eye, making it too late for the former. He said something to the others he was with and they approached Ricki and her friends as a group. 'Jason tells me you're the one who sounded the alarm about the fire,' he said to Olivia.

Her shivering increased. 'I didn't see flames at first, just smoke.

I called Jason and he didn't answer, so I called nine-one-one just to be safe.'

'I'm a heavy sleeper,' Jason said, embarrassed.

Blaine took off his leather jacket and placed it around Olivia's shoulders. 'Your call helped contain the fire. And may have saved Lakshmi's life.'

'Terrible.' Mooni cast her eyes on the action still playing out. Nat muttered agreement.

'When this is over, you best believe we'll find a way to thank you.' Ricki could tell Blaine was sincere, despite the fact he delivered the pronouncement like it was a line from a *Code Name: Blue Heron* movie.

Olivia, self-conscious, shrunk closer to Ricki. 'No problem. Whatevs.'

Zellah, who'd peeled off, reappeared, along with Mordant. 'We set up food and coffee in the Bon Vee kitchen. Y'all come with me.'

Sensing Zellah wasn't about to take no for an answer, everyone trooped after her. Ricki hung back. The gate Blaine had installed between the estates was wide open to allow firefighters additional access to the fire. The rolling flats making up Blaine's moveable maze lay toppled on their side, the cornstalks blackened or burned to nubs. The fortuneteller's tent had been reduced to a smoldering pile. 'When I go home tonight,' Ricki heard one firefighter tell another, 'I get to tell my kids I almost couldn't get to a fire because I got stuck in some movie star's crazy maze.'

The other firefighter chortled. 'I know, right? The guy should set up a barbeque to go with all this roasted corn.' He pushed a flat aside with his boot and resumed checking for hot spots.

Ricki started for Bon Vee, then paused. She saw detectives Nina and Sam conferring with the fire chief. Nina must have felt Ricki's stare because she turned towards Bon Vee. Nina removed her phone from the back pocket of her jeans. Seconds later, Ricki received a text: **Don't let anyone from BV or DS leave.**

An hour later, the firefighters were on their way, having done their job and been feted with food and profuse thanks. To Ricki's relief, it hadn't been hard to lock down the others in Bon Vee's family room, which was off limit to tours. With its large stone fireplace and preponderance of comfortable chairs and sofas, the room proved to be a refuge, especially since news crews had replaced the fire trucks on Persephone Street. Jason and Olivia busied themselves sending out alerts to their respective patrons, with Jason spreading the news that the haunted house at Duncan-Sejour was no more and Olivia sharing with Bon Vee visitors that the estate would be closed for the day but open for the evening's haunted house tours.

'Knock, knock.'

Nina and Sam stood in the doorway of the family room. 'Come in,' Ricki said, glad to see the law enforcement officials for a change. 'There's coffee, tea, sweets, and sandwiches. Unfortunately, we drank through our liquor supply.'

'We're good,' Nina said.

'I could eat,' Sam said simultaneously.

Sam took a plate and helped himself to snacks while Nina took a seat on a counter stool, positioning herself above the others. Ricki knew the seating choice was intentional.

'Do you know what happened?' Blaine asked.

'It's too early for a final analysis, but we've got enough information to make an educated guess.'

'How is Lakshmi?' Ricki asked.

'In critical but stable condition.'

The lighting in the room was too dim to make out anyone's expressions but Ricki noted that she and not the spiritual advisor's Duncan-Sejour housemates put the question to Nina, and the detective's answer didn't elicit any sighs of relief from them.

'Ms Berkenflaum suffered serious burns, so she's looking at a stint in rehab.'

'Berken-what?' Blaine said, confused. 'She has a last name?'

'Yes,' Nina said. 'And a first. Mary. According to her driver's license. You didn't know?'

'It's my job to act. It's their job to know stuff like that.' He directed this in an accusing tone to his team.

'We did know.' Nat said this through gritted teeth, making Ricki wonder if he was finally ready to blow up at his self-involved brother. 'And you didn't need to know. Lakshmi is her spiritual name and we'll handle this.'

Blaine sat back in the well-cushioned side chair, still aggrieved.

'So, what's your analysis?' Ricki asked. Buzzing with fatigue, she was eager to get the conversation back on track so she could go home and catch at least a few hours of sleep.

Sam weighed in, sharing information between hefty bites of a turkey po'boy. 'Ms Berkenflaum said she fell asleep in the tent after a long day and night of work. She woke up to the tent in flames. From what the fire department investigator could determine, an overloaded generator fell on the tent, sending sparks that ignited it.'

'Fell or was purposely knocked over?' Zellah asked the question Ricki was thinking.

'That shouldn't matter because according to the production designer, the generator was positioned at a safe distance from the tent and the maze,' Nat said, his jaw tight.

'Fire her,' Blaine ordered.

'For what? If the production designer did observe the safety protocol, and I can't imagine why she'd lie about it, someone else moved the generator from its approved location to one closer to the tent.' Ricki admired the patience in Mooni's voice. 'Besides, she can't be fired. She already finished the job.'

A strangled sound came from Jason. 'Oh, man. Oh, no. Oh, man.'

Nina raised a brow. 'Are you choking on hot sauce or do you have something to add to the conversation?'

Jason gave a weak nod. 'When you brought up the generator, you made me realize something. Because we had to direct as much power to the haunted house as possible, we had to turn off other electricity drains during the tour. Like the security cameras. I was supposed to turn them on after the tour ended. I was so busy doing everything else I forgot to do it.'

'We were curious about why the security system seemed to be conveniently turned off,' Nina said. 'I appreciate the explanation.'

'One less thing to investigate,' Sam said in a cheery voice as he bit into one of Zellah's homemade pecan hand pies.

Jason dropped his head. 'I'm fired, aren't I?' His voice was so husky Ricki thought he might cry – if he wasn't already.

'No.' Blaine sounded weary. 'I don't have it in me to break in another assistant.'

'There's something else you should know,' Jason said, hastening to add, 'but it's not about me. Lakshmi or Mary or whoever she was – is – was selling some of the towels she used to wipe you down after a massage on the internet. Miranda found out and wanted a piece of the sales in exchange for not telling. I was going to bust them both, but then Miranda . . .' he trailed off.

'File that under something *we the detectives* should know.' Nina scowled at Jason, who wilted further.

'It's not a big deal for A-listers,' Blaine said. 'Not in my world. People bidding on a towel with my sweat on it? You can't buy that kind of publicity.'

'You can if you factor in the price of the towels.' Worn out, Ricki snapped this, earning a snort of laughter from Nina.

'One last question.' Nina swiveled in her chair to face Olivia. Her tone softened. 'Olivia, honey, you called in the fire. Did you see anyone in this room near either Bon Vee or Duncan-Sejour at the time?'

'No, ma'am. I mean, yes, ma'am, I mean no, I didn't see anyone out front or come out of the house. I stuck around until the fire department showed up because I saw the smoke turn into flames and I was scared. I couldn't just leave. I didn't know what else to do. But I couldn't see into the backyard, so I don't know if anyone was there. Like, if someone hopped the fence behind Duncan-Sejour into the other yard or something. I don't know.'

Olivia sounded plaintive. Her voice wavered to the point where Ricki feared her young cousin might break down. 'I think we're done here,' she said, ready to fight with anyone who disagreed, including the detectives.

'Like I said, that was my final question.' Nina hopped off the counter stool. She went to Olivia. 'You did great. You saved a woman's life tonight.' She faced Blaine and said in a tone much less gentle, 'Mister A-lister, buy this girl a very nice thank-you gift. Like, awards-show basket big. I've read about what y'all get for winning awards or even giving them out, and that is some major swag.'

Ricki walked the detectives out of the family room to the back door reserved for employees. 'I didn't want to mention this in front of everyone because I can't verify it,' Ricki said in a low voice. 'But I'm pretty sure Lakshmi has a drinking problem. I've noticed her unsteady on her feet and slurring her words. And I smelled liquor on her breath when I went by the tent to have my fortune told. The fortune also came with a threat.'

She relayed it to Nina and Sam, who exchanged a look. 'When was this?' Sam asked.

'Last night. I went from there to the Freret Jet.' She addressed Nina. 'On the way home, I talked to you about my DNA connection to Miranda. Then I went to bed and woke up when Olivia called about the fire.'

'Explains why she was "asleep" when the tent went up,' Sam said to his partner.

Nina nodded. 'More like passed out.'

The three continued out of Bon Vee towards the detectives' patrol car. 'Lakshmi told me Blaine's house is a dry house,' Ricki said. 'It's because he's in recovery. Anyone living there caught with alcohol would be fired. Maybe Miranda found out about Lakshmi's secret drinking and was going to narc on her. Maybe Lakshmi killed her, then felt guilty about it, started drinking more heavily, and accidentally stumbled into the generator during a binge. The thing is, though, she's built so small it's hard to imagine her lifting Miranda onto the crypt resting place at Bon Vee, like you said before. But she does have strong hands from being a masseuse and is pretty strong in general.'

Ricki couldn't stop herself. She was on a roll. 'Oh, I know, maybe *two* people were involved. Or maybe Lakshmi knew something about the real killer and let them know and they tried taking her out. Or maybe—'

'Does she always give you a big old headache?' Sam asked Nina.

'Pretty much. She's like one of those kids in school who were like, "Pick me, pick me!"' Nina shot her hand in the air and waved it to imitate an overeager student.

Sam's retirement countdown alarm sounded. He checked his

phone. 'Yes ma'am, another day towards retirement ticked off.' He shot Ricki a look. 'After a night like tonight, it can't come soon enough.'

TWENTY-FIVE

The detectives' teasing embarrassed Ricki, but she didn't blame them. She'd come across as an overly enthusiastic amateur . . . *which is what I am,* Ricki thought glumly on her ride home. The late hour and the evening's dramatic events caught up with her. She felt bone-weary and desperate to see Miranda's murder solved so life could get back to normal – if life in The Big Easy could ever be considered normal. Ricki was still determined to do whatever she could to move the case along. *But to be taken seriously, I need to* not *sound like a blithering idiot,* she scolded herself.

With the following day devoid of updates on the fire or Miranda's murder, Ricki decided to finally pay a visit to the woman's grudge-carrying ex-boyfriend Chess Villeneuve, at Home Supply, the big box hardware store where he worked. She arranged with Lyla to have a docent open Miss Vee's and run it until Ricki got there, then wrote up a fake shopping list she could use to initiate a conversation. The list turned real as she evaluated a few repairs her charming but shabby abode would benefit from. New bathroom fixtures, LED lightbulbs, a special cleaner to buff up the marble fireplace mantel, and more – all would go towards making the rental feel more like her home. She saw something skitter across the floor and added one more item: cockroach traps.

Ricki left the shotgun cottage for her car. As she got in, she glanced down the street and saw the back of Virgil, who was walking Thor and Princess toward the river. They made a left onto the next block and disappeared from view. Ricki got a pang of loneliness. She loved having kitten Red at her shop but eventually she'd go back to her family. At home, she missed fur babies Thor and Princess and the comfortable pet co-parenting routine she and Virgil had established before he left town for weeks on the road with his show. She understood being a judge on *America's Next Top Southern Chef* was a demanding job, but she also knew his radio silence stemmed from more than judging duties. Yet here he was, back home and out of nowhere declaring to the world that she was his girlfriend. 'I swear, solving murders is easier than trying to figure out what's going on with that man,' she muttered, firing up the car's engine.

On the drive to Home Supply, Ricki went over possible ways to introduce Miranda into the conversation she planned on initiating with Chess. 'Excuse me, can you tell me where the toilet paper holders are? Chess, wow, what an unusual name. I had a friend who dated someone named Chess. Did you know a Miranda Fine?' She settled on this as the best segue into the topic.

She found a parking space not far from the store's entrance, taking a picture of the spot so she didn't lose her car to the massive lot. She sucked in a few breaths to steady her nerves, adding a couple of affirmations for good measure. Then she walked up to the store entrance, where the large automatic sliding doors parted for her.

Ricki generally avoided big box stores, finding them generic in quality and overwhelming in size. The minute she stepped into Home Supply, she felt overwhelmed. Shelves stood two stories high and the aisles looked like they stretched into infinity. She began the journey of tracking down Chess at the left end of the store. She trudged down one aisle after the other, grateful she'd chosen footwear for comfort, not style. Her white sneakers were getting a workout.

She'd reached an aisle dedicated to what seemed like a thousand variety of nails when she recognized Chess. He wore a handyman's apron over his store-issued red polo shirt and was in the middle of helping a customer. Ricki hung back until they'd finished.

'Here you go,' Chess said to the customer after using one of his long arms to effortlessly reach a box of nails teetering on the edge of a high shelf. 'One-inch, fifteen gauge with a three-sixteenth head diameter.'

The customer thanked him and left with their find. Ricki was about to move in when a heavyset man she'd noticed hovering nearby beat her to it. Ricki suppressed a gasp. The man was Robert 'Bobby' Grimes, private investigator to the stars. Or at least one star: Blaine Taggart.

Ricki stepped back, ducking behind a tall roll marked 'Attic

Insulation.' Determined to eavesdrop, she slowly moved the insulation roll closer to the men while maintaining cover behind it, earning odd looks from passing customers. She'd drawn close enough to overhear the conversation when music blared over the store's PA system, followed by an announcement of a sale on shop vacuums in aisle seven, drowning out the men. Ricki silently cursed.

She peered around the insulation roll and saw Bobby throw his arms around Chess in a bear hug, a gesture that telegraphed familiarity between the two. He released Chess, who appeared despondent. Bobby said something that must have been encouraging because Chess managed a smile. Bobby then moved his fists back and forth like he was cheerleading, earning a small laugh from Chess. The private eye gave him another, quicker hug and left Chess to deal with a customer.

Ricki made a snap decision to postpone her conversation with Chess and trail Bobby instead. Wherever he led her might reveal the mysterious connection between Miranda's ex-boyfriend and Blaine's current PI.

She dashed off, moving so fast that she sent the insulation roll tumbling down the aisle into a couple of nonplussed customers. Once outside, she put a hand to her forehead to block the sun and scoured the parking lot for Bobby. She located him in a spot not far from her own car and drew in a breath. Bobby got into a black sedan with heavily tinted windows and a dent in the left front fender – the car that had followed Ricki to the Freret Jet.

Ricki raced to her own car and jumped in. Luckily, traffic out of the parking lot was backed up thanks to a red light, so Ricki made it out of the lot only a few cars behind the PI. She kept him in her eye line down Carrollton Avenue. He obeyed the school speed zone signs, to her relief. She assumed that like most locals, he knew to take the zones seriously. Ricki had earned a couple of pricey tickets herself for going a mere mile over the school zone speed limit.

Bobby made a left onto St Charles, a right onto Broadway, and a left onto Magazine Street, bumping along a section of road that was in constant need of repair, like a majority of New Orleans' streets. Ricki was sure he was simply headed to Duncan-Sejour when he reached a yellow light at the intersection of

Jefferson and Magazine. He shot through the light as it turned red, leaving Ricki two cars behind. She willed the light to change as he made a sharp right on to Leontine Street. By the time the light changed and she made it to Leontine, Bobby was gone. She drove around the neighborhood aimlessly, then gave up. Discouraged, she drove towards Bon Vee.

As she crossed Louisiana Avenue, the car behind her honked. Annoyed, she ignored it. The car honked again. 'What is your problem . . .' Ricki glanced at her rearview mirror and trailed off. Bobby Grimes waved to her from his black sedan.

'Oh, sh . . .' Ricki gulped. Heart racing, she clutched the steering wheel. She maintained a rigid pose as she continued the drive to Bon Vee. But instead of parking there, she stopped in front of St Aquilinus. Familiar with the church's schedule, she knew an AA meeting would be letting out momentarily, giving her the safety of numbers.

Bobby parked behind her. She watched from her rearview mirror as he got out of his car and sauntered her way. Ricki double-checked to make sure all four doors on her Prius were locked. Bobby tapped on the driver's side window. Ricki lowered it two inches. 'Yes?' she asked politely, doing her best to feign innocence.

'You need a few lessons in surveillance, chere,' Bobby said, leaning an elbow against the door frame. He chuckled. 'Rule number one. Dress in black or nondescript colors. Half your skirt was sticking out from the side of the insulation roll you were "hiding" behind.'

Embarrassed, Ricki glanced down at the explosion of bright orange and pink flowers on the yellow background of her 1950s skirt. 'Noted. In my defense, I wasn't planning on spying on you. It fell into my lap. The lap of my extremely colorful skirt.'

'Now that you happened on me and my nephew, Chess—'

'Nephew?'

'Yup. I never knew Miranda, I only knew of her. When she was looking for someone to spy on Bon Vee, a lotta PIs wouldn't take the job. The Charbonnet name means something in this city, plus you want to do your best not to cross Eugenia. She's a—' He policed himself. 'A you-know-what buster. I try to keep it clean for the ladies.'

Deciding it was best not to call him out on the sexist comment, Ricki simply nodded.

'Miranda was grateful to hire me. Gave me the opportunity to work both sides of the fence. Literally.' He pointed first to Bon Vee and then to Duncan-Sejour. 'Spy on you folks and also on Miranda to come up with leverage I could use to make her pay back Chess what she took from him. It'd help him get some satisfaction and move on with his life.'

'Did you ever find anything on her?'

'She made the woo-woo lady cut her in secret sales of Taggart's sweaty towels,' Bobby said, telling Ricki what she already knew. 'I was on the trail of another possible side hustle when she got called – or sent – to her maker.'

'What?'

Bobby put a finger to his lips and went, 'Shh.' He dropped his finger. 'You never know when it's gonna pay off to follow a lead. In the meantime, my lips is zipped. Blaine's kept me on for security and surveillance—'

'Like tailing me,' Ricki fumed. 'Blaine flat-out lied when he said it wasn't one of his cars tailing me the other night.'

'More like a half-lie,' Bobby said, unfazed by her ire. 'It was my car, not his. But I am paid to keep an eye out for you. And who doesn't like those nice, fat movie star entourage paychecks?' He leaned in, his proximity making Ricki nervous. 'Blaine's got no idea about Chess being my nephew and I mean to keep it that way. I don't wanna say I know people, but . . . I know people.' He straightened up and plastered on a big smile. 'Y'all have a nice day.'

Bobby strolled back to his car. He put it in reverse and drove backwards across the street to Duncan-Sejour, earning honks from displeased drivers.

Ricki didn't move. She struggled to rein in her emotions, which ricocheted back and forth between fear and defiance. It was no fun being threatened by at last count, three of Blaine's entourage. On the other hand, she was tired of letting them intimidate her. She'd vowed not to withhold anything she learned from Nina, which meant refusing to give in to fear.

She put her car in reverse. The door to the church community room opened and the AA meeting let out, so she braked before pulling out to make sure none of the members chatting with each other were crossing the street behind her car. She checked her rearview mirror. What she saw made her heart race.

A man had his back to her as he conversed with other meeting members and she instantly recognized the distinctive infinity logo on the back of his leather jacket. It belonged to the man she'd seen lying semi-conscious in Blaine's side yard the night of Miranda's murder.

The man turned around.

It was Nat Luna.

TWENTY-SIX

Nat. Blaine's half-brother. The one member of Blaine's entourage with an alibi. Or a supposed alibi.

Nat crossed behind Ricki's car and she slid down in case he glanced in her direction. She blessed the fact she'd gone with a boring but environmentally correct, heat-reflecting white Prius and followed her dad's practical advice to skip bumper stickers. 'They're h-e-double-hockey-sticks to get off the bumper when you wanna sell the car,' Luis insisted. Ricki had never been gladder she listened to him. The two choices meant there was nothing to identify the car as Ricki's.

She craned her neck to see if she could catch Nat's reflection in her side view mirror. He appeared to have gone through the Duncan-Sejour front gates. She raised her head enough to look back at the house and watched him go inside. After counting to ten to ensure he was truly gone, Ricki sat up. She pulled out into the street, made a U-turn, and drove past Duncan-Sejour to Bon Vee.

Anxious to share this crucial development with Nina, she placed a call to Nina from the privacy of her car rather than inside the house, where anyone wandering by Miss Vee's might overhear her. 'I have news,' she blurted before Nina could get out a hello. 'Less important stuff first. Blaine's PI, Robert 'Bobby' Grimes is the uncle of Miranda's jilted boyfriend Chess and took the job so he could spy on Bon Vee and Miranda to see about getting retribution for his nephew.'

'That's less important?' Nina sounded perplexed. 'It actually sounds like a pretty good lead.'

'You'll see why in a minute. Also, I hope it's a lead that goes nowhere because he said he knows people, the kind you don't want to know, and I believe it.'

'OK, filing that under potential witness intimidation. Go on.'

'Here's the critical update. Remember how I saw a man lying on the Duncan-Sejour side yard the night of Miranda's murder? I know who it was. Nat Luna.'

Ricki waited as Nina took this in. 'Nat Luna,' the detective repeated after a beat. 'As in "I have an ironclad alibi" Nat Luna.'

'Yes. I recognized his jacket. And the logo on the back.' Something dawned on Ricki. 'The logo. It looked familiar and I'm pretty sure I know why. Hold on.' Ricki opened the search engine on her phone and typed in the address for a movie database website. When the site opened, she typed in Blaine's name and scrolled down his list of credits. 'There. *The End Times*.'

'Are you saying they're here? Because at this point, I believe it.'

'No. It was the title of a science fiction movie Blaine made. He was unhappy because the studio wound up releasing it straight to streaming during the pandemic, so the movie came and went. But the logo was an orange ombre infinity symbol. The one on Nat's jacket. Here.' She held up the phone as if Nina could see it, then caught herself. 'What am I doing? Sorry. It's been a morning.' She pressed the arrow to forward the movie's website page to Nina.

'Got it. Huh. I imagine there's not a lot of swag for movies that come and go.'

'No. Especially not expensive leather jackets.'

'Looks like we'll be extending an invitation for a second interview to a certain Nat Luna. I'll also have someone here make discreet inquiries into Bobby Grimes, but we'll keep you out of it. Oh, and Ricki . . . not bad.'

'Thanks.' Ricki glowed. At this point, she knew Nina well enough to know that reluctant, tepid praise from the detective was as good as it got.

'Happy great sales morning!' the life-size daisy trilled to Ricki.

Benny and Jenny greeted dressed in complementary as opposed to identical customers: Jenny was the human inside the daisy costume while Benny was kitted out as a bumblebee. 'We've been all a-buzzzzz here,' Benny said with added sound effects. 'A Garden District tour bus blew out a tire out front right about opening time, so we invited the occupants in. They were here for about an hour waiting for the tire to be fixed and boy, did we do a honey of a business.'

He flitted around the store showing Ricki many empty spots on the shelves. 'You guys are the best,' she said, thrilled. 'How can I thank you?'

'You can start by saying "y'all" instead of "you guys,"' Jenny said reproachfully. 'Do I look like a guy to you?' She did a pirouette in the middle of the store, her petals floating in a circle with her.

'You do not,' Ricki said, properly chastened. 'You look like the prettiest flower in the bouquet. And let me rephrase my compliment. *Y'all* are the best. This really takes the "sting" out of a tough morning.'

'A sting pun! Madame, I bow to you.'

Benny did so, taking a deep bow that pointed his costume stinger straight at the ceiling.

After the twins left, Ricki did a quick inventory check. Red strutted alongside her from bookshelf to bookshelf. The tourists with time to kill had done a run on everything from community cookbooks to the kitschy vintage salt and pepper shakers Ricki was always on the hunt for. They'd also bought half of her Christmas and Hannukah-themed cookbooks. She balanced tending to the rest of day's customers with internet searches for new stock until closing time.

She joined her friends for an early and quick dinner break at Zellah's café before prepping for the evening's first haunted house tour. Ricki told everyone about Nat, eliciting a cry of '*Nooooo!*' from Cookie.

'I like him,' she said, bummed. 'We were developing a thing. I was expecting him to ask me out any day now. It can't be him.'

'You also said it can't be Britni because she'd including you in the Westwego friend group,' Ricki reminded her.

'I'll trade Nat for Britni. Murder solved. You're welcome.'

Theo took a thoughtful if huge bite of his roast beef po'boy. He mused while chewing. 'If you want a man's perspective—'

'Sure,' Zellah said. 'Let us know when one shows up.'

Theo rolled his eyes. Their relationship, which had been contentious in the past, had settled into occasional teasing. 'That joke is so old it's on Medicare. As I was saying before I was so rudely interrupted, here's the deal. The police think Miranda's murder wasn't premeditated. It might even have been an accident. To me, Nat seems like the kind of guy who'd own what he did and turn himself in. And if the fortuneteller tent fire was deliberate, he sure doesn't seem like a guy who would resort to killing someone to cover his tracks.'

'Those are *really* good points, Theo,' Ricki acknowledged.

'So good,' Cookie said, 'that I'd like you to be the man-of-honor at my wedding to Nat.'

'Two out of three compliments.' He put down his po'boy and folded his arms in front of his chest. 'Zellah?'

He stared her down. She stared back and then caved. 'Fine. It's three outta three.'

'Yaaaas!' Theo fist-pumped, then yelped and grabbed his arm. 'Ow. I increased my weights too much and pulled my bicep muscle.'

'There is someone else who's easier to picture as a suspect.' Ricki filled her friends in on her run-in with Bobby Grimes. 'When he was being fake-nice to me, it felt like in a TV crime show when a mob boss is being fake-nice. He could have cornered Miranda and gotten tough with her about the money she owed Chess.'

Zellah rubbed her temples. 'I'm losing track of all these murderous white people. Can we make a list? It'd help me keep track.'

'Sure. It would help me too.' Ricki began typing. 'Duncan-Sejour suspects first. Blaine, because he hired someone who lied to him and was doing deals behind his back. Nat and Mooni, his only family who would do anything to protect him. Jason, who directly benefited from Miranda's death. I'm adding Lakshmi because she initiated the sweaty towel scam Miranda glommed onto. Then there's skeevy PI Bobby Grimes, who wanted revenge on the part of his nephew. His nephew Chess, the wronged boyfriend. And Britni, Miranda's frenemy who's been obsessed with Chess for years.' Ricki paused, and then added another name. 'Gordy Fine. Miranda's brother. I haven't discovered any way he might have gained from her death, but that doesn't mean there isn't one we don't know about.'

'If you're distantly related to Miranda . . .' Zellah trailed off.

Ricki finished the sentence for her. 'It means I'm related to Gordy. And if he killed her, to a murderer.'

The friends finished their meal in silence. They were about to leave the café when Ricki's phone sounded a text alert. Ricki read it. 'Huh? No. It can't be.' In a state of disbelief, she re-read it.

'What?' Impatient, Cookie tried to make out the text over Ricki's shoulder but the evening's darkening sky made it impossible.

'It's from Nina.' Ricki read the text to the others. 'Nat Luna released as a suspect. Mooni Benson has confessed to being responsible for the death of Miranda Fine.'

TWENTY-SEVEN

The Bon Vee crew contemplated this somber development. 'I know she did bad things in her past and scared you, Ricki,' Zellah said. 'But to me, she seemed like good people. You just don't know, do you?'

The others murmured agreement. Cookie gazed across the yard at Duncan-Sejour. No one had turned on a light there and the massive home stood shadowed in gloomy darkness. 'I feel bad for Blaine,' she said. 'Nat told me Mooni was more of a mother to him than his own mother. Same for Nat, even though by the time she got out of jail, he was on his own. She's been the only stable force in their lives. Nat and Blaine always came first, no matter what. Her whole life was about supporting and protecting them.'

'Hmmm.'

Zellah eyed Ricki. 'Uh oh. I know that "hmmm." It comes with a look in your eyes that says "Or maybe . . .'''

'I do have an "or maybe,'" Ricki confessed. 'Cookie said "protect." Is there a chance Mooni admitted to Miranda's death to protect someone else from being accused of the crime? Like Blaine or Nat?'

Cookie scowled. 'You leave my Nat alone.'

Ricki started to respond but Theo interrupted. 'We better put a pin in this debate. We've got our own haunted house up in thirty.'

The four dispersed. Ricki returned to Miss Vee's, where she changed into her witch's costume. She double-checked the cauldron, which emitted the requisite bubbling sounds and simulated smoke, much to Red's ongoing delight. Ricki was about to turn on the projections that transformed the room into a forest when someone rapped on the shop's French doors. To Ricki's surprise, Blaine stood on the other side of the door.

'Blaine?' She opened the door and let him in.

The actor looked terrible, although his terrible was still an average person's handsome. His face was gaunt, his eyes puffy. He smelled like cigarette smoke. Instead of product, Ricki suspected the shine to his hair came from lack of a recent wash. 'Sorry for barging in on you.' He paced as he talked. 'I know you've got a tour soon. But I needed to talk to someone. Real bad. Someone I can trust. That's you, Ricks.'

'I'm sure there's someone closer to you,' Ricki said. As the witness who exposed Nat's lie and turned him into NOPD's prime suspect, which had snowballed into the current calamity, she couldn't have felt less trustworthy.

Blaine shook his head almost violently. 'No. No. It has to be you.'

Ricki summoned the strength to confess what she'd done. 'Blaine . . . I saw Nat on your side yard the night of Miranda's murder. I didn't realize it was him until today. I'm the one who reported it to the police. I'm sorry but I had to.'

Blaine froze in place. He stared at her. Then he began pacing again. 'Wow. OK. You know what, I get it. Thank you for telling me. You didn't have to. You're an honest person. That's why I can trust you. It's weird. I pay a ton of people for their trust. Agents, lawyers, publicists. And I don't trust any of them.'

Blaine's manic state alarmed Ricki. 'Maybe we should sit down.'

She motioned to the reading area by the bay window. Ricki grabbed a water bottle from the mini fridge behind the shop desk. They each took a seat in one of the club chairs. Ricki handed Blaine the water bottle. He used more force than necessary to open it and downed the bottle in a couple of gulps. He wiped his mouth with the back of his hand. 'My lawyers are arranging bail for Mooni. I wanted to be at the station myself but NOPD asked me not to. Between fans and paparazzi, they were afraid there'd be chaos.'

'They're probably right.'

Blaine leaned forward, pain etched on his face. 'Nat's alibi was a lie. I know what really happened. He did go to Delcambre the afternoon of Miranda's death. But he fell off the wagon and got drunk with the shrimp boaters there. He's my sober companion and was desperate not to have me find out. Mooni drove to Delcambre and got him home that night. The security cameras showed him leaving the house but never showed him returning, thanks to Mooni, who was trying to protect him. She paid the boaters to say he'd spent the night there and snuck him in under the range of the security cameras so I wouldn't see him drunk. They were both afraid I'd feel betrayed and it would send me on a bender if I saw my brother – who is also my bestie, my right-hand man, my role model – fail.'

Ricki bit her lip to control herself. The man she'd seen sprawled on the ground of Duncan-Sejour's side yard was a man battling his demons and trying not to drag his beloved kid brother down with him. 'Oh, Blaine. I'm so sorry.'

'Mooni confessed so Nat wouldn't have to. They're trying to protect me.'

'From falling off the wagon.'

'No.' Blaine squeezed his eyes shut. 'They think I did it. Killed Miranda.'

Ricki opened her mouth and shut it, unable to find the right words in response. Yes, Blaine was on her suspect list. But if she was honest with herself, it was pro forma. She never truly believed him capable of violence. 'Did you?' she finally asked, her finger discreetly hovering over the emergency alert on her phone in case he answered in the affirmative.

Blaine stared at her, appalled. 'You too?'

'It's a legitimate question.'

Blaine didn't argue with her, but he also didn't look happy. 'No. Of course not. Miranda was just a person who worked for me. Not my first assistant, not my last. I kept trying to tell Nat and Aunt Mooni I didn't have any reason to kill her, but they wouldn't believe me.'

'Why not?'

Blaine stood up. He began pacing again. 'They thought I had a thing with Miranda.'

Is this what it's like when Nina interviews a suspect? Ricki wondered, pulse racing. *Because if it is, I have even more respect for her. It's hard and incredibly scary and I may throw up when it's over.* 'Did you have a thing with her?'

'No! Never.' Blaine gave his head another violent shake. 'She's totally not my type.'

Given the dismissive tone in his voice, it took a massive amount of willpower for Ricki not to call him out on it.

'But Miranda did her best to let them *think* we'd had a thing. I don't know what her end game was but Nat and Mooni were convinced she was going to turn this into a threat she could use to blackmail me. That's what drove Nat to relapse.'

And maybe murder, Ricki thought. Nat no longer had an alibi. The possibility existed that he'd sobered up, come across Miranda, and confronted her.

Blaine collapsed into the chair. 'I don't know what to do . . . how to feel . . . about any of this. Should I be angry at them for lying to me about Nat's slip? Be angry they believed Miranda? Forgive them? Worry about what happens when all of this becomes public?'

'A hard no on the last one. So not an important concern right now.'

'Right. That's what crisis management teams are for.'

'Oh, *please*.'

Ricki couldn't stop herself from exclaiming this with more than a little disdain, but Blaine didn't notice. He dropped his head into his hands. After a moment, he raised it and gave Ricki a beseeching look. 'I need help to work this. With Lakshmi out as my spiritual advisor . . .'

'Wait, what? Me?' Ricki responded with disbelief. 'Blaine, I can give you my opinion as a . . . friend.' She hated giving their fraught relationship any legitimacy but decided this wasn't the time to quibble about it. 'Nat and Mooni are your family. Your only family. Whatever they did for you, and hopefully it doesn't include murder, they did out of love. The three of you need to work through what happened together. And if you have to have a spiritual advisor, this city is packed with all kinds of them. Tarot card readers, voodoo priestesses. I have some cards practitioners have dropped off at the shop.' She went to her desk, pulled out a small stack of business cards, and handed them to Blaine.

Muffled sounds of conversation came from the hallway. Ticket holders were arriving for the evening's first haunted house tour. Blaine stood up. 'I better go. Thanks for listening.'

He walked to the door, then turned around. 'And thanks for being a friend.'

TWENTY-EIGHT

Whether Mooni was guilty or not, her confession shut down NOPD's investigation into Miranda's death and the fortuneteller tent fire. Blaine picked up the tab for his aunt's bail bond, which teetered close to seven figures because the judge had taken Mooni's past criminal record into account when setting it. Ricki had watched Blaine's reunion with his aunt and half-brother through her shop's bay window. The three clutched each other in a tight hug, then disappeared into Duncan-Sejour. She hadn't seen any of them since.

The countdown to All Hallows' Eve was on. The Bon Vee staff decided on a whim to schedule the last haunted house for four p.m. on Halloween proper, two hours earlier than usual, and follow the tour with a party for the local kids. They came to this decision on October thirtieth, which gave them a day and a half to pull it all together.

Ricki and Zellah sat at a café table, coffee and croissants on hand for sustenance as they went over details for the party. Ricki picked up one of the cookbooks from a stack on the table and turned to a page she'd marked with a sticky note. 'I love these mummy hot dogs.' She showed Zellah a photo from a circa-2000 cookbook showing hot dogs wrapped in dough cut into strips to create the illusion of a mummy wrap. 'We can have chips and other salty snacks for the kids, and these as the main course.' She grinned. 'If you can call mummy dogs a main course.'

Zellah nodded approval. 'Yes to that.' She typed it into a document on her phone. 'What about dessert?'

'Cupcakes for the kids. They can decorate them to look Halloween-y.'

'I'm on it.' Zellah rubbed her hands together with relish. She loved anything that tapped into her artistic talents.

Ricki flashed a mischievous grin. 'If we want to scare everyone at the party, we could do a creepy gelatin mold. Here's a picture from one of my cookbooks. You think it would make a good screensaver?'

She showed Zellah a photo of a whole fish encased in aspic, its eyes staring out from its gelatinous tomb. Zellah recoiled. 'This should be on a giant poster with the tagline, "Go Vegan!"'

There was a sudden bout of screeching from Gumbo and Jambalaya. The peacocks hurried past, aiming angry squawks at Red as the kitten amused herself by running back and forth between them.

'Not again. Red, no!' Ricki jumped out of her chair and rescued the critter before Gumbo took a peck at her.

'That kitty's a character,' Zellah said, chuckling.

Ricki returned to table. She settled into her chair with Red in her lap. 'She can't go on torturing those two forever. I've dropped the ball on finding her family. I need Olivia to print out more flyers and expand the area where she puts them up. We never got a response to the ones we posted locally.'

'At this point, I think we can assume she's the offspring of one of the neighborhood feral cats.'

'Probably.' Ricki stroked the kitten's fur, earning a happy purr with each stroke. 'But I want to give it one last try.'

'I think we're good here, party-wise.' Zellah rose and Ricki followed suit.

'I could use more of the battery-operated votive candles,' Ricki said. 'Do you know if Mordant is planning a hardware store run?' As she asked this, something slipped through her mind before she could land on it.

'He's not,' Zellah said. 'I'm hoping he's free by tomorrow for Halloween. Don't worry, we're good,' she added, reacting to Ricki's expression of concern. 'It's his new venture. He's keeping it to himself until he's ready to share. We have to respect that.'

'We do. As long as you're OK, I am.'

Ricki gave her friend a hug, then they went their separate ways. Miss Vee's wasn't set to open for an hour, which gave the shop owner time to make a quick run to the local hardware store to pick up the ersatz votive candles herself.

On the walk to her car, Ricki's phone rang. She saw the caller was Lyla and answered. 'I'm glad I caught you,' Lyla said. 'The Bon Vee hot water heater died. Our plumber is rushing a replacement over, but we have to postpone opening for a couple of hours. I've sent out a notice to our tour ticket holders. Benny and Jenny are making a sign for the front door. Do you want them to make one for the shop?'

'Yes, thanks. I'm on my way to the hardware store.'

'While you're there, pick up some nails I can accidentally run over. Four flat tires would give me a great excuse to miss this weekend's volleyball tournament.'

Nails. The elusive thought wandering through her mind finally made itself known. She'd never returned to Home Supply to check out Chess Villeneuve, Miranda's ex. Bon Vee's delayed opening gave her the window of opportunity she needed to trade a trip to the local hardware store for one to Chess's workplace.

'Ricki, are you still there?'

'Yes. Sorry. I got distracted. On my way to the store but not buying you nails. You love your daughter, volleyball tourneys and all.'

'True dat,' Lyla said with a sigh. She signed off.

Ricki got in her car and pulled out into the street. As she drove off, she couldn't stop herself from glancing over to Duncan-Sejour. Two security guards sat on the porch, eyes on the street. She recognized one of them as PI Bobby Grimes. He seemed to sense her and cast an eye at her car. Ricki instantly looked away, eyes back on the road. No way would she give him any opportunity to intimidate her into rethinking her plan.

Bobby Grimes may not have intimidated Ricki but the mammoth size of Home Supply did, as usual. She scanned the rows of aisles, trying to decide where to begin her search for the store employee and possible murder suspect.

'Can I help you?'

Ricki turned to see what kind employee asked this and found herself face-to-face with Chess Villeneuve. 'Agh!'

'Sorry, didn't mean to scare you. But you looked lost.'

She quickly recovered and thanked the universe for the stroke of luck. 'I am. I need battery-operated votive candles. I know you sell them here but I have no idea where.'

'They're in our seasonal department. Follow me.'

The two walked past one aisle after another, which tasked

Ricki with trying to keep with Chess's long, loping strides. The seasonal department appeared to be at the opposite end of the store, which gave her the time she needed to bring up the real reason for her visit. 'You look familiar to me and I think I've finally figured out why. Weren't you at the memorial for Miranda Fine?'

Chess's pace slowed. His face darkened. 'No. I mean, I was. But only for a minute.'

'I went to college with her,' Ricki said, harkening back to her original lie. 'She was a piece of work.'

'Mmm hmm.' Chess picked up his pace, increasing it to the point where Ricki had to practically jog to keep with him.

'How did you know her?' Ricki considered this as a logical question and asked in the most innocent tone possible.

'Long story,' was Chess's terse reply. His phone pinged a text. He read it and typed a quick response. 'Here's what you're looking for.'

They'd reached the seasonal section. Chess pointed to a shelf holding a scant supply of candles, obviously a popular holiday item.

'So many choices,' Ricki murmured, trying to draw out her time with him.

He gave her a look. 'There are like, three boxes left.'

'I meant in general.' Ricki waved her arms. 'So many choices of decorations.'

Chess shifted to the persona of polite store employee. 'Do you want the candles? I can get them for you.'

'Yes, thank you. I'll take all three boxes.'

As Chess retrieved them, someone called his name. Ricki joined him in looking towards whoever it was. Ricki's eyes widened but she managed not to gasp. Waving to Chess as she hurried his way was Miranda's frenemy and longtime pining-for-Chess-er, Britni. 'Hi,' she greeted him with a flirty smile, slightly breathless from the hike through Home Supply.

Ricki opted to play into the moment. 'OMG, this is such a coincidence! First Chess, now you. I'm Ricki. From the limo ride. I'm the one who went to college with Miranda. UCLA.' She added the last for an extra dollop of authenticity.

'Right, hi.' Britni barely managed to mask her displeasure at running into Ricki. She focused on Chess, purring, 'Y'all ready to go? We don't wanna be late.'

Chess checked his watch. 'Break just started.' He addressed Ricki. 'You can take those to the cashier or do self-service checkout.'

'Got it. Thanks again. Nice running into you both.'

Neither responded as they took off for the exit.

Ricki counted to five, then reached up on her tippy toes to replace the votives. She raced-walked out the door to the parking lot, where she saw Chess helping Britni into the passenger side of his Jeep Wrangler Sport. Ricki dashed to her Prius and hopped in. She put two cars between them as she followed Chess and Britni out of the parking lot. *I'm getting pretty good at this*, Ricki thought, giving herself a mental pat on the back.

Chess pulled onto I-10 and Ricki did the same. Instead of staying on the interstate, Chess took the fork onto US-90 Business Route, which crossed over the Mississippi via the Crescent City Connection bridge. They stayed on US-90, passing the welcome sign to Westwego. Chess eventually exited US-90 to local streets. The route was familiar to Ricki. She'd taken it to Gordy Fine's place of business, Mardi Gras Motorworks . . . which to Ricki's surprise proved to be Chess and Britni's destination.

Chess drove into the used car lot and parked in one of the visitor spaces. Ricki drove past the lot. Two blocks later, she made a U-turn. She found an open parking space behind a utility van, which conveniently blocked her car from the lot's direct view. Ricki slipped out her car and scurried behind the utility van. She peeked around the front of it and saw Gordy Fine come out of the lot showroom. He shook hands with Chess and hugged Britni. Then the two followed him into the showroom. The last thing Ricki saw before the door shut behind them was Britni's self-satisfied smirk as Chess placed a possessive hand on the small of her back.

Ricki darted back to her car. NOPD might think they had captured the criminal responsible for Miranda's death and Lakshmi's serious injuries, but Ricki wasn't so sure. She sensed a damaged, sensitive soul under Nat's gruff exterior, which made it hard to perceive him as a possible killer, and chalked up Mooni's confession to a willingness to do whatever it took to protect her nephews. On the other hand, Britni, Chess, and Gordy all despised Miranda, albeit for different reasons.

Ricki whipped out her phone and texted what she'd witnessed to Nina. **The three of them are definitely up to something,** she wrote at the end of the text. **The question is . . . what?**

After pressing send, Ricki put her car in reverse and sped away, not wanting to risk being seen by the three if they came out of the showroom.

A weariness descended on her as she drove home. Whatever happened, she took comfort in knowing she'd done everything within her power to help solve Miranda's murder. She murmured her favorite affirmation: *I am having a safe, uneventful journey.*

It was time to actually have one.

TWENTY-NINE

Halloween finally arrived, although it was hard to tell since New Orleans' predilection to party made every day in October feel like Halloween. The weather couldn't have been more perfect; sunny with brilliant blue sky and a hint of crisp coolness to the air.

Ricki woke up early, excited about spending her first All Hallows' Eve back in New Orleans in twenty years. The holiday had the added benefit of superseding all the recent troubling events. She hopped out of bed and showered. Eager to get to Bon Vee and kick off the day's festivities, she nuked an egg white bite and slipped on her witch's costume.

She'd swallowed the last bite of egg when her phone rang with a call from Nina. 'I have an update from Westwego for you,' the detective said, skipping the niceties.

'Great.' Ricki sat down at her kitchen table, ready to hear how her report on Chess, Britni, and Gordy's activities had paid off.

'Britni Sanchez got a great deal on her new car.'

'Huh?'

'It appears that was the very logical reason behind her trip to Mardi Gras Motorworks.' Nina's acerbic tone made Ricki squirm. 'Westwego PD interviewed all involved. Ms Sanchez found a newer model of the Jeep Sport her friend Chess Villeneuve already owned. He agreed to accompany her to the car lot to check it out. Apparently she was nervous about driving such a sporty vehicle, but Villeneuve agreed to help her learn how to handle it. Salesman Gordon Fine is on record as saying he wasn't sure who was more excited about the purchase, Ms Stockley or Mr Villeneuve.'

The way to Chess's heart isn't through the kitchen, it's through his set of wheels, Ricki thought glumly. *Well played, Britni. Well played.*

'According to the Westwego detective I spoke to, the lot has some great deals. But as to solving the recent crimes at Duncan-Sejour . . .'

'It's a non-starter.' Ricki finished Nina's sentence for her.

'I'm afraid so.'

'I'm sorry,' Ricki said, mortified she'd led the detective down the road to another dead end.

'It's not a total loss. I'm in the market for a new car. I may take a looksee at the Mardi Gras Motorworks inventory myself. In the meantime, we have a confession from Mooni, so I'm taking today off to enjoy Halloween. I recommend you do the same. Speaking of which, thanks for invitation to the Bon Vee party. My kids are looking forward to it.'

'See you this afternoon.'

The call ended, and with it Ricki's investigation. She'd yet to produce a remotely useful clue, serving only as a gadfly buzzing around the NOPD with theories that went nowhere. *When it comes to sleuthing, it's emphasis on the 'amateur' for me*, she thought as she tugged on her black leggings. *I'm done. Finished. Finito.*

Determined to follow through on this vow to shelf sleuthing, Ricki concentrated on applying witchy makeup. She impulsively slathered on a green base, which she'd bought but yet to use. After adding black eyeliner and red lipstick, Ricki admired herself in the bathroom mirror. *I look terrible, which is perfect.*

She was about to leave when the doorbell rang. She put her eyeball to the peephole and saw a rakishly handsome pirate on her doorstep. Ricki opened the door and the pirate's first mates barked and yapped joyfully as they jumped up and down. 'Babies!' Ricki fell to her knees and hugged them.

Virgil lifted up the eye patch covering one of his eyes. 'I thought you'd get a kick out of seeing them in costume.'

'I love it.' Both dogs rolled over for tummy rubs and Ricki obliged, dedicating a hand to each tummy. 'Isn't it a little early for costumes?'

'We're on our way to the New Pawlins Howl-oween fundraiser.' Virgil had replaced his mother, who suffered from Lewy body dementia, as board head of New Pawlins Critter Krewe, an animal rescue she'd founded.

'Right. I forgot. I made a donation online, though.'

'Thank you.'

The dogs rolled over and back onto their feet, knocking their costumes askew. Ricki straightened each dog's bandana and first mate's cap, then stood up. She and Virgil stood in awkward silence. 'We're gonna be home tonight, giving out candy,' Virgil finally said, 'if you wanna stop by.'

'I can't. We're going down to the Quarter for the Krewe of Ghouls parade, then Bar None afterwards for the final Halloweenie Challenge.' She didn't know why but felt a need to explain further. 'It's my first Halloween in New Orleans since I was eight. I want to experience as much of it as I can.'

'Sure. I get it. Well . . .' Virgil paused. An awkward silence ensued. 'Have fun.'

'You too.'

Virgil left with the pups. Ricki dropped down onto the arm of the living room sofa. Her heart ached in a way it hadn't in a long time. She hated being so conflicted about her feelings for Virgil. They both had a history of failed relationships. Ricki still carried the wounds from her doomed marriage; Virgil had two broken marriages under his belt.

'It's not meant to be.' Ricki said this out loud, hoping verbalizing the feeling would confirm it. She stood up and grabbed her tote bag. As she head out the door, she caught a glimpse of herself in the mirror and winced. *Still, I really wish I wasn't wearing this hideous green makeup when he stopped by.*

Once at Miss Vee's, Ricki was glad she'd gone all in on her witchy look. Customers got a kick out of it, especially when she promised a cackle with each sale and then delivered. She was sucking on a throat lozenge when Olivia dragged herself into the shop. 'If your costume is hungover college student, you nailed it,' Ricki wryly commented.

Olivia wrinkled her nose and glowered at her. 'I'm not hung over anymore.'

Ricki raised an eyebrow at the 'anymore' but didn't say anything.

Olivia dropped her backpack on the floor and flopped down into one of the armchairs in the reading nook. Red leaped into Olivia's lap and made herself comfortable. 'I'm whipped. I still can't find a topic for my internship paper. I was up late hanging with Jason. We were supposed to brainstorm topics but there's a chapter of his frat at Loyola and they were having a party.'

'Well, throw cold water on your face to wake up. We've got twenty-five kids descending on the place in half an hour. Also, I made more flyers for Red. We can put them up tomorrow.'

'Whatevs,' Olivia grumbled.

She lifted Red off her lap and placed her on the floor. The kitten saw a bird fluttering in a tree outside and shot out the open bay window. Olivia hefted her backpack and dragged herself over to the shop desk. She shoved the backpack under the desk. A slip of paper fell out and floated to the floor. Ricki picked it up and handed it to Olivia. 'Here. Make sure you pay this. Parking tickets add up in this city.'

Olivia waved her off. 'Jason said his dad'll take care of my tickets.'

'Tickets.' Ricki repeated. 'As in plural.'

'They call Jason's dad a fixer,' Olivia said, impressed. 'He can fix anything. There was this whole hazing thing with Jason and his frat little brother and the frat brother's family threatened to sue but Jason's dad made it all go away.' She yawned. 'Jason says he can score me Adderall easy peasy. Maybe I should let him.'

'No!' Ricki said, alarmed. 'No Adderall. And why would he do that? He was the one who told you a friend died taking Adderall.'

'No, a pill they *thought* was Adderall. It's different. Jason still feels bad about it.'

'Wait,' Ricki said, confused. 'I thought Miranda was responsible.'

'It's complicated.' Olivia groaned. 'This conversation is giving me a headache. I need to eat something. I'm going to the café and see if Zellah's got a spare mummy dog. Cookie said they're delish. She's already snuck two of them. Back in a sec.'

Olivia's offhand, even complimentary, comments about Jason set off alarm bells for Ricki. She scurried to the shop door to make sure Olivia was gone, then zipped back to her desk, where she wrote 'Jason Bergen' into her search bar. Nothing came up. Which made Ricki suspicious. With a job for a movie star and a famous Hollywood lawyer as a father, Jason's name should have come up even peripherally, especially if there was the threat of a lawsuit at some point. She checked a couple of social media sites and only found a few carefully curated images. Ricki had been around Hollywood insiders enough to know that what was available of Jason online smacked of being monitored by a professional hand.

Ricki thought for a moment. Then she searched her contacts and tapped on the number for the last LA contact she could think of who might take her call. A sunny voice answered. 'Ricki? Oh my gosh, *hi*.'

'Liza, hi.' Liza worked as a publicist at one of LA's biggest publication relations agencies. She and Ricki had struck up an acquaintanceship when Chris was trying to woo Liza to be his publicist. She let Ricki know the wooing was sexual as well as professional, bonding the two women.

Liza's enthusiastic response assuaged Ricki's guilt about falling out of touch with her. 'I'm sorry I've been MIA. It's just that with Chris and Lachlan and the move . . . life's been a lot lately.'

'Don't worry about it. It's always good to hear from you. I miss you, girl. How's New Orleans and when can I visit?'

'It's wonderful and whenever you want to. But I'm calling for a reason. Have you ever heard anything about Jason Bergen?'

'Jason Bergen.' Ricki could practically feel Liza's eye roll. 'The worst kind of nepo baby. Someone with the right connections but everything else is wrong about him. Or that's the gist of what I've heard. Let me see if I can get you more deets. Call you back.'

While Ricki waited for Liza to get back to her, she readied for the party, planting hand wipes and sanitizers throughout the shop as encouragement for parents to wipe their kids' sticky mitts before letting them touch the merch. She could hear squeals of delirious joy through the shop windows. The guests were starting to show up.

Fortunately, she didn't have to wait long for a callback from Liza. 'I earned a dinner from you at one of New Orleans' fine restaurants because it turns out one of the assistants here went to college with Jason. Girls at her sorority were warned to stay away from him. He had a reputation for trying to doctor their drinks. He got in big trouble for breaking frat rules and hazing a pledge. He got him drunk, then dumped him outside a known gang house in South LA wearing only his pants. Kid got robbed

and beat up. The family was going to sue but Jason's father shut
it down with piles of money. Jason also started a campaign against
affirmative action on the campus that specifically targeted students
of color on scholarship. It came complete with racist leaflets.'

'I'd say why wasn't he expelled but let me guess. Father not
only a lawyer but an alum and big donor to the school.'

'You know this town so well.'

'And I don't miss it one bit. Thanks a ton. You earned two
dinners here. Book a visit.'

Liza signed off. Ricki used the reverse camera function on her
phone to check her makeup. She touched up her lipstick and
angry black brows, then locked up the store and headed to the
backyard.

Like their parents, New Orleans' kids knew how to party. The
Bon Vee yard was awash with superheroes, monsters, unicorns,
and princesses, with the occasional outlier, like the little boy
dressed in gray from head to toe who announced to Ricki, 'I'm
thunder.' She congratulated him on his originality, then went on
the hunt for Olivia, ducking under a ghost piñata, and maneu-
vering around an obstacle course of apple bobbing, bounce house,
and general mayhem. She found her young cousin at the table
where kids were decorating sugar cookies cut into Halloween
shapes.

'These are good,' Olivia said, holding up the half-eaten ghost
cookie she was snacking on. 'Especially if you load 'em up with
frosting.'

'We need to talk.'

Olivia gave her a questioning look but stood up. Ricki motioned
for her to move away from the kids. 'A couple of things you
mentioned about Jason worried me, so I called an old friend who
might know more about him. What she found out isn't good.'

'You spied on him?!' Olivia delivered this with a combination
of disbelief and outrage.

'Olivia, we're family. And even if we weren't, I love you and
will do anything to protect you. So hear me out.' Ricki shared
what she'd learned from Liza. 'She was able to dig all that up
in a few minutes. I'm sure there's things we don't even know
about. Bottom line, Jason has a bad track record.'

Olivia steamed. She had about four inches on Ricki's five-three height, which enabled her to look down on the shop owner. She crossed her arms in front of her chest and fixed a glare on Ricki. 'I cannot believe you snuck around behind my back and tried to ruin my relationship with Jason. I don't care about his "track record."' She mimed exaggerated air quotes and heaped sarcasm on the expression. 'I trust him way more than I trust you.' She grabbed a handful of cookies. 'I am done here.'

Olivia stormed off. Ricki sunk to the stone bench. She hadn't even mentioned her biggest fear to Olivia: that bad-news Jason's background made him a prime suspect in the crimes at Duncan-Sejour.

'Ricki?'

She looked up to see Nina standing next to her. The detective wore jeans and a snug-fitting black T-shirt emblazoned with an orange witch flying over the word 'Hallowqueen.'

'Oh. Hi. Welcome to the party.'

'Thanks. My son just split open the piñata. The boy's got a swing that could take him to the majors.' Nina eyed her. 'You OK? Or just trying to adjust to seeing me in my civvies?'

Ricki opened her mouth to reveal what she'd uncovered about Jason. *Speaking of crummy track records, mine as an amateur sleuth sucks. I've got nothing here but gossip about Jason. I cannot send Nina down another dead end.*

'I'm fine,' she said, mustering a smile. She rose to her feet. 'I could use a mummy dog. Would you like one? I hear they're delish.'

THIRTY

The entire Bon Vee staff except for Lyla, who was at yet another of Kaitlyn's games, pitched in to clean up the estate after the party. The sooner it was done, the sooner all could disperse to their own Halloween events. Eugenia planned on wearing her ghostly wedding dress as she distributed candy to kids who dared trod the path to her home a few blocks from Bon Vee. Benny and Jenny, each dressed as half of an open pecan, were doing the same in their Carrollton neighborhood. Ricki, Theo, Cookie, and Zellah were going to the Krewe of Ghouls parade on Canal Street, then moving on to their favorite French Quarter bar, Bar None, which was hosting the season's final Halloweenie Challenge.

Ricki passed on dinner with her friends. Instead, she made a pitstop at home. First, she texted a question to Liza, her LA friend. Then she changed into a surprise costume. She'd fashioned two large sheets of oak tag paper into a sandwich board. One side, she'd painted the cover of a 1967 edition of *The New Orleans Restaurant Cookbook*, which featured a tureen of gumbo set against the backdrop of a lacy cast-iron balcony. Not a natural artist like Zellah, she'd spent so much time on the cover illustration that the oak tag slung over her back just read 'Happy Halloween!'

She put the costume in her car and drove to St Charles Avenue to pick up the streetcar to the Quarter, saving the twenty minutes it would have taken to walk there from her house. She passed families where the parents were as costumed as their kids and houses that were so decked out in spooky décor and doings they could have been an amusement park attraction.

A streetcar clanged its way down St Charles. Ricki parked and managed to reach it just in time to board. She hadn't put much thought into navigating in her sandwich board, which proved tricky. She turned sideways and climbed up the stairs onto the streetcar, which was parked with Halloween revelers, all in costumes. Ricki maintained her sideways stance, trying to protect her flimsy sandwich board from being accidentally mauled by a raucous group of Zombies singing and dancing to Oingo Boingo's song, 'It's a Dead Man's Party.'

The streetcar arrived at Canal Street and emptied its full load of merrymakers. Ricki carefully made her way to her friends' assigned meeting place at the corner of Canal and Bourbon Street. Cookie, who'd gone with a Sexy Alice in Wonderland costume, saw Ricki and waved. Theo and Zellah were with her. Theo was dressed as a vampire; Zellah had transformed herself into one of the city's storied oak trees through the magic of trompe l'oeil painting, complete with Spanish moss dangling from her arm-branches.

Her friends reacted to her new costume with the appropriate enthusiasm. 'Love the book cover,' Zellah said. 'Especially the touch of the shrimp hanging over the edge of the tureen. Let me see the back.' Ricki turned around. 'Ha. Somebody ran outta steam.'

'Yup,' Ricki said with a vigorous nod. 'Somebody who isn't Zellah-talented and never will be.'

Theo impatiently craned his neck to see down Canal Street. 'Where's the parade already? This cape is hot.' He used the edge of his cravat to wipe sweat from his face, removing a swatch of makeup with it. 'It's a good thing vampires were already dead because wearing a getup like this in New Orleans humidity would've killed them.'

'Where's Olivia?' Ricki searched the crowd. 'I don't see her. She was going to meet us for the parade, then go to some parties on campus after.'

'It's barely six thirty,' Zellah said. 'She'll be here.'

Ricki frowned. After her confrontation with Olivia about Jason, she wasn't so sure. She texted her. **At Canal and Bourbon. Where are you?**

With Jason came the instant reply, along with an anger emoji.

This was Ricki's worst fear. She could envision Olivia sharing Ricki's suspicions with Jason out of anger about how farfetched they were in her eyes. But if they weren't so farfetched, her cousin could be in danger. 'Hey everyone, keep an eye out for Olivia.' Ricki yelled to be heard over the cacophony of enthusiastic parade-goers. 'She's with Jason and I don't trust him. I think he might have something to do with Miranda's death.'

A rumble from the crowd drowned Ricki out. 'There!' Cookie pointed to a few blocks down, where a marching band was rounding a corner. 'It's coming!'

The band marched down Canal Street towards Ricki and her friends, followed by a float designed to look like a giant skeleton. The crowd shouted their approval. Ricki was jostled as they tried to beat each other out for the treats and prizes being thrown by the float and those that came after it. A strap on her sandwich board came loose and she reattached it.

Less interested in the parade than in making sure her young cousin was OK, she called to her friends, 'I'm going to look for Olivia.' They responded with nods, more focused on scoring throws from the floats.

Ricki did her best to protect her sandwich board as she threaded her way through the sea of humanity. She alternated glances at the endless entertainment offered by the Krewe of Ghouls with scanning both sides of the street for Olivia. She heard someone call her name. Hoping it was Olivia, she looked around and then realized the call was coming from her landlady Kitty, whose marching dance troupe, the ABBA Dabba Do's, was dance-marching up Canal Street.

Kitty was dressed in the troupe costume that was half disco and half Wilma Flintstone. The sixty-plus hospice nurse wore a sequined one-shoulder leopard print top over tight white satin bell bottoms. Tiny disco balls hung from her ears, while her bun was held in place by a large fake bone. She also carried a plastic bone club, which she wielded like a baton as part of the troupe's dance routine.

She used the club to motion to Ricki. Not sure what else to do, Ricki joined Kitty in the parade. 'You know how you asked me what I remember about the time around your birth?' Kitty made a disco move with the club, aiming it up on an angle and then down on the diagonal.

'Yes,' Ricki tried copying the move in a lame attempt to look like she belonged to the troupe. Her bulky sandwich board made mirroring the dance moves even harder. 'Did you remember anything new?'

'I did. I remembered that when I showed up to take the shift where I looked after your birth mama, I asked the girl – and she was a girl, maybe sixteen years old – who the father was and if we should contact him and she mumbled, "He's fine." I assumed she meant it in a general sense and was evading my question. But what made me think of it is I was reading about the poor girl at Duncan-Sejour who was found deceased and how her last name was Fine. So it got me thinking, could that have been his name?'

'Kitty, this is incredible.' Ricki twirled along with her landlady. Her sandwich board knocked into the ABBA Dabba Do next to Kitty, who shot her a dirty look. 'It turns out I'm related to Miranda. As a third or fourth cousin, which seems a much more distant connection than if my birth father was named Fine.'

'Not necessarily.' The music switched from ABBA's hit 'Waterloo' to 'Dancing Queen.' Kitty swayed back and forth in rhythm to the song. Ricki did the same, her sandwich board swinging with her, earning more dirty looks from the other troupe member. 'The DNA connection between you and her could have been through a cousin of his, not a sibling. That would account for the less direct genealogical connection.'

'True. I didn't think of that. The irony of my ancestry search is I'm terrible at it. But thank you so much. This is awesome.' She reached to hug Kitty but the sandwich board came between them.

Ricki stepped out of line, to the relief of the ABBA member next to Kitty. A Day of the Dead float trundled by, followed by the Krewe of the Rolling Elvi comprised of people of all ages dressed as Elvis Presley. There were more floats, including one featuring a large snapping alligator, more bands, and more dance troupes – basically, more of everything. The last float finally rolled by and Ricki gave up on finding Olivia. She texted her friends she'd meet them at Bar None.

By the time Ricki reached the bar, she deeply regretted her costume choice. It made negotiating the packed streets of the French Quarter nearly impossible and earned more odd looks than compliments. She soldiered on through the dense clutch of barflies, relieved to see her pals had scored a table.

'You just made it,' Cookie said. 'The Challenge is going to start in a minute.'

'All I want to do is take this off, sit down, and have a drink.'

'Did you ever find Olivia?' Zellah asked.

'No. And she hasn't responded to my texts.'

Ricki began to lift the sandwich board over her head. Theo glanced over to the bar entrance. 'There she is now, making use of her fake ID with that guy Jason.'

Ricki dropped the sandwich board back onto her shoulders. She looked to the front of the bar. What she saw was worrisome. Olivia and Jason appeared to be in a heated conversation. 'I'll be right back.'

She muscled her way through ghouls, goblins, vampires, and sexy nurses-firefighters-policewomen, ad infinitum before plowing into a ringmaster.

'Ricki, there you are.'

It was Blaine, at the bar with Nat. Surprisingly, the actor wasn't surrounded by fans. Ricki chalked this up to the costume serving as a temporary disguise. 'Out of my way.'

'I thought you'd be here. We need to—'

'I said, out of my way.'

She pushed him aside. A sting of music erupted, followed by a DJ. 'It's time for the Bar None Halloweenie Challenge. Assume positions for the Freeze Dance Challenge. Welcome to . . . the Sixties!'

The dance floor filled, blocking Ricki's path. Chubby Checker singing 'The Twist' blasted from the speakers. The dancers began twisting. Ricki stood up on her tiptoes to see over people's heads. 'Olivia!' she cried out.

'Freeze!'

All but a few dancers froze, allowing Ricki the opportunity she needed to zero in on Olivia. To her horror, the girl was struggling to free herself from Jason, who had a tight hold on her arm.

'Unfreeze!'

'Surfing USA' blared. Ricki elbowed dancers out of the way who were exiting the area because they'd lost the challenge.

'I love this song,' Blaine declared. He jumped onto the dance floor, earning exclamations of delight as people recognized him.

Ricki reached Olivia and Jason. 'Let go of me, Jason,' Olivia pleaded.

'To turn me in?' Jason snarled. 'Forget.'

'Please.'

The terror in her voice propelled Ricki. 'Let her go!' She grabbed Olivia by the waist and struggled to pull her back.

'Freeze!'

The music stopped and the dancers froze. Ricki and Jason continued their tug o' war over Olivia. 'The way this works is y'all are supposed to stop when the music does,' a dancer explained, trying to be helpful.

Jason, propelled by the power of fear and anger, was gaining ground. The music ramped up again. Ricki felt her hold on Olivia slipping. She cried out for help but she was drowned out by the Beatles' cover of 'Roll Over, Beethoven.' Gyrating dancers jostled her, dislodging the sandwich board, which blocked Ricki's face. She ripped it off and threw the boards aside. A board hit Jason on the forearm.

'Ow, you gave me a paper cut!' Distracted, he released one hand to tend to the tiny wound. Ricki used both hands to yank Olivia away from him. In an instant, Nat tackled Jason and the two were on the ground.

'That's my stuntman,' Blaine said proudly.

Olivia collapsed sobbing into Ricki's arms. Cookie, Zellah, and Theo ran to them and the Bon Vee friends embraced in a group hug. Meanwhile, Nat grabbed the whip from Blaine's costume and wrapped it around Jason to secure him until the police arrived.

The bar patrons surrounded Jason and all chorused as one, 'Halloweenie!'

THIRTY-ONE

T he Bayou Backyard had closed at midnight but at twelve thirty, Ky reopened it solely for the Bon Vee friends to convene. He served drinks and snacks on the house while everyone waited for Ricki.

She dragged herself in shortly after one a.m. After Jason's takedown, Ricki spent hours at the NOPD Eighth District Police Department on Royal Street but had promised her friends an update on the evening's dramatic events. She was too wired to sleep anyway.

'For you.' Ky delivered a full pour of Chardonnay to her as she collapsed onto one of the benches fronting the bar's indoor picnic tables.

'You're my favorite person.' A grateful Ricki took a slug of wine.

'How's Olivia?' Zellah asked, brow creased with concern. 'She must be traumatized.'

'Her parents were already waiting for her at the police station, along with Eugenia. I think she was more in shock than anything. They took her home.'

'Pure luck Nina was at the parade with her kids and ex,' Theo commented. 'Sidebar, she made a great Catwoman. Very hot costume.'

Cookie swatted him. 'Not. *Now.*'

'Aside from her costume enabling Theo's crush, we did luck out having her show up,' Ricki said. 'Because she was lead detective on the Duncan-Sejour cases, she got to interview Jason.'

'I doubt she got much out of him,' Zellah said. 'If there was ever anyone who lawyered up fast, it'd be an entitled white kid like him.'

Ricki refreshed herself with another swallow of wine. 'Oh, he lawyered up. But not fast enough. By the time his defense attorney arrived, Jason had already tried to defend himself by claiming Miranda's death was an accident, along with details of how he insists it happened.'

Ricki's friends leaned forward simultaneously as if choreo-graphed. 'Spill,' Cookie demanded.

'I'm starving. I need sustenance first.' She inhaled a mini crawfish pie while the others waited impatiently, washing it down with another swig of wine. 'Much better. OK, so Olivia once mentioned to me that Jason told her a lot of overworked assistants used Adderall. Yesterday, she told me Jason said he could score her some if she needed it and it got me thinking. I texted a friend in Los Angeles who works in publicity. She'd already tapped into the assistant network and uncovered a few episodes from Jason's background his father had tried to cover up. This time I asked if she could connect not just Jason but Miranda to the distribution of the medication.'

'And she did,' Zellah said, transfixed.

Ricki nodded. 'Other assistants were involved, but Jason swears Miranda was the ringleader. Remember, she was older and had more life experience than him. He says he wanted out, which is why he was so happy when Blaine bought a place here. It put distance between him and LA.'

'But then how did Miranda wind up dead here?' Cookie wondered. 'And on Bon Vee property?'

'I can finally answer that question,' Ricki said. 'Jason saw Mooni turn off the security camera when she was trying to protect Nat, and he used this for cover. He and Miranda heard about the assistant who'd died from ingesting a drug marked as Adderall that turned out to be fake and fatal, and they panicked. They needed a private place to figure out a game plan in case their names came up in the investigation into the assistant's death and chose our crypt. It wasn't hard to avoid the Bon Vee security cameras, which haven't been reliable since the hurricane in September. Anyway, Miranda told Jason if the drugs were traced back to them, she was going to point the finger at him because he had a rich father who could get him off. They got into a fight, he shoved her, in self-defense, according to him, and she slipped on the bat tray and took a fatal blow to her head on the marble bench.'

'Ah, the old "self-defense" defense,' Theo said knowingly.

Zellah snorted. 'Says the man whose legal expertise comes from watching TV crime shows with a dinner tray on his lap.'

'It may work for him,' Ricki said. 'The detectives weren't happy when Jason's lawyer did show up. Apparently Barry Becker is the best money can buy in this city.'

'But what about Lakshmi?' Cookie asked. 'Does NOPD know if Jason tried to kill her or was that an accident?'

'No idea. Maybe Nina can tell us.'

Ricki gestured to the bar's open-air entrance. Nina walked to them carrying a small bag.

Theo jumped out of his spot on the bench and offered it to the detective. 'Thanks,' she said, taking a seat. 'I'm still not interested in dating you.'

'Yet,' Theo said with an impressive dose of un-earned confidence. 'Bourbon neat, right? Be right back.' He strode off to get her a drink, ignoring the chuckles from his friends.

'I had to stop by Bar None and check in with our team there,' Nina said. 'They gave me this for you.'

She handed Ricki the bag. Ricki reached in and took out a T-shirt decorated with logo of a hot dog wearing a pumpkin costume and giving two thumbs-up. The tagline beneath him read 'I'm a Hallo-winner.' 'It's the shirt they were going to give the winner of their challenge,' Nina said.

Ricki held up the T-shirt. 'I love it but I didn't even do the challenge. I was trying to help Olivia.'

'The manager said you'd earned the T-shirt, no matter how many Halloweenie bars you went to. I don't disagree.'

Ricki took in the compliment from Nina. Rather than push her luck with the prickly detective by sharing how much it meant to her, she opted for a simple 'Thank you,' then returned the shirt to the bag and changed the subject. 'We were wondering if you found out anything new about what happened with Lakshmi.'

Nina shook her head. 'By the time we got to her, Jason's lawyer showed up and shut him down. So the fortuneteller tent fire is still under investigation.'

Theo returned with Nina's drink. He grabbed a chair from another table and positioned it close to her. 'If you need another, say the word. I know it's been a rough night for you.' He reached out as if to place a reassuring hand on her arm.

'I'm trained in Krav Maga,' Nina said, sipping her bourbon. Theo instantly pulled his hand back.

'I can't stop thinking about Olivia,' Ricki said. 'How scared she looked when Jason wouldn't let go of her. She never should have been dragged into this.'

'She owes her life to you, Ricki,' Cookie said. The others voiced fervent agreement.

Embarrassed, Ricki waved them off. 'I knew entitled kids like Jason in Los Angeles. I think he's a coward at heart. I can't see him going through with anything violent. He would have chickened out, released her, and tried to make a run for it. But I hate that he fed Olivia lies to deflect attention from himself. And me too, like saying Blaine was shopping for homes in countries without US extradition treaties. I have a little trouble picturing Blaine in Angola or Azerbaijan.'

'No kidding,' Zellah said with a laugh.

Ricki passed her wine glass from one hand to the other, avoiding eye contact with her friends. 'I feel like what happened with Olivia and Jason was my fault. Olivia told him I'd warned her against them spending time together. When she saw how this spooked Jason, she realized I was right. He knew she was onto him and that's what set him off.'

Cookie reached across the table and put her hands on Ricki's shoulders. 'Look at me.' Ricki reluctantly did so. 'I said it before and I'll say it again. You. Saved . . .' Zellah, Theo, and Ky joined in and all four finished the sentence, 'Her. Life.'

Ricki managed a smile. 'Y'all are amazing friends.'

Nina did a double-take. 'Excuse me, but did she just say "y'all?"'

'She sure did.' Zellah winked at Ricki. 'Which means y'all are one of us now.'

THIRTY-TWO

Over the next few days, Halloween decorations disappeared in New Orleans, replaced by Christmas with an occasional nod to Thanksgiving. Kaitlyn's volleyball team qualified for the state playoffs, causing Lyla to alternate between pride for her daughter and whimpers about the amount of volleyball-watching involved.

And the mystery of the fortuneteller tent fire was finally solved, thanks to a stray kitten.

Prior to Bon Vee opening for the day, Ricki filled in everyone over coffee in the staff lounge. 'You know how Jason said he forgot to reactivate Duncan-Sejour's security cameras the night of the fire? He left them off on purpose so he wouldn't get caught doing what he did.'

'Which was?' Eugenia prompted. Now that all her employees were in the clear, the doyenne was all in on murder updates regarding the doings next door.

Ricki poured a cup of coffee, then began. 'Lakshmi told NOPD she had trouble sleeping the night of Miranda's death. The third floor rooms at Duncan-Sejour get stuffy, so she opened a window and happened to see Jason hurrying up the front walkway from the street in the middle of the night. She thought this was strange but didn't plan on saying anything because she was afraid if he knew she was sneaking liquor into the house, he'd bust her.'

Cookie's hand shot in the air. 'Pee break!' She dashed out of the room. The others took the opportunity to refill their coffee cups and help themselves to breakfast pastries. She dashed back into the room. 'OK, continue.'

'Anyone else need a pee break?' Ricki asked.

Eugenia pulled a face. 'That's rather gauche. Perhaps in the future we can go with something like "I'll be right back." We don't need specifics, do we?'

'No, ma'am,' Ricki and Cookie said together while their friends snickered.

'Now, continue please, Ricki.'

Ricki took a breath, then picked up where she'd left off. 'Jason discovered her flask when he was helping to set up the fortune-teller tent for the Duncan-Sejour haunted house. He told her she'd be fired and she shot back that she'd seen him sneak back to the house after Miranda died. So the night of the tent fire, when no one was looking, Jason moved the generator, which was sparking, closer to the tent. Then he kicked it over, which ignited the fire. He also moved the corn rows to make it more difficult for the firefighters to reach the tent.'

'How does Red factor into this?' Theo asked.

'She's our accidental hero. Jason thought he'd managed things so he was in the clear. But Red scampered up the vine on the side of Bon Vee to get away from Gumbo and Jambalaya after she teased them one too many times. She bumped into the security camera on the side facing Duncan-Sejour and knocked it askew. The camera recorded every move Jason made.'

'My takeaway here is one of our security cameras actually worked,' Zellah said.

'Thank goodness it did,' Eugenia said. 'Barry Becker might have been able to pull off a self-defense plea in the case of that poor Fine girl but good luck to him getting the charges in this case knocked down from attempted murder.'

'Aunt Eugenia, you sound like a tough character from one of my TV police procedurals,' Theo joked.

'Don't be silly. But,' she added with a flinty expression, 'I would not recommend running into me in a dark alley.'

Benny and Jenny appeared in the lounge doorway, or rather half of each of them did. 'Can we come in?'

'Of course.' Eugenia gestured for the twins to join the others and they came into the room.

While still dressed matchy-matchy, they wore professional attire of beige chinos, crisp white button-down shirts, and navy blazers. 'Eugenia, we're here to give notice,' Benny said.

'And invite all of you to our going-away party Friday night,' Jenny added.

'I'm sorry you're leaving us,' Eugenia said.

'You're like the least weird tour guides we've ever had,' Cookie

said. Zellah cleared her throat as a subtle warning, to which
Cookie responded, 'What? It's true.'

'Where are you going?' Ricki asked.

'LaLaLand!' Benny announced in a sing-songy voice while
throwing his arms open in a theatrical gesture.

'Blaine told his agent about us,' Jenny explained. 'She said
there's been shows about twins before but never with differently
gendered senior adults. She thinks we "have something," so we're
going out to Hollywood to "take meetings." If a project moves
forward, Blaine will be a producer.' She beamed.

'We wish you all the best,' Eugenia, ever gracious, said.

'And if you do a series set at a culinary house museum set in
New Orleans, I want a say in who plays me,' Cookie declared.

With Halloween over and holiday shopping yet to kick in, foot
traffic was light, so Ricki spent the next morning packing away
leftover Halloween merchandise. 'That's the handy thing about
vintage holiday merch,' she said to Red, who was curled up on
one of the gift shop armchairs. 'It's timeless. What doesn't sell
this year I can put out next year.'

Her cell phone rang. She lifted the phone from its perch atop
a stack of books and answered the video call. The face of a
woman in her mid-seventies popped up, weathered but cheery.

'Ricki, hi. It's Diana Todd from down the street.'

'Hi Diana.' Ricki recognized the caller as the senior who was
always gardening in the front yard of her pink stucco house with
an elaborate three-story cast iron gallery that made it a darling
of social media posts.

'I'm calling because my daughter Erin saw your flyer about
the kitty. I've been at Erin's place on the Northshore recovering
from a knee replacement.'

Considering the amount of time Diana spent on her knees
puttering with her plants, the replacement came as no surprise,
but Ricki responded politely, 'I'm sorry about the surgery. I hope
you're healing well.'

'Yes, thank you. The reason I'm calling is that prior to the
surgery, Erin and I were trying to trap a feral cat and her kittens
who were living in my crawl space. We were able to rehome all
of them except one who slipped from our clutches.'

'Red.'

'Yes. The kitty whose pet parents you've been looking for. Thank you for taking care of her. Erin and I would be happy to find the kitty a home.'

Ricki cast a fond glance at the kitty, purring contentedly on the chair. 'No need, Diana. I really appreciate you solving the mystery of where she came from. But she's found her home.'

'I was hoping you'd say that,' Diana said, her faded gray eyes twinkling. 'She's a ginger, just like darling Miss Vee was. She was meant to be at Bon Vee.'

Ricki ended the call with a promise to keep Diana updated on the kitten. Red meowed. She stretched, then padded over to the window and batted it, emitting a disgruntled meow when it didn't open. Ricki was keeping the window closed to ward off more kitty-peacock confrontations. Of course, that wouldn't prevent the agile kitten from streaking out of the shop the minute anyone opened the door. Now that Ricki had committed to adopting Red, she'd have to do something about that. 'And we need a better name for you,' she said to the kitty, pulling her off the window frame where she'd attached herself.

Olivia trudged into the shop and deposited her backpack under the shop desk with a sigh. 'How are you doing?' Ricki asked, feeling for her.

Olivia shrugged. Her light-brown eyes, usually bright and cheery, were shadowed. 'My parents are calling what happened a learning experience. When they're not saying, 'What were you thinking?' in a voice that makes me feel like the world's biggest dummy. Oh, they took away my fake ID.'

'About time for that.'

'At least I have a theme for my internship paper: "From Intern to Assistant to Killer: Lessons Learned the Hard Way."'

Olivia's lower lip quivered. Ricki held out her arms. 'Come here.'

Olivia went to her and they hugged. Ricki could feel the girl's ribs under her oversized T-shirt. The trauma of the last few days had taken a physical toll on her.

Olivia pulled away. She wiped her cheeks with the back of her hand. 'I need to see if Zellah has everything I need for the kids' class this afternoon. I picked up those extra cookie cutters

Lady was holding for you at Good Neighbor. The kids will love cutting their cheese sandwiches into animal shapes.' She removed a bag from her backpack and handed it to Ricki.

'Liv,' Ricki said, 'why don't you take the afternoon off? I'll take over the class and make sure you still get the internship hours.'

'That would be great,' Olivia said. 'Thank you.'

She impulsively threw her arms around Ricki for another hug, then retrieved her backpack. 'I think I'll take a nap in Grandmama's office.'

'Eugenia would love that. Now is the time for family.'

Red sidled up to Olivia. As if sensing the girl's trauma, she rubbed against Olivia's leg and purred. Olivia picked her up. 'Is it OK if I take Red Beans with me?'

Ricki stopped pricing books. 'Is that what you call her?'

'I started calling her Bean because that's what my gen calls things we love. Then it became Beans, then Red Beans.'

'Perfect.' Ricki looked out the window, where the peacocks were strutting their stuff. 'We have Gumbo, Jambalaya, and Red Beans. Beans for short. Much better than Red. Sure, take her with you. But I'm thinking I may eventually bring her home with me. The peacocks won't have a feather left if she continues teasing them.'

Olivia took off with the kitten and Ricki followed her out, hanging the vintage sign she'd found that read 'Back in Five Minutes' in a very 1950s font from the shop's French doors. She made her way outside to the café, where she confirmed the cooking class supplies with Zellah. She was about to return to Miss Vee's when Blaine came through the gate between Duncan-Sejour and Bon Vee.

Ricki noticed his eyes, like Olivia's, were shadowed and his fine lines seemed to have deepened. *The last couple of weeks aged everyone*, she thought.

Blaine greeted her with a 'Hey,' then took a seat at a café table, implying Ricki should do the same. Curious about what motivated his visit, she sat down opposite him.

'I'm leaving New Orleans for Bulgaria tonight,' he said. 'Pre-production for *Code Name: Blue Heron 6*. No idea when I'll be back. If ever. Mooni and Nat are staying here, though.'

'Nat's not doubling or stunting for you?'

Blaine shook his head. 'He told me we need a break from working so close with each other. I get it. He wants to do his own thing. He has this idea about opening a non-alcoholic bar and restaurant here. Mooni would create the menu for it and start off as the head chef. I think it's a winner and talked him into letting me invest.'

'I'm glad they'll still be around.' *But not as glad as Cookie will be*, Ricki thought.

'There's something else I needed to share with you. It's what drew me here. To Duncan-Sejour. To you. I've been waiting for the right time but if there's anything that hit home for me these last few weeks, it's that there is no right time. So I'm just gonna go for it.'

Blaine leaned forward, radiating a level of movie star charisma so strong it felt like a force field stripping Ricki of her powers to push back against him. She felt herself start to succumb.

Blaine's crystalline eyes bore into Ricki's hazel orbs. It was almost as if he could see straight down into her soul. He reached for her hands and said in a husky voice filled with emotion, 'I want to buy the rights to Chris's life. I wanna play him in a movie.'

The force field instantly dissolved. Ricki yanked her hands out of his. 'I knew it!' she exclaimed, simultaneously triumphant and furious. 'I knew you had an ulterior motive for coming here!'

'Hear me out. Please.' His hands now free, Blaine clasped them together, pleading. 'Chris was my best friend. I knew him better than anyone, even you. Someone is gonna make a movie about him, you know it. Let it be me. I promise I'll give you input. Maybe even a producer title.'

Ricki stood up and turned to Zellah. 'Did you hear this?'

'Oh yeah.'

'There's a word for you, Blaine. What is it? Hmm?' Ricki pretended to puzzle over this. She lit up. 'Oh, I remember. Zellah, wanna say it with me?'

'You betcha.'

'Halloweenie!' the two women yelled at the top of their lungs, then burst into laughter.

'I guess that's a no,' Blaine said, deflated.

'Oh, it's a *hella* no.' Ricki went to the gate and yanked it open. 'Here's the door. *Do* let it hit you on the way out.'

Blaine got up. He trudged through the gate. He stopped and turned around. 'Ricki, are you sure you—'

'Goodbye, Blaine. Hopefully forever.'

Ricki slammed the gate shut.

EPILOGUE

R icki and Zellah were cleaning up after the kids' cooking class when Mordant showed up. His gangly frame was clad in black pants and a gray T-shirt under a black jacket. With his long face and perpetually doleful expression, he reminded Ricki of a human Eeyore.

'Milady.' Mordant bowed to Zellah, then handed her a bouquet of black roses he'd been hiding behind his back.

'You know me so well.' Zellah favored him with a kiss on the cheek.

'Hi Mordant,' Ricki said. 'We've got a few extra pimiento cheese sandwiches, if you're interested and don't mind they're shaped like rabbits.'

'Maybe later. I'm here for you, actually.'

'Me?'

Ricki cast a questioning glance at Zellah, who shrugged and said, 'No idea.'

'If you're free, can you take a ride with me?'

'OK, let me finish up,' Ricki said, still puzzled. 'Although I have to say, that sounds very mobster-y.'

After locking up Miss Vee's, Ricki met Mordant at the hearse he'd transformed into a vehicle for transporting tourists around the city on haunted history tours. Ricki pressed him to explain what was going on, but his only response was, 'You'll see.'

Mordant took St Charles Avenue to Business 90, from where he merged onto I-10, exiting at City Park Avenue, then making a right onto Canal Street, where he pulled a U-turn. He backtracked and made a right into a cemetery.

Ricki leaned out the car window to read a sign. 'Alrighty, I'm in a hearse in the Dispersed of Judah Cemetery. Nothing strange here at all.'

Mordant continued his vow of silence. He parked the hearse on side of a lane winding through the expanse of tombs and crypts. He got out of the vehicle. Ricki did the same. Mordant retrieved a giant bag from the back of the hearse. 'I hope you're not planning to bury me in that,' Ricki said.

This elicited the hint of a smile from the man. 'Follow me.'

'He speaks!' Increasingly frustrated, Ricki didn't bother to curb the sarcasm.

The two trod a path through the silent, hallowed grounds. Mordant came to a stop in front of a simple above-ground tomb, its only decoration a Star of David. Carved under it was, 'Benjamin David Fine, 1931-1955. Beloved son and brother.'

Overcome with emotion, Ricki placed a hand over her mouth. She squeezed her eyes shut to blink back tears and slowly lowered her hand. 'Is that . . .'

'Your great-grandfather? The father of Genevieve's baby? Everything I've uncovered leads me to believe the answer is yes.'

'How . . . what . . . when did . . .' The situation felt surreal, leaving Ricki at a loss for words.

Mordant reached into the bag. He extracted two portable beach chairs and set them up facing the marker. He sat down and Ricki followed his lead. 'I've been working on earning my private investigator's license. I've only told one person about this in case I wasn't able to pull it off. But I did. And one of my assignments was finding your birth family.'

'How?'

'I got in touch with Miranda's brother Gordy. He's an OK guy. And has some excellent deals should I decide to go hearse-less. Anyway, once I explained my goal had nothing to do with Miranda's death, he proved helpful. We worked together to come up with a password Miranda might have used on her cell phone. She was rarely in touch with him but we found an old email she signed as "Mogul in Training." It didn't work as a password at first but then Gordy had the idea to add dollar signs and we did. The hardest part was figuring out how many. When we hit six, we unlocked the phone, which Gordy finally got back from NOPD.'

'What did you find on her phone?'

'An unfinished family tree. Which eventually led to you.'

Ricki couldn't take her eyes off the headstone. 'He was so young when he died.'

'I know. I was curious about that, so I researched and found his obituary notice. He died of . . . give me a minute, I have to look it up.' Mordant removed his phone from his jacket pocket and checked it. 'Familial Hypertrophic Cardiomyopathy.'

Ricki stared at him. 'I have that. I'm on medication for it. And I have to keep my weight down. Which hasn't been easy since I moved here.'

'David was on a path to becoming a rabbi. He was living in an apartment in the Quarter when he passed away.'

Ricki turned her attention back to the marker. 'I bet he met Genevieve at Charbonnet's. He died the year Genevieve gave birth. She did it out of state. I bet he never knew she was pregnant. Her family was – is – devout Catholics. If David was studying to be a rabbi, his family must have been devoutly Jewish. No wonder they kept their relationship a secret in New Orleans in the early 1950s.'

Mordant gave a somber nod. 'He didn't live long enough to marry or have children, so there are no direct descendants from him.'

Ricki pointed to the headstone. 'It says, "beloved brother." A sibling. There's the family bloodline.'

'Yup. That's what I've been working on. From the unfinished family tree Gordy and I found, so was Miranda.'

Ricki contemplated this. 'Although it won't tell us anything about who adopted the baby. We don't even know if Genevieve gave birth to a boy or girl, who would have been my grandparent.' She had a thought. 'What about whoever maintains the gravesite? It must be a family member. Maybe someone knew about Benjamin and Genevieve's relationship and passed the secret down through the generations.'

'When Benjamin died, his family paid for care in perpetuity, so it's in the hands of the cemetery employees and has been for decades. I checked.'

'Oh,' Ricki said, disappointed.

The two grew quiet. The only sound came from birdsong. The air was fragrant with the scent of lilies paying homage to loss at the grave next to Benjamin's. Ricki felt a drop of a salty tear on her lip. Mordant wordlessly handed her a pack of tissues and she wiped her eyes. 'If Benjamin had lived, I think Genevieve would have married him,' she said. 'She was a rule breaker. I think love would have won out.'

'I don't know. It's tough to break society's rules in New Orleans. Even today. And Genevieve did lie about the father of her baby when she confessed to Eugenia. There was no "Irish busboy."'

'True,' Ricki acknowledged. 'But she might have been protecting Benjamin and his family. Mindful of old prejudices that are still around, like you said.' She paused. 'Thank you, Mordant. I'm so grateful for this. I feel like there's a clue here somewhere. I'd like to hire you to keep searching.'

'You don't have to. I've already been hired. By Eugenia. She was looking for a PI and when I told her about my interest, she put me on the case. I'd never take a penny from you anyway.'

Ricki stood up, hovering over her great-grandfather's resting place. The tears she shed dripped down, giving the impression the gravestone itself was weeping.

On a day rife with life-changing surprises, Ricki found one more waiting on her doorstep.

Virgil sat on the top step, flanked by Thor and Princess.

'Can we talk?' he asked.

Ricki didn't answer right away. She wanted nothing more than to process the revelation about Benjamin Fine and do a deep dive into anything she could discover about him on the internet, minimal as Mordant warned her it would be. But that was all about the past. And Virgil was here, now, in the moment. Past, present . . . future? If nothing else, they needed to come to an understanding that would allow them to successfully co-parent the pooches and have a decent relationship as neighbors. 'Is there room for me on the stoop?' she asked.

'We'll make room.'

Virgil pulled Princess closer to him and Ricki sat next to the German shepherd, welcoming the happy doggy's licks and pets.

'Ricki,' Virgil began. 'I've told you before I'm a bad bet. I've been married twice. Both times, total disaster. I have two kids I know about. I'm out of town more than I'm in it and in recovery for substance abuse. My second wife swears I have OCD. But when I do commit, I commit with every inch of my being. And I'd like to commit to a relationship with you.'

Ricki gave him the side eye. 'Seriously? That's your idea of selling yourself?'

'I wanted to be honest with you,' Virgil said, abashed. 'I probably should have toned down the honesty and ratcheted up the romance.'

'That would have been my recommendation,' Ricki said. 'Of course, if this was a movie rom com, the woman would ignore all those red flags and fall into the hero's arms.'

'And in the non-movie version?' Virgil sounded tentative but hopeful.

Ricki looked down at the ground. 'Those endings work because romantic as they are, they're also real. Believe me, I speak from experience. I thought I was so smart because I went into my marriage knowing I couldn't change Chris and I didn't intend to. What I didn't factor into the equation is that *I* would change.' She lifted her head and met Virgil's eyes. 'So, if we have any kind of relationship, I'll never expect you to change. But I can't promise I won't.'

'Understood,' Virgil said. 'I can't promise I won't change either. For the better. I want a future that makes up for my past. I'm hoping that future is with you.'

Virgil placed a finger under Ricki's chin and lifted her lips towards his. Thor let out an impatient yip, then began pawing at Ricki's door, blowing the romantic moment. The couple laughed and broke apart.

'I think Thor's making her priorities clear,' Ricki said. She stood up.

'No more stoop for her.' Virgil also stood. He handed the dogs' leashes to Ricki. 'They're all yours until I get back.'

She hesitated. 'Would you like to come in?'

'Yes,' he said. 'I'd like that very much.'

Ricki unlocked and opened the door and the dogs bounded inside. 'Oh, and by the way,' she said as she and Virgil went inside, 'we're getting a cat.'

RECIPES

Cookbook: *Betty Crocker's Cookbook for Boys and Girls* **(1981 ed.)**

The first edition of this book came out in 1957. I have a 1965 edition that belonged to my younger brother and it's fascinating to see how the recipes evolved over the years, inspired by food and health trends, although there always seems to be some form of recipe for hot dogs, lol. It's also interesting to see how ingredients change over the years. This 1981 recipe calls for a 16 oz. can of pumpkin. A can of pumpkin today only contains 15 oz. of the ingredient. Luckily, the missing ounce doesn't affect the loaf's flavor.

The recipes are designed to be made by kids, so they're kept as simple as possible. But that doesn't make this pumpkin loaf any less delicious. In fact, it's wonderful!

GOLDEN PUMPKIN LOAF

Ingredients:

1 cup sugar
1 egg
1 can (15 oz) of pumpkin
3 cups biscuit baking mix, aka/Bisquick baking mix
1 teaspoon pumpkin pie spice
½ clove
½ teaspoon nutmeg

Directions:

Heat oven to 350 degrees. Liberally grease a 9x5x3 loaf pan. Beat 1 cup sugar, 1 egg, and the pumpkin in a mixer bowl on medium speed around 30 seconds, until well combined. Gradually add the other ingredients and beat until the batter is smooth.

Pour the batter into the greased pan and bake for 50 minutes to an hour, or until a wooden toothpick inserted into the loaf's center comes out clean.

Cool the loaf, then remove it from the pan and cut into serving slices.

Servings: 8 full-size pieces or 16 half-size pieces.

Cookbook: *Adventures in Good Cooking and the Art of Carving in the Home: Famous Recipes, A Duncan Hines Book* **(1948 ed.)**

Unlike Betty Crocker, a fictional character created in 1921 for a Saturday Evening Post contest, Duncan Hines was a real person: a traveling salesman who compiled a list of restaurants he'd eat at during his travels that he shared with friends. This turned into a book and a food column. Eventually, he licensed his name for baked goods, hence the Duncan Hines mixes we know today.

This recipe for Pumpkin Chiffon Pie is from a long-gone restaurant called The Dinner Bell in Oakland, CA. I was fascinated by the confusing way the recipe is laid out in the book: i.e., a bunch of ingredients on the left, then directions telling you to 'put in double boiler,' leaving the reader to decipher exactly what goes into the double boiler. And a 'baked pie shell' isn't even included in the ingredients! Apparently, this isn't unusual for recipes from past decades, but it was new to me.

I've simplified the directions and made sure all necessary ingredients are listed.

PUMPKIN CHIFFON PIE

Ingredients:

1 cup brown sugar
3 eggs, separated
1 and ¼ cup pumpkin
2 tsp. cinnamon
½ tsp. ginger
¼ tsp. allspice
½ tsp. salt
1 T. gelatin
¼ cup cold water
2 T. sugar
10' baked pie shell

Directions:

Place brown sugar, egg yolks, pumpkin, cinnamon, ginger, allspice, and salt in a double boiler. Mix ingredients and cook until the mixture begins to thicken, then turn off heat.

Soak the gelatin in the cold water for five minutes. Add it to the hot mixture, stir until it's thoroughly dissolved, and cool.

Beat the egg whites until they form stiff peaks, then beat the sugar into the egg whites. Fold the egg whites into the cooled mixture.

Pour into the baked pie shell and chill. Serve garnished with whipped cream.

Servings: 6-8.

Cookbook: *Marian Tracy's Complete Chicken Cookery; Marian Tracy* **(1953 first ed.)**

Given that red meat was the predominant protein in the 1950s, I found the notion of a 1953 cookbook entirely devoted to chicken recipes unusual. However, rather than rely on my instincts, I checked with my 97-year-old mother, who married in 1952. She confirmed that chicken was still an entrée outlier at the time and a cookbook comprised of recipes solely for it was indeed unique.

Since oysters figure so prominently in New Orleans cuisine, I gravitated towards this incredibly simple recipe for chicken and oyster soup. It's almost too simple: feel free to play with it by adding seasonings, plus chopped scallions and parsley. On the other hand, its simplicity does allow the flavor of the oysters to shine.

CHICKEN AND OYSTER BROTH

Ingredients:

4 cups chicken broth
1 pint oysters and their liquor
½ cup heavy cream
¼ - ½ tsp. salt *
½ tsp. paprika *

Directions:

Whip the cream until stiff, then season with the salt and paprika.

Make sure the oysters can be evenly divided between four servings. Cut the oysters into large pieces if necessary.

Heat the chicken broth on a medium flame. Add the oysters and their liquor. Cook until the edges of the oysters begin to curl or ruffle. If you like your oysters cooked firmer, let them boil for around four to five minutes.

Place a spoonful or two of the whipped cream in the bottom of four soup bowls. Pour the oyster and chicken soup over it and serve immediately.

Servings: 4.

*Since no specific salt or paprika measurements were listed in the original recipe, I created my own. Feel free to adjust the measurements, although you probably won't need more salt if it's already an ingredient in the chicken broth you use.

Cookbook: *Betty Crocker's Party Book* **(1960 ed.)**

Under the auspices of General Mills, Betty Crocker's library of cookbooks included a handy selection of spiral-bound hardcover themed cookbooks like this 'Party Book' with the cover quote reading 'More than 500 recipes, menus, and how-to-do-it tips for festive occasions the year 'round.' (Other books included *Betty Crocker's Cooking Calendar, Outdoor Cookbook,* and *Dinner for Two Cookbook.*)

The chapter on recipes and party tips for Halloween included this recipe for popcorn balls. I couldn't resist including it, separating the ingredients from the directions, which are combined into one paragraph in the book.

POPCORN BALLS

Ingredients:

1 cup sugar
⅓ cup water
⅓ cup light corn syrup
1 tsp. salt (not necessary if you use salted, already-popped popcorn)
¼ cup butter
1 tsp. vanilla extract
7 cups popped popcorn

Directions:

In a heavy saucepan, mix the sugar, water, light corn syrup, butter (and salt if you're using it as an ingredient).

Cook the mixture to 250 degrees or until a few drops form a hard ball when dropped into cold water.

Remove the pan from the heat and stir in the teaspoon of vanilla.

Place the popcorn in a large bowl. Pour the liquid mixture over the popcorn in a thin stream, stirring constantly to mix well and coat the popcorn.

Butter your hands to lessen stickiness and shape the popcorn into balls. Chill to firm up.

Servings: approx. 12 balls.

Cookbook: *Frightfully Fun Halloween Recipes* **(2000 ed.)**

As I mention in *French Quarter Fright Night*, cookbooks dedicated to a specific holiday didn't really take off until the 1990s.

This collection from Favorite Brand Name Recipes came out in 2000. It's the kind of paperback booklet you'd find on a supermarket endcap or the checkout stand. Along with recipes, it contains useful entertaining and craft tips in sidebars labeled 'Haunted Hint.'

I'll point out something I noticed regarding a newer recipe – one that's only twenty-plus years old versus fifty, sixty, or even eighty or more years old. There's an attempt to make ingredient lists much clearer. For example, this recipe not only specifies two cups of shredded Cheddar cheese, it notes that two cups is equivalent to 8 oz. However, the attention to detail can backfire. The second ingredient specifies '1/2 (8-ounce) package cream cheese softened.' Does the recipe call for half of eight ounces, which would be four ounces, or ½ of a sixteen ounce brick? For the sake of the recipe in this case, I'll assume it's the latter.

JACK-O'-LANTERN CHEESE BALL

Ingredients:

2 cups (8 oz.) shredded Cheddar cheese, mild or sharp
½ package cream cheese, softened
¼ cup solid pack pumpkin
¼ cup pineapple preserves (if these aren't available, use apricot preserves)
¼ tsp. ground allspice
¼ tsp. ground nutmeg
1 pretzel rod, broken in half
1 slice pumpernickel or dark rye bread
Black olive slices
Assorted crackers

Directions:

Beat shredded cheese, cream cheese, pumpkin, pineapple preserves, and spices in a medium-size bowl until as smooth as possible. Cover and refrigerate for two to three hours, or until the cheese is firm enough to shape into a ball.

Shape the cheese mixture into a round pumpkin. Place it on a serving platter. Use a knife to score evenly placed vertical lines on the cheese ball to make it resemble a pumpkin.

Place the half-pretzel rod into the top of the ball so that it resembles a pumpkin stem. Cut two small triangles from the bread slice and place them on the pumpkin to create eyes. Cut the olive slices in half and place them on the pumpkin in a small line to create a smile.

Cover and chill until serving time. Serve with the crackers.

Servings: a lot – it's a spread.

Cookbooklet: *What Mrs Dewey did with the NEW JELL-O!
48 Fascinating New Recipes* **(1933)**

I'm going to start off by saying something you've never seen
before in a culinary mystery: **don't make this recipe!**

In a mystery that revolves around Halloween, it's fitting to
have one recipe that sounds downright scary and in the annals
of culinary cuisine, few recipes are as frightening as those for
savory aspics. Thank me for sparing you Mrs Dewey's recipes
for Ham and Celery Loaf and Jellied Salmon Loaf!

This ninety-year-old postcard-size gem is an advertorial give-
away from the Jello-O Company, 'a division of General Food
Corporation.' The booklet kicks off with a two-page story about
the fictional Dewey family's excitement when Mrs Dewey brings
home containers of Jell-O in 'bright new boxes.'

When I read the ingredients and instructions, I was concerned
the addition of additional liquids would make it difficult for the
mold to solidify. I was proven right when I took a stab at recre-
ating this recipe. The result was a gelatinous blob. I decided to
include it anyway because any ninety-year-old recipe is at least
of historical interest and I'm fascinated by twentieth century
fondness for savory molds.

CREAMY PIMIENTO RING

Ingredients:

1 package Lemon Jell-O
1 and ½ cups warm water
½ tsp. vinegar
½ tsp. salt
½ cup milk
¼ tsp. paprika
1 tsp. minced onion
½ cup mayonnaise
½ cup grated American cheese
⅓ cup pimiento, finely chopped

Directions:

Dissolve Jell-O in warm water. Add vinegar and salt. Put in refrigerator to chill.

Add milk, paprika, and onion to mayonnaise, and whisk to blend.

When Jell-O is slightly thickened, beat in the mayonnaise mixture, then fold in the cheese and pimiento.

Transfer mixture into a ring mold and chill until firm.

Unmold and garnish with watercress.

Servings: 6.

Acknowledgments

Profuse thanks to everyone at Severn House for making the publication of my fourth Vintage Cookbook Mystery such a great experience. Additional thanks to my wonderful agent Doug Grad for the publisher matchmaking.

Huge love and thanks for my fellow blogmates at Chicks on the Case, my group mates at the Cozy Mystery Crew Facebook page, and my Fearless Foursome. And a shout-out to my NOLA crew! Your support and insight inspires me, as does our beloved Crescent City.

As always, a ton of love and gratitude to my husband Jerry and daughter Eliza for their patience and endless support. I truly couldn't do this writing thing without you. And to my late mom and dad, two voracious readers who passed on their passion for books to all three of their children. I will miss sharing this book with you.